# SUTHERLAND'S CROSSING

## A BEAU CRENSHAW DETECTIVE NOVEL

# GWEN KELLY

## ALSO BY GWEN KELLY

Life Lessons of Lucy Lu – Children's Book – Ages 4 to 9

# DEDICATION

*I dedicate this book to Craig, a special soul
forever etched in our hearts.*

*And I dedicate this book to all animals who suffer, have suffered
or continue to suffer at the hands of humans. May we one day
get to a place in human's advancement where we all recognize
good common sense and realize animals are not commodities or
there for our pleasure or entertainment. May we one day realize
that spaying and neutering is as important in keeping the pet
overpopulation under control, as brushing our teeth every day
or that crimes against animals are equally as grotesque as those
done to humans so the punishment needs to fit the abuse.*

## SUNDAY, JUNE 18, 1995

A slight breeze caressed the Spanish moss draped over the limbs of the live oak trees—majestic portraits of southern charm—holding secrets of the past tightly embedded in every vein of their massive frames. Oh, the stories they could tell. A voice echoed brazenly through the forest walls.

"Come out, come out wherever you are."

The salty air was oddly silent, yet noticeably dense. As the late-afternoon sky set in motion its dark descent, the billowy softness of the pure white clouds shifted against the backdrop of the periwinkle-blue sky, causing fragmented glimpses of the sun poking through the clouds. Staring long enough, the mind could take hold and contort the images into characters as if watching a movie, but in a flash these clouds contorted the mind into a new scene, forever in motion and constantly twisting the narrative. Audra knew her narrative was about to become twisted.

"I know you're here."

The screech of cicadas came from every direction as they started up their early-evening songs of the South, intermittent with katydids in a much higher staccato-style pitch, frogs croaking to the beat. As if silently orchestrated, birds harmonized their ballads to make magic. It was a classic June afternoon in Charleston, South Carolina, known for its relentlessly humid subtropical climate, and yet for Audra, this day would be anything but typical. She had to carry forward, somehow. *Think, Audra, think,* she told herself, *and breathe, for God's sake!* Every second counted. From here on, every decision would have a life-altering effect. As an introvert, acting impulsively was as uncomfortable to her as orbiting the moon.

Today all her senses were elevated, her nose first detecting the rotting flesh of a dead animal nearby, its odious stink compounding by the potent smell of jasmine, which by itself is a beautiful aroma, unless commingling with the foul stench of death. Her eyes feasted on the scene before her to force the scent from her mind, but Audra's nostrils couldn't escape the wicked unpleasantness.

"Come on. This is ridiculous. Where are you?"

She shuffled forward and grabbed onto the weathered porch railing, stumbling with each step. Sweat beaded on her brow, and her drenched clothes stuck to her body, the material creasing and pinching her skin when she moved, its restriction only adding to her sensation of constraint. Droplets of briny sweat would land on her upper lip unnoticed. Every so often, a piece of the paint flaked off the porch railing and stuck itself to her wet skin. Pieces of her thick, shoulder-length brunette hair glued itself to her face, and when she raised a hand to swipe the stray strands from her skin, the saturated hair resisted leaving the flawless complexion.

The cawing from a trio of black crows jerked Audra back to reality as they flew past her, their tone first eerily piercing but eventually softening as they glided into the periphery, then disappeared entirely from view. Their departure left behind the sound of her heart beating madly in her chest. Each thump sent a chilling echo throughout her.

Why did everything have a sensation of being so exaggerated? She wanted to scream. And yet . . . there was still a drive in her pushing her forward . . . to get to the finish line. Like the sensation on a roller coaster as it creeps ever so slowly to the top . . . *click clack . . . click clack . . . click clack.* Finally, it reaches the top, and for a moment, is suspended in an odd weightlessness, with no way of turning back. You are now relying on the metal bar lying across your lap to keep you tucked in place, preventing an escape, forcing on, and providing a false sense of security. And as it crosses the threshold, the coaster picks up momentum, and that sinking feeling in your stomach begins an uncomfortable dance. The weightlessness is amplified until everything catches up. Then the nervous laughter begins, and you embrace the triumph of conquering the beast. The lines become blurred between normal excitement and what is deep-seated agony.

She spotted her twin sister, Abby, now, less than a 100 yards away, but Abby couldn't see her. She was fiercely looking for her, though, and now mad as a rabid dog, screaming out into the swamp to an audience of no one.

"I know you're there, Audra. Come out, and let's talk about this. Grow up and face me for once in your life. Come on, Audra. Stop this."

Audra felt conflicted. How was she going to protect herself? Everything was rushing forward like a dam that had broken. She needed to settle down, to think clearly. But the panic wouldn't let go. The horrible panic. Oh, how she hated that word. She was sick of its grip on her, of its being in charge of her life knowing that panic held the cards for what the day would bring. She was so sick of it all. What a strange existence. Maybe death was the best end.

At only thirty-three years old, Audra didn't want to deal with this, to experience this kind of torment. A ripple of strength overcame her, and Audra knew what she needed to do. She needed to finish the ride. She turned around and gasped as a voice broke against her stillness so close she could feel the warmth of the breath.

"Hello, sister. It's been awhile."

## WEDNESDAY, JUNE 21, 1995

Beau lumbered up the stairs leading to the back door of the 1950s-style bungalow. His right hand yanked on the handle of the screen door, the screeching hinges reminding him how desperately they needed WD-40. Making a mental note, he stepped inside. The overpowering scent of Fleecy in the air announced it was laundry day. His eyes darted from the kitchen to the living room and back again. "Kathleen, where are you?"

No reply.

"Kathleen? I don't have time for games today. Kathleen?" Beau's voice boomed louder on the last few syllables.

"I'm right here, for God's sake," Kathleen muttered, her left foot stepping off the last of the squeaking basement stairs and onto the kitchen floor, all the while drying off her hands with a dish towel. "Stop yelling."

"I'm hardly yelling. You didn't answer me."

His bulky stature overshadowed her narrow frame. Beau wasn't fat but had the body type that big-and-tall stores would market to. Although average looking, there was a certain charisma to him. Maybe because of his size, you felt safe when he was near. He was a gentle giant. It was as if his birth development became rushed and no thought given to providing him definition, so everything on him seemed square. Large and square. Square head, square jaw, square shoulders, square hands.

Beau had no desire to be fashionable, likely attributed to his size. He found a few mainstays and stuck with that. A navy linen suit, with white short-sleeved shirts during the summer months, returning to a black suit with long-sleeved white shirts and ties for the winter months; ties that looked as though they were passed down from his father, as they often had snags or holes in them and were definitely not the current fashion trends. Now and then, he would mix it up with a tweed jacket. On cooler days, he wore a black rumpled trench coat that had two middle buttons missing, buttons he had no interest in replacing. His home attire was a faded stretched-out polo shirt, khakis, and time-worn deck shoes. His only notable style was his collection of hats. That, he seemed to have a passion for. Felt fedoras in the winter and straw Panamas in the summer. Perhaps that was a feel-good connection to his past, a sense of comfort and familiarity when he would go with his father to the hat shop. Perhaps he wanted to keep the tradition going, or maybe he just liked hats.

"What's so important that I had to come rushing up from the laundry?"

Beau hesitated before answering, taking stock of the woman before him. He loved her look, always did. He loved how she could transform a fifties housedress to an elevated style for the nineties. Every day was a different apron, most of which she had sewn herself. Today was a freshly ironed pink-and-white gingham. A scalloped edging sewn around the perimeter and pocket area added to the gingerbread charm. The pearled brooch and simple pearl stud earrings were the finishing touches. He couldn't remember a day she didn't wear a brooch and earrings. Unlike so many other women, who caked on enough makeup to look like exaggerated renderings for Madame Tussauds wax museum, Kathleen could mute her makeup, accentuating her best features, which were her eyes and smile. It brightened her youthful appearance, giving her a fresh glow, but it was her hair he loved most. It had a natural whimsy that fell in a tousle around her face in a playful, feminine way. If only they didn't have to talk with each other. Conversing is what got them into trouble.

"I got a page and need to head out."

"You can't be serious," she said, continuing to dry her hands on the dish towel even though they were already dry. "We're having dinner and playing cards with the Millers tonight. I've been looking forward to this for weeks."

"I guess the corpse didn't get the memo to die on a different day when we didn't have plans with the Millers."

"No need to get sarcastic about it," Kathleen said with a huff.

"Well, no need to challenge me on it. There's nothing I can do about it. Do you think I want to spend my day off looking at a stiff? Especially at this time of day? I'd much rather be back in the shed finishing my birdhouse. And as much as I hate spending time with the Millers, I would actually take his droning on about how he met some rock star backstage in 1972 for the eight hundredth time. One of these days, though, I'm going to tell him no one gives a shit about the fact that he peaked in high school."

"Don't be crass," Kathleen muttered. "Well, what time do you expect you'll be home? Can you join us later?"

"How the hell should I know? I mean, seriously, Kathleen, we've been married for how long, and you're still asking me a stupid question like this? You don't wrap up a body in an hour or two. I don't even know who or how they died."

"Too long. That's how long we've been married."

"Oh, come on, let's not start down that path again. I'm frustrated, that's all. I'm tired of this," Beau said in a softening tone, not wanting to get into it with her.

"You should have thought about that before you gambled and drank our money away. You got us into this mess," Kathleen snapped.

He knew she would think it was the job he was tired of, but really, it was the bickering.

"And there it is. You want to talk about *our* money? Like you worked a day in your life. You don't know what it's like out there going to a job day after day, month after month, year after year, constantly having someone control you only to come home to a consistently pissed-off wife. I'm the one paying the bills around here, if you hadn't noticed. Why don't you get a job so I can quit mine and then I'll happily make birdhouses for the rest of my days and listen to the Millers drone on about their stupid lives while we serve them food at our table and play fucking poker with them? How's that sound?"

"You're an ungrateful bastard, you know that? You think taking care of the house isn't working? How dare you? I'm the one stuck in this haunted hellhole," Kathleen said spewing her words, her once tear-filled eyes now shooting daggers.

"Yep, that's right. I'll take it. I'm an ungrateful asshole, and I totally own the poor decisions I've made, but the memory that haunts you haunts me too,—every day. I've been paying for it ever since, and it appears that I'll be paying for the remainder of my life, because you'll keep reminding me every opportunity you get. God forbid we should stop living in the past."

"And you don't remind me? You hate me for it. I can see it in your eyes, Beau Crenshaw. I see how you look at me," Kathleen screamed out between sobs, gesturing at him with her index finger. "Just go solve someone else's mess instead of looking at your own. Anyway, being a cop is what you love the most."

"For Christ's sake, Kathleen, I don't hate you. Let's not go there." He wanted to de-escalate his heated words, so he leaned forward to touch her arm.

"Don't take the Lord's name in vain, and don't you touch me. I'm not doing this dance with you today. Just go. I'll pray for you." Her body recoiled and stiffened as she raised her hand in a gesture not to come any closer. "Just go."

"Better add yourself to that prayer, because the last time I checked, it takes two to tango," Beau said with a snarl, angry at the rejection of his touch. He hated it when she threw religion into the mix, too, as if tattling to Daddy was going to absolve her of her part in the argument.

At that, he turned and walked away, knowing that if he stayed, they would continue to spit venom at each other until it transformed into a full-blown screaming match. She would end up crying uncontrollably and he would wind up being frustrated and alone, apologetic for the mean things he'd say, but angry that she poked him to say the things he did. He was already aggravated enough about the long night ahead of him, and he didn't want to dwell anymore on their deteriorating twenty-eight-year-old marriage. He'd leave that for the marriage counselor.

Quickly changing into his work attire, attire Kathleen had given up ironing long ago, he snatched up his badge and gun and left without a parting word. He wanted out of the house now and away from his miserable existence. He was agitated and annoyed that things had escalated yet again, but he didn't have time to dwell on any of it.

Slumping into the driver's seat of his city-issued Crown Vic, he took a big breath, let out a sigh, and glanced down at the pager to get the address of the crime scene. Putting the car in reverse, he paused for a moment, wondering whether he should go back and at least say goodbye. Knuckles whitening on the steering wheel, the anger now shifted from Kathleen to himself. He hated leaving like this. It would ruin her day as well. He hated their arguments. He didn't want her to be upset. She had already been through enough. Why did he have to go there? Why did he say those cruel things to her? Would they ever be able to get over what happened? He hoped so. Deciding it could go either way now, he didn't have time to continue with the war of words, so he took his foot off the brake, loosened his grip, and continued backing up, but not before slamming his fist down on the steering wheel.

"Fuck! Why does it always have to end this way?" Beau belted out.

With that out of his system, Beau continued backing out of the driveway and, putting the car in drive, shot off, kicking up dirt and rocks high into the road. His focus was needed elsewhere now.

It was an address on the edge of town. Traffic was light at this time of the day, so he figured it should take him about twenty minutes to get there. All that came across the pager was that a body was found in a car in a swamp. His job now was to unravel the steps leading up to how and why it got there. Was it an accident? Intentional? Murder?

## TWO HOURS EARLIER

"911. What is the nature of your emergency?"

"There appears to be an object in the swamp at 582 Seacroft Lane," the anonymous caller said in a muffled voice, as if cloth were placed over the receiver.

"Can I please have your name and the phone number you are calling from?"

"There's something shiny in the water. Nothing shines in the swamp. You'd better send someone to check it out. Could be a car," the anonymous caller said.

"May I please have your name and phone number?" the 911 operator asked again, her tone now striking a high level of agitation.

"You'd better check it out." There was silence, then a dial tone.

"Ignorant prick. 'Shiny object.' Like that's an emergency. This better not be some stupid prank," the operator said out loud, but knowing all calls had to be investigated, she sent out the radio request.

"Calling officers in the area of 582 Seacroft Lane. There's a possible 302. Please respond if you are in the vicinity. Over."

"Dispatch, this is car 216. We're in the area and will respond to the possible 302" came the reply.

"Car 216, strange call, so maybe nothing. No further details were provided other than a shiny object spotted in the water and possible 302. We have traced the call back to a guest phone at the Preston Hotel. Could be a prank, but proceed with caution, Eddy."

"Ten-four. We're on our way," Eddy replied.

It was close to noon on a predictably hot and muggy Charleston day as Bruce and Eddy turned onto 582 Seacroft Lane, a long private drive off Bailey Grove Highway, their eyes seeking anything that might seem suspicious. The crunching of stones under the tread of the tires, as the patrol car crawled up the driveway, nearly drowned out the faint sound of cicadas and katydids in the distance, which was already a gentler, softer pitch in the daylight hours compared with their evening melodies.

"I'm sure this is going to be an easy way to end our shift," Bruce said. "Likely some kids decided to go for a joyride, and the fun got out of hand."

"Hope you're right," Eddy said.

Both transplants from other states, the two officers had been riding together for a few years now and were friends outside of work, the differences in their personalities enhancing their connection instead of hindering it. They first became acquainted in the academy as young men. Both men were married, and while Bruce would say his was a satisfactory union, Eddy was deep in the throes of an ugly divorce.

Bruce was a frumpy, not-so-tall, wiry man with pointed features, and while only in his thirties, his hairline took on that of a much older gentleman. No amount of food would encourage his skeletal frame to fill in and cover his bony structure. Eddy was the six-foot pretty boy with cobalt-blue eyes and dark wavy hair that was meticulously kept in place with the aid of a multitude of hair products; his body was ripped. Add the cop uniform, and women threw themselves at his feet. Bruce knew Eddy's charms played a part in why Eddy was going through a divorce, but he didn't pry about the actual reason for the split, because he really didn't want to know.

On either side of Seacroft Lane was open marshland, a whooping crane visible with its stark white, contrasting against the golden hues of the reeds, its eyes alert, patient and ready, waiting for lunch. Continuing down the lane, the landscape turned from marshland to swamp, from tall grasses to an often-misunderstood complex ecosystem so intense and uninterrupted that without it, human life would be affected.

The tall, gangly trees covered in Spanish moss dripping down from the crooked limbs immediately darkened the heavenly blue sky. Against the backdrop of the swamp, the occasional openings offered a shimmering light show with only hints of sunlight peeking through. The driveway ended at a cleared lot beside the swamp's edge, where a wood-paneled cottage stood, painted a pale pastel yellow with Charleston green shutters and a green tin roof, built on stilts because of the possibility of flooding, which was common in the low country. Overall, the place was in decent condition. The only items on the screened-in front porch were two weathered wicker rocking chairs and a small, rickety, unpainted wooden table.

Behind the cottage and to the left, the grounds were forested with planted pine trees, and to the right was the swamp. Theirs was the only vehicle present.

"Kind of a dreary place to notice a 'shiny object,'" Bruce mused aloud. Already suspicion loomed in each of their minds, especially since the 911 operator had mentioned that the call was odd.

They parked to the left of the driveway area and slowly got out of the patrol car, guns ready to be drawn and used if necessary.

"You hate snakes and gators as much as I do," Eddy said. "So, if one of those comes near us, I'm shooting it."

"Hell yeah. Sometimes I wonder why I moved to a place littered with 'em, until I think back to shoveling snow in January," Bruce said.

The men noticed evidence of tire tracks leading into the murky water, the mud holding onto the imprints while the weeds were forced over by the weight of the tires. They stood for some time, letting their eyes follow the tire tracks, scanning the swamp water. After a few minutes, Eddy noticed an object barely out of the water gleaming back at him.

"Hey, check out over there," Eddy said as he pointed ahead. "Does that look like what I think it looks like? I believe we found the shiny object."

"Yup, looks like part of a taillight," Bruce said. "I'm going with my original theory that a joyride got out of hand. Wonder whose car it is, though? Rental or Mommy and Daddies? Wanna make a wager?"

"Yeah, right. Or have you forgotten I've got a divorce to pay for?"

"Good point," Bruce said, then cocked his head to speak into his radio. "Dispatch, this is car 216. Based on what we can see, we have what looks like a car in the swamp and will need a tow truck and some divers to hook it up. See whether old man Walter is close by."

"Ten-four, car 216. I'll get back to you once the tow truck

and divers are heading your way. I'll check with Walter first to see whether he's available."

By now, Eddy had started assessing the area and taking pictures. "Why'd you ask for old man Walter? There's no way he'll get close to that water," Eddy said chuckling.

"Because he's the best there is, and he'll be the first to arrive. You want this dragging on? There's a game on tonight, and I'd rather be kicking back with a cold one and not in this morbid swamp."

"True that," Eddy said.

Bruce moved the patrol car out of the way so the tow truck would have plenty of room to maneuver, while Eddy took pictures of the tire tracks, the surrounding area, and where the unidentified vehicle seemed to have entered the water. It appeared the vehicle came up the driveway and straight into the swamp. The area would soon be compromised once the tow truck and divers arrived, so they wanted to get as many pictures as possible.

"Doesn't seem like anyone's home, but lets check," Bruce said as both men walked toward the cottage.

"God, I hope this isn't someone's full-time house. Who in their right mind would want to live in a swamp?" Eddy said.

"Ya got that right. In decent shape, though, so someone's keeping it up. I'm surprised there's not more mold or moss. Hardly even a cobweb. Must have been pressure washed recently," Bruce said.

"Shit. What the hell is this? Almost twisted my ankle. Figure I'd find this to step on."

Bruce was already on the bottom two steps of the porch as he turned around to see Eddy pick up a hand-carved wooden cross, about twelve inches high, that was hidden in the taller grass. The force of Eddy's weight had snapped the cross in half.

"Man, someone took their time carving this. Shame I broke it.

Wonder why it's out here in the grass?" Eddy said, turning it around in his hand, admiring the craftsmanship.

"Yeah, look at the detail. A lot of work went into that. I'd just leave it on the porch so they can see it. Maybe they can have it fixed."

Bruce knocked loudly on the door. No one answered. He continued knocking and identified himself as the police. Still no answer. They looked in the windows but saw nothing out of order. It looked like a sparsely decorated home, neat and tidy. Bruce tried the front door. It was locked. Without cause, they couldn't enter the home even if the door were open, but he was prepared to yell inside if it were, and, because of the nature of their visit, it could fall under extenuating circumstances.

"Let's take a walk round back," Bruce said.

Finding all in order there, they started around the side of the cottage when Eddy pointed straight ahead of him.

"Hey, tire tracks over there in that parking area. I'll get some pictures. They look pretty fresh. Didn't we have a storm a few days back?" Eddy said.

"Something like that. Looks like there has been a car here since then. They don't seem the same as the swamp tire tracks, though, do they? A little more rugged, like a truck tire?"

While Eddy was taking pictures, Bruce stood nearby and looked around at the grounds.

"Looks like a roadway leading back into the pines. I see some sort of building. You done?" Bruce said.

"Hang on. Just a few more," Eddy said.

Minutes later, Bruce and Eddy walked a couple of hundred feet and came upon an old, run-down trailer that looked as though someone had recently visited, based on the footprints near the door. Overgrowth had been cut back, which would indicate more than a single visit. Otherwise, why bother.

"Hunters might stay here," Eddy said.

"Likely," Bruce said.

Bruce banged on the door and announced they were police. No answer. Bruce banged a couple of more times. Still no answer. They looked in the windows of the dingy trailer but saw nothing out of sorts.

"From the looks of things, the cleaning lady hasn't been by recently," Eddy said chuckling. "What a shithole."

"It's killing you to see this, Mr. Over-the-Top Clean, isn't it?" Bruce said.

"Hell yeah it is. There's no need to live like this. Soap's cheap."

They headed back toward the cottage and continued checking its perimeter but, not detecting any type of suspicious activity there, walked back to the swamp to wait for the rest of the crew.

"Maybe the car in the swamp belongs to whoever lives here," Eddy said.

"I wish they'd hurry up already. This place gives me the creeps," Bruce said.

"Don't you find it odd that someone would leave a car in the water?" Eddy remarked, unable to let it go now. "Maybe they couldn't afford to have it towed out, or maybe it's a junk car and rather than leave it sitting out to rot, they decided to put it in the water to erode there, thinking it would happen faster."

"What would happen? You think it's going to turn to dust overnight? You say some of the craziest shit sometimes, man. It's scary, actually."

Bruce cocked his voice to one side as he spoke into his radio.

"Dispatch, this is car 216. Do you have an ETA on the divers and tow truck for Seacroft Lane?"

"Car 216, checking on ETA."

17

"Ten-four."

Less than ten minutes passed when dispatch came over the radio.

"Car 216, divers and Walter are enroute. ETA fifteen minutes."

"Ten-four."

"This place is eerie, man," Eddy said. "And I can't imagine why anyone would want to live here."

"I know. You've already said that many times."

"It's not like you can fish or enjoy the water. And this place is crawling with snakes and alligators that you would constantly be on the lookout for."

"Yeah," Bruce said chiming in. "I sure wouldn't want this as my vacation spot. Give me the mountains or a golf course any day, but this place? Hell no."

"I thought you were a cruise man," Eddy said playfully.

"Cruise ships suck. You'll never find me on one of those. I don't care how cheap they are. Way too many people and those buffets. Can you imagine all the people coughing and spitting all over the food? Kids grabbin' food with their hands and puttin' it back. No thanks."

As the minutes ticked away, Bruce and Eddy caught up on the sports scores, and then, like clockwork, they both started talking about Walter. It was hard not to. Everyone who grew up in Charleston knew the story. As it got passed down, it became more and more embellished so that the only people who really knew the truth were the people involved that day.

Walter had been the department's preferred towing specialist for nearly thirty of his forty years towing. It wasn't Walter's charming personality that kept them talking about him, but his devastating story and the grief this man was holding on to. It was so traumatic that the minute his name was brought up, the memory of that dreadful day, several years earlier, flooded in fast and furious like a pop-up storm.

Bruce lifted his head, motioning as he said, "Speak of the devil. Here comes old man Walter now." The front end of the 1978 GMC tow truck was now visible as it chugged up the drive.

Walter hopped out of the truck and hobbled toward the two officers. A tour in Vietnam left a permanent limp in his gait, a limp for which he never offered an explanation. He was still sporting long-outdated sideburns and a permanent five-o'clock shadow, and his thinning gray hair was tied in a ponytail that needed a trim years ago. He wore the same dark green work shirt tucked into dark green work pants, and an overused leather belt was the only separator between the two monotone pieces of clothing. Heavy steel-toed, tan-colored work boots were his usual form of footwear, and he always had a tire-pressure gauge tucked in his shirt pocket. The man always talked with a cigarette in the corner of his mouth, which danced like a marionette. Everyone wondered whether his skin was permanently stained with engine oil, as he was covered from head to toe in it. His hands and nail-bitten fingers had dark grease carved into every line.

"You two good-for-nothings got nothing better to do than sit around in your car in a mosquito-infested swamp?" he said grunting. "Dragging me out to this godforsaken mud pit. I'm gonna be retiring soon, boys. You keep doing this to me. Time to throw in the towel, like they say. I should be dealing with only the easy jobs now. I've done my time."

"You're too damn miserable to give this up, Walter, no matter what kind of job it is. Who else you gonna torment?" Bruce said jokingly.

"Miserable, I'll give you that," Walter said. "Yup, definitely give you that."

Eddy pointed toward the swamp and said, "Looks like some sort of vehicle took a splash, Walter, and looks pretty fresh."

"Why'd you say it's fresh?" Walter asked.

"I don't know," Eddy said.

"You've got the brains of a fart, don't you, boy?" Walter said.

Bruce broke into laughter, while Eddy just smiled, not really understanding the joke.

Looking over to where the car was positioned, Walter asked, "Now how in the hell did it get in there? And you know I won't be gettin' in that godforsaken water."

"How it got there is what we're meaning to find out. Someone called it in," Bruce said as a noise caught his attention, causing him to glance back toward the lane. "Don't worry, diving team's on its way. In fact, I bet that's them coming up the drive now."

"What kind of crazy bastard wants a job where he ends up swimming in a swamp? Shit for brains, I tell ya. I'll never figure that out, but better them than me," Walter muttered under his breath and went about getting the truck positioned and the winch set up, and out of habit, he grabbed the shovel from behind his toolbox. It had been known to come in handy a time or two. All this while Bruce and Eddy stood by like audience members waiting for the show to begin.

After a few minutes of small talk, the dive team suited up, giving the officers and Walter time to catch up on typical man conversation—politics, the weather, and sports.

Walter got the tow hook ready to hand off to one of the divers, making sure he understood where to hook it. Both divers entered the water cautiously and approached the car.

Walter went back to his conversation with Bruce and Eddy.

A yell from one diver stopped Walter in mid sentence.

"There's a body in the driver's seat."

Things just got more complicated.

"Ugh," Bruce said. "Not how I wanted today to go. Gonna be a long night," he said out loud then turned to his radio. "Dispatch, this is car 216. Divers have confirmed a body in the car at 582 Seacroft Lane. Will need a detective and medical examiner on site."

"Car 216 will contact a detective and ME and advise on ETA."

"Ten-four."

"Looks like you're on overtime, Walter," Bruce said. "Eddy, continue taking pictures of the car and the area. I'm gonna tape off the area back at the trailer and the tire tracks up at the cottage."

"I'll be in the truck taking a break. Holler when you need me," Walter said as he flicked open the lid of the classic chrome lighter, his thumb striking the wheel enough to produce a flame. With one quick puff, the cigarette was lit, and the lighter's lid was snapped closed. He returned it to his pants pocket and hopped into the truck to settle in.

Over an officer's radio came an update from dispatch. "Car 216, we have an ETA on a detective and ME. On the way and approximately thirty minutes out."

"Ten-four, dispatch," Eddy said.

"Good. Gives us plenty of daylight still," Bruce said. Next, he yelled over to the divers. "Boys, might as well come out for now. It's gonna be thirty minutes for the rest of the gang to get here."

One of the divers acknowledged with a wave, and at that, both men started the slow walk back to dry land, the weight of the water and sludge suctioning them down like quicksand as if gravity had tightened its grip and was beckoning them toward the center of the earth.

# WHAT LAY BENEATH?

Beau drove up Seacroft Lane, his mind pushing his argument with Kathleen to the side so he could focus on the dead body. A suspicious death investigation involves many elements that require a clear and sharp mind. Pulling up next to the patrol car, he mindlessly put the car in park and turned off the engine. Before exiting, he briefly took a mental image of the scene, and played with a toothpick. His replacement for cigarettes.

Pine straw rustled and crackled under Beau's feet as he headed toward Bruce and Eddy. "You boys got nothin' better to do on my day off than dredge up trouble?"

"Trust me, if we'd known this was going to go on, we may not have been so quick to answer the call," Eddy said jokingly.

Bruce banged on the driver's-side door of the tow truck. "Beau's here, Walter. Break's over."

"How far behind do you think Doc and CS are?" Beau asked, totally ignoring Eddy's comment.

"Dispatch said you were both thirty minutes out, so they should be here any time now."

"What's the deal here?"

"Dispatch got an anonymous call about a shiny object in the water. We thought it could be a prank, but the divers found a body in the car."

"Did you notice anything out of the ordinary when you searched the grounds?"

"Doesn't seem like anything is out of place. No one's home now, but tire tracks up by the cottage look fresh within a few days. There's an old trailer on the grounds too. Possibly used by hunters. It's pretty grim, but I doubt they would care."

Both men turned toward the drive area, hearing a vehicle coming up the lane.

"There's the man with all the answers. Good timing," Beau said.

Doc stepped out of his car and waved toward Beau and the officers. Crime-scene investigators, or CSI, were quietly organizing their work paraphernalia.

"I'll be right there!" Doc yelled over. "Let me talk to CS and get suited up first."

"Take your time," Beau said. "Body's not going anywhere." Beau wished he had kept that last comment to himself. Still unnerved by his confrontation with Kathleen, his tone was still sharp, but needed to show some respect for the dead.

Doc had been with the medical examiner's office for over twenty years, so he had a long working relationship with Beau. A short, pudgy man with a thick head of silver hair and beard accompanied by round, frameless glasses and jolly red cheeks made him resemble Santa Claus, who should grant wishes and hand out gifts instead of dissecting human bodies to determine their cause of death. He briefed CS on who would handle what and then went to the trunk of his car to suit up before meeting up with the others. Suiting up for him was as natural as brushing his teeth.

"Walter, wanna get her brought up?" Beau said.

"You got it."

Directing his attention back to the divers, Walter handed the tow hook off to the closer one and this time said, "Make sure you boys put the tow hook behind the back bumper and not on it. Otherwise, that bumper will pop off that car like a face on a hot stove."

At that, he turned around and walked back to the truck, muttering under his breath, "Ya gotta tell these stupid bastards everything."

"Gentlemen, whatta we have today besides the obvious?" Doc asked, walking up to the group. He snapped the latex glove, indicating that he was fully suited and ready for action.

"Divers just confirmed one body, deceased," Beau said.

"Interesting place to end up," Doc said.

"Yeah, and on my day off too," Beau said. The words no sooner left his lips than he regretted the comment. Flashback to Kathleen again. *Get a grip, Beau,* he thought to himself.

Doc paid him no mind. Beau was known to make off-the-cuff remarks and had been nicknamed "Crude Crenshaw" years ago from the crew that worked alongside him, but Doc didn't figure Beau much cared what they called him. Doc had defended him many times. What people didn't understand about Beau was that he had a heart of gold and would do anything to help anyone. He kept it hidden inside his tough armadillo shell.

A thumbs-up from the divers meant the car was ready to be hauled out. Everyone stood in silence as the winch churned and chugged along, slowly dragging the car to the surface, water raining down like a fountain exposing a 1991 four-door Mercedes-Benz S-Class sedan. The noise of the water first pounded down to the ground with a powerful vengeance, then moved toward a tranquil trickling sound, eerie amid the sight before them. As the car emerged from the murky swamp, the group saw the body of a woman slumped over the steering wheel, pale blue skin (what scientists call vascular marbling) looking toward them, an icy, frightened stare with opaque eyes wide open, all color now gone. Now on dry land, the water was draining much slower now, but still leaching from every crevice of the vehicle.

"Walter, you gonna keep it hooked this way to tow to the lab, right?" Beau asked.

"Yeah, it's at a good angle."

"Good, drop it down on all fours, then, so we can get good access."

"Down she comes," Walter said, a new cigarette miming the words with him.

"Bruce, Eddy, tape off the area where the car came out while CS gets what they need from the car, then stand by," Beau said.

"Roger that," Eddy and Bruce said in unison.

Turning his attention back to Doc, Beau said, "First thoughts, Doc?" Both men were now peering through the windshield and driver's-side window.

"Looks to be late twenties, early thirties," Doc said. "I can't give a professional opinion until we clean the body and perform the autopsy, but from looking at her through the windshield, it appears that there are bites on her arm and face, which have caused swelling. See it there? Notice the round ring of red and then the two bruised puncture areas? It resembles a snakebite. Odd, though, since the car windows are shut. A snake couldn't easily get inside, and what's also strange is that water moccasins lie around on the limbs of the trees during the afternoon and late afternoon, catching the sun's heat. As the day cools, they drop into the water. A water moccasin would be the most obvious snake to bite.

"Oh, and look. There appears to be other trauma to the body. Looks like blood on her skin and her clothes. Interesting. And she's wearing her seat belt. Odd indeed."

Doc paused, frowning, shook his head, then returned his thoughts back on the snakebites. "Well, I'm assuming the car went in the water recently during the daylight hours, so disregard that thought. We know never to assume anything. We don't actually know when the car went in the water. Will definitely need to investigate this theory further. These snakes are not easily provoked, so if the car hit the water, it is unlikely they would have come toward the car, but rather would venture away from it unless the car had been in the water for a while. Then the snake could have slithered up easily inside the engine block and gained access that way, but why the biting then? She would have already been dead. Or was she? Did the car enter the water but was not completely submerged for a while? The weight of it slowly pulling it under? Are these actually snakebites? Mercy me. What torture did you go through, woman?" Doc pondered as he subconsciously took his thumb and index finger, rubbing them back and forth across his forehead.

"Just me thinking out loud, Beau. I guess how it got there is on your list of things to figure out. We'll know more once we start the autopsy about what really killed her." Doc muttered away to himself, still intrigued by what he was seeing.

Beau yelled over to the CS team, "You boys getting any fingerprints? Hopefully, the water hasn't washed them all away. Let me know when you get pictures of the car and the surrounding area so we can start opening doors and moving things around. Get underneath the car as well. Tie off as many areas as possible to preserve what we can. Be sure to photograph and measure every imprint you find—tires, shoe prints, everything. Oh, and take an imprint with pictures of all our shoes so we can eliminate them. And there are some tracks over at the cottage, along with a trailer behind it. Get imprints and fingerprints on the handrails and doorknobs. Take too many pictures."

Beau began his walk of the property, starting with the cottage. On the porch he noticed the broken cross just as Doc yelled out they were ready to open the doors of the car, so he quickly hustled back. Beau approached the driver's-side door and tried to open it. Locked. He attempted to open the back door, but it was locked. He walked around to the passenger side, locked as well.

"Hey, Bruce!" Beau yelled. "Can you get the Slim Jim? Let's try it before breaking a window."

"Sure thing," Bruce said.

As Bruce wriggled and battled with the door opener for over twenty minutes, he finally heard a pop and uttered a sigh of relief, knowing he had released the door lock. By now, everyone was standing around him, relieved he was successful.

"Good work," Beau said.

As Beau opened the driver's-side door, he screamed out, "Son of a bitch!" He jumped back and out of the way of a four-foot water moccasin slithering out, angry as hell and coming his way fast and furious. Its head was up and ready to strike out at anyone that got in its way. It was looking to escape from being trapped in the car and didn't care what direction it took; it just wanted to return to its natural habitat. Doc, CS, and Bruce all collided as they jumped out of harm's way.

Quick to respond and relying on his trusty shovel, Walter stormed in and, with force unlike anything the others had seen, was on the snake as fast as lightning. He first whacked it across its head, knocking the snake unconscious, and then chopped the snake in half and continued chopping it persistently, crushing its head into small pieces, cursing the entire time.

"Hold on, Walter! Let me get the head. We'll need it for a venom sample," Doc said.

Walter stopped long enough for Doc to reach over and stuff the snake's head into an evidence bag, then flung the rest of the remains into the swamp.

"Jesus, I hate snakes." Walter said with a bark as he returned to the truck, still cursing under his breath but going on about his business as if this were all in a day's work. Walter scraped the shovel on nearby grass to get any remnants of the snake off his lethal weapon and stored it back on the truck.

"Damn, I guess you really do hate snakes," Beau said with a scoff. "Jesus, you were like a honey badger out there, but thanks for reacting. You likely saved me a visit to the hospital today, being pampered by a pretty nurse and all that." The minute he said nurse, he wished he hadn't.

Walter turned and walked away without a word as Doc and Beau cautiously approached the car, shining a flashlight inside, exposing the dark shadows and what might be lurking in them. They looked at the slumped-over dead body. Beau wanted to get a firsthand look before CS removed the body from the car.

"This would explain where these bites came from, then," Doc muttered out loud.

CS removed the body from the car to place her into a body bag.

"Beau, come over here!" Doc yelled, now hovering over the body.

"Good God Almighty, this woman has been through a lot of trauma, so it will be hard to tell exactly what killed her. Some madman has done some pretty grotesque things to her body. See the cuts around her chest area? When I went to do a temperature check, look at what I found. It goes all the way from her chest to her pubic area. What hell you must have endured."

Dumbfounded, Beau couldn't believe what he saw. It was like stepping back in time. This woman had been sliced and diced, then sewn together with what looked like a fishing line just like Mary, Walter's wife.

"Doc, this is just like Mary. Don't let Walter catch one glimpse of this."

"I know, I know. I need to get her back to the lab and check for similarities. How could it be, after all these years, that he's still out there?"

"I can't believe this, Doc. I'll let you finish up here while I check out the car."

Beau walked back over to the car, his mind racing, and approached cautiously, being sure not to touch anything, since CS was still gathering evidence. He also wanted no more surprise snake encounters, so he took things slowly.

The thoughts were rapid-firing now. *Who was she? Why was she back here? Mercedes-Benz. Expensive car.* The last word had no sooner left his lips than he froze for a moment, putting everything he now knew together. Mercedes-Benz, a woman in what appeared to be her early thirties.

Suddenly Beau muttered under his breath, "No, no, no, no. Please, God, let this not be Audra Barrington," as if saying it to himself would change the outcome, but his gut was telling him otherwise. He walked over to the woman's body, which had already been placed in a body bag. Pulling down the zipper enough confirmed that the lifeless face staring back at him resembled the pictures Oliver, her father, had given Beau of Audra Barrington, missing since March 1995, a striking resemblance to Oliver only in a beautiful female form with a flawless complexion, auburn hair, medium build, and wearing a flowered buttoned-down shirtdress with strappy sandals. Such a happy outfit to wear for such a dreadful event.

Beau yelled over to Eddy in a commanding voice, "Eddy, do we know who owns this property?"

"Nothing confirmed yet, but I called in both the VIN number of the car and the property address."

Beau waved an acknowledgment and continued his thoughts while checking the exterior of the car for clues. *Audra's been missing since March, and she shows up dead now? It doesn't look as if she has been in the water since March. Where have you been all this time, Audra Barrington? Where have you been? Is Mary's death tied to this one?*

He noted the vehicle was in excellent condition except for an area at the front grille where several scratch marks were noticeable in a six-by-six-inch area. *That's odd*, Beau thought. *"What would make those types of scratches confined only to this area? The rest of the car is immaculate, so how did this happen, and when? The car doesn't look as if it has been in the water for a long time. No rust is present."*

Beau turned back around, looking toward the swamp. Something caught his eye, only for a fleeting moment, and then it was gone as the clouds passed over the sun, darkening the sky. Thunder clapped in the distance. Charleston was preparing itself for a pop-up rainstorm. Beau stayed focused on the area but had to wait until the sun peeked out from under the clouds, flickering its light through the trees. His eyes scoured the area, up and down, side to side, and then he saw a cable coming out of the water about fifty yards away.

"Boys, let's check this out before the rain gets here!" he yelled over to two of the CS investigators.

As the men approached, Beau pointed to his left near the edge of the swamp, and they all headed toward the area. Moving up to the other side of the swamp, they could see footprints in the moist, fertile soil.

"Hold it here, boys," Beau said directing the others. "Let's get some pictures of these footprints first, an imprint, and then rope this off." Looking at one man, he beckoned and said, "Let him take care of that, and you can come with me. We'll go around the other way."

The footprints looked like adult feet, but it was difficult to tell whether they belonged to a man or a woman. As they carried on, they discovered a portable winch attached to the tree, camouflaged by dead leaves and debris loosely covering it.

"Well, well, well, look what we have here," Beau remarked. "See what you can get from this, then send it along with Walter," Beau said.

They all knew this just changed the course of the investigation, and perhaps this was not the act of a trapped, deadly snake and a frantic woman, but a premeditated murder.

While Bruce was waiting for dispatch to provide information about the car owner, Beau resumed examining the car for any signs of foul play. He noticed that all the manual door locks had been removed, and someone had jammed them with some sort of compound. He recorded his findings and then yelled out to Bruce, "Hey, wanna take a crack at this back door and see whether you can get it open?"

"Sure thing," Bruce said, glad to be doing something instead of just standing around.

After several minutes, Bruce could hear the pop of the lock and slowly opened the back door, standing behind it in case there was another snake needing to escape. Walter stood nearby, ready with shovel in hand and cursing under his breath. Both were relieved there were no more surprise snake sightings. A CS investigator went in first to gather whatever evidence there might be.

"I found a handbag," he cried out. "It was tucked under the back seat."

The investigator placed the handbag on the hood of the car taking a series of pictures, then removed the remnants of the bag, one by one taking pictures of each of the contents.

"Here's a wallet. We'll get prints before we start removing anything."

Beau stood off to the side. He wanted to get right in there but knew he had to wait his turn. Pulling out a piece of chewing gum from his suit pocket, he unwrapped it meticulously, then placed it in his mouth, putting his toothpick back in his suit pocket for another time. As he slowly chewed, he looked down at the piece of foil wrapper. He first folded it in half and then rolled it up as tightly as possible. He did this whenever he felt nervous energy. The distraction gave him time to collect his thoughts. He had a gut feeling he knew to whom the handbag belonged to. The secret of the missing Barrington daughter was now partially solved, at least. He knew the news was going to be devastating for Oliver. He would have to choose his words carefully.

CS handed the wallet to Beau, who found the driver's license, which confirmed what he already suspected. Audra Barrington. There she was. A hopeful woman with a bright future now deprived of life.

"Audra Barrington?" Eddy said out loud. "Isn't she the woman who's been missing for a few months? This body doesn't look it's been in the water for any length of time."

Beau said, "Yeah, she's the one. Daughter of Oliver and Charlotte Barrington."

The search of the car's interior did not provide any further clues. There was no garbage, no cigarette butts; even the glove box housed only the car owner's manual. There was not even a box of tissues. The purse, too, held very little. It was a plain taupe leather clutch with a fold-over, envelope-style flap and snap closure. All the wallet contained was the driver's license, one credit card, a health insurance card, and a library card. Inside the purse was a hairbrush, comb, compact mirror, a couple of Band-Aids, and some Wrigley's Extra chewing gum. As one of the CS bagged and documented the purse and its contents, the other CS zipped the body bag closed, tagged it as AZ783H904F, and loaded it into a van.

"Beau, we're taking off now!" Doc shouted. "Given how late it is and the preparation we need to do with the body, why don't you stop by the lab around noon tomorrow? I should have some information for you by then."

Waving his hand in approval, Beau yelled out, "I'll see you then, Doc."

Beau surveyed the area once more and advised Bruce and Eddy to wait until the medical examiner and CS had gone.

Walking to the beginning of the tire tracks, Beau measured the distance to the water's edge. Then he walked over to where he found the winch and timed how long it took him to reach there. He recorded his results then radioed dispatch to give an update and that he was heading back to the station shortly.

Until he could get some answers from Doc, he would review the missing person report again. The Barrington family was a wealthy and well-known family in Charleston. Could this have been a kidnapping gone wrong? Beau kept coming back to that theory.

"Beau," Bruce yelled out. "We got confirmation that the car is registered to Oliver Barrington."

"Thanks, Bruce. I figured as much," Beau said.

Bruce and Eddy looked on as Walter did a final walk around the car that was now hooked up to the tow truck, checking the tow bar and chains to ensure all was securely fastened before towing the car to the lab for forensic testing. The winch had also been loaded onto the back of the truck, and, as Beau had suspected, a tow hook was on the end of the cable. Walter looked over at the men as he headed toward the driver's-side door of the truck.

"You're good to go, Walter, and thanks again for your help today with the snake."

"My pleasure. Hate the sons of bitches."

"We could tell. Drive safe, old man."

"I'll catch you good-for-nothin's later," Walter said grumbling.

"Have a good one, Walter," Bruce shouted back, his hand gesturing a farewell at the same time.

Intermittent raindrops started falling.

"Hey, Beau, you need us for anything more? Otherwise, we're heading back to the station."

"No, all good. I'm right behind you. See you back there," Beau said.

Bruce and Eddy got into the patrol car to head back to the station. They drove slowly down the gravel lane, their minds now consumed with the recent events of the day, their eyes also scouring the area with the last bit of daylight, looking for any clues that might now be important to the investigation.

When they reached the end of the lane, Eddy radioed dispatch to update their status. "Dispatch, this is car 216. We are leaving the location and heading back to the station."

Dispatch promptly responded. "Ten-four, 216."

After several minutes, Eddy broke the silence by saying, "Man, what a day this turned out to be."

"You got that right. I think today warrants an extra few brewskis tonight," Bruce said.

In a hurry to beat the rain, Beau realized they hadn't bagged the broken wooden cross. He put the car in reverse and backed up to the cottage. He would get this to Doc on his way to see the Barrington's.

What was uncovered today would certainly lead one to believe that the mystery of the missing Barrington was no longer a mystery. But Beau had a feeling the mystery was just heating up.

The questions started flying into his head, fast and furious. *Where have you been, Audra Barrington? Right here in Charleston? Right under our noses? Or were you brought back here? And if so, from where?*

## THREE MONTHS EARLIER - THURSDAY, MARCH 9, 1995

# THE DISAPPEARANCE OF AUDRA BARRINGTON

All eyes diverted to the man who entered the Charleston Police Department's front door. Dressed in a heather-gray Armani suit with a crisp white French-cut shirt, accented with a Salvatore Ferragamo blue silk tie, mother-of-pearl cuff links, and vintage Testoni leather lace-up shoes, he approached the front desk with an air, but not with arrogance. The overtly handsome man with a chiseled face, wavy raven-colored hair dappled with silver highlights, and intense blue eyes was no stranger to those in his view. Everyone in Charleston knew who the Barringtons were.

He approached the front desk. "My name is Oliver Barrington, and I would like to report a missing person," he said nervously, after clearing his throat.

Gerald Steinborn, the out-of-shape sergeant on desk duty that day, took immediate notice of the name and thought this would be better handled by a seasoned cop than a rookie, since this was the upper echelon of Charleston.

"Mr. Barrington, please have a seat. Someone will be right with you."

Oliver hooked a finger into the knot of his tie and gave a tug to loosen it. Taking a seat in the metal chair, he wiped his manicured hands on his Armani pants. Crossing his legs, he looked about, nervously wringing his hands until finally sensing his excessive behavior, he clutched his hands together, interlocking each finger, then placed them on his ever-so-slightly bouncing knee. He gazed around the drearily painted cinder-block walls, his eyes fixating on the wall clock that was overtly crooked. He had a strong urge to straighten it.

The sergeant walked back to Beau Crenshaw's office and poked his head inside.

"Hey, Oliver Barrington's here. Said he would like to report a missing person. He seems more on your pay grade, or do you want me to handle it?"

"Oliver Barrington? Missing person? Sure, I'll handle this," Beau said. "I'll be right out."

Gerald walked back into the waiting room observing the town celebrity sitting in front of him. He knew the customary facial expressions of someone who was deeply distraught. Oliver stood up, hands in his pant pockets, and paced back and forth.

"Someone will be right with you, Mr. Barrington. Can I get you anything to drink?" Gerald said as he rubbed his left eye.

"Thank you, no," Oliver said, dropping his gaze back to the floor.

Beau stood up from his desk, running his hands down the front of his body. Maybe his hands would iron away the many wrinkles. Taking a deep breath, he walked out of his office toward the waiting room. As he approached Oliver, he extended his large, rugged hand.

"Mr. Barrington, my name is Beau Crenshaw. Let me take you back to one of the interview rooms so we can talk about how I can help you today."

The two men walked in silence until Beau stopped at a room with a door and a glass window and said, "After you, Mr. Barrington. Please have a seat."

Beau closed the door, noticing the hint of a man's cologne that he knew would be well beyond his salary. Sitting across from Oliver, he launched into his rehearsed spiel.

"Can I get you anything to drink, Mr. Barrington?"

"No, I'm fine, but thank you for asking," Oliver said, noticing how sparse and cold the room was. Same off-white-painted concrete-block walls as the lobby, and an old beat-up wooden table accompanied by two equally aged chairs were the only furnishings in the room. *Not a place to comfort people. Criminals and people reporting missing loved ones should not have to share the same space,* he thought. There was a window, if only looking out into the hallway, but it at least broke the monotony.

"Mr. Barrington, how can I help you today?"

"I would like to report a missing person. My daughter, Audra."

"And how long has she been missing?"

"It appears to be from Thursday."

"Appears to be?"

"I got a call from her employer yesterday afternoon that she did not show up for work. They tried calling her throughout the day but got no answer. This is when they called me, as I'm her emergency contact number. They asked whether I knew of her whereabouts and whether she was okay. I said I hadn't heard from her but that I would go by her apartment. I drove there, but because I don't have a key, all I could do was bang on the door. The curtains were drawn, so I couldn't see inside the windows. Her car was gone. I stopped by the landlady's unit, but she was out. I left a note asking her to call me, but I haven't heard from her. I know there is a time you have to wait to file a missing person report, but I don't have a clue how long she has really been missing. They said she was at work on Tuesday."

"Is this why you waited until this morning to report her?"

Oliver's eyes looked about the room nervously.

"Why would you ask me such a stupid question? I don't have a rule book on missing people. Listen, I didn't mean to snap, but this is my daughter we're talking about."

Beau sat back in the chair knowing it didn't matter what the policy was for a missing person; when it came to Oliver Barrington, policy was going straight out the window, although Oliver likely didn't realize he was entitled to special privileges. Mr. Barrington was an influential man in Charleston, employing a good number of the townspeople, and his reputation preceded him as a generous and fair employer. His family also donated to many of the local charities.

Observing the distress in the man's eyes, Beau said, "We'll file a report today, since you don't really have the exact date she went missing. Let me get a clean tape in the recorder so we can begin."

Beau placed a new tape into the recorder, pressed record, and then said, "Testing, testing."

He rewound the tape and listened. "Testing, testing" replayed back to him clearly. Hitting record again, he said, "This is Thursday,

March ninth, at 8:52 a.m. I am here with Oliver Barrington, who is filing a missing person report. Let's get the minutiae out of the way. Oliver, can you please state your name for the record and provide your home address."

"My name is Oliver Barrington. My address is Sutherland's Crossing, 1102 Five Oaks Drive, Charleston."

"Mr. Barrington, you mentioned your daughter is missing. Can you please state her full name?"

"Audra Eileen Barrington."

"And her address?"

"1384 Tradd Street."

"Date of birth?"

"May 17, 1962."

"Okay, so she's thirty-three."

"Is she really? How time flies."

"Who does she work for, and who did you talk to?"

"She works full-time at the Newhaven Medical Clinic as a clinical psychiatrist. I talked to Lana Montgomery in HR."

Beau nodded his head as he said, "Impressive occupation. Now I need to get a description of her."

"Well, she's about 5 feet 6 inches, has straight dark shoulder-length hair, pale complexion, hazel-colored eyes, and weighs around 135 or 145 pounds. Dresses casually, mostly in jeans and T-shirts."

"Glasses?"

"No."

"Any skin markings, such as scars, birthmarks, piercings, tattoos?"

"None that I am aware of."

"Was she seeing anyone special?"

"She has never mentioned having a boyfriend and certainly has brought no one home to meet the family."

"Do you know the names of her friends?"

"No. Maybe her coworkers will know more about her private life and whether she was seeing someone. Audra never had many friends growing up and even as a young child, she was more of a loner, but surely now she has outgrown that."

"Mr. Barrington, Oliver, when was the last time you saw Audra, and why do you suspect she is missing? Do you believe this is a miscommunication with days off and she went away for a few days?"

"You'd have to ask her boss that question."

Oliver's posture was regal, but his hands were fidgety. They searched frantically over the perfectly manicured fingers knowing they would find that one loose piece of skin that could be worked on, pulled on, tugged on, and eventually ripped away. He was only semiconscious of his obsessive actions but knew enough to stop before he ripped the skin off, drawing blood to the open wound. His mind suddenly realized how embarrassing it would be for him to ask for a Band-Aid because he couldn't stop picking away at a hangnail. *Stop now,* he told himself, *enough.*

When Beau didn't proceed with another question, Oliver continued: "It's been about a week since I last saw her at a family dinner. My son Jamie was visiting from out of town. I'm not saying it's impossible but very unlike Audra to mix up her days. She's good about stuff like that. Not only is she one of the most organized people I know, but she also takes her job seriously. No, she wouldn't just fail to show up for work. I really wished I had asked her for a key now. Why didn't I ask her for a key? Something is wrong," Oliver said, lowering his head into his hands.

Quickly he became very agitated and told Beau to stop the tape. First slamming his fist down on the table, then getting up all while wagging his finger madly at Beau, he yelled, "You don't understand.

Get your thoughts away from my daughter just randomly not showing up for work. She's not like this. Don't you get what I am trying to tell you? She knows how important it is to keep a consistent routine with her patients. It could be detrimental to their well-being. These are people facing mental health issues. Audra chose the profession to help people. She is a qualified doctor. Missing appointments could kill her career and could kill somebody. She may have her quirks and be difficult, but she would not do this. This unexplained absence is way out of character for her. Something is wrong. Something is terribly wrong. Help me. Please help me."

Hastily Oliver regained his composure, sat down, and put his head in his hands, shaking his head back and forth. With a kind of moan, he said, "Detective, something is wrong. I can sense it. Something is terribly wrong."

Beau took the toothpick out of his mouth that had been placed there at the beginning of the interview and twirled it between his thumb and index finger. He spoke with compassion as he said, "Oliver, I understand this is very upsetting for you, and I am sorry I have to go through all this with you. There are going to be some tough questions ahead, but I have to ask them so we can determine what has happened here. I am coming into this blind, so I need to get as much information as possible so I can help you. We will do everything in our power to find your daughter. Do you need to take a few minutes, or are you ready to proceed?"

Oliver motioned to carry on.

Beau paused for a moment, giving Oliver enough time to settle, turned the tape back on, and then said, "So, tell me about the last time you saw her. Did you notice anything different about her? Did she seem withdrawn or aloof? Was she agitated at all?"

"Dinner started at around 5 p.m., and she likely left around 8:30 or

9. She seemed her normal self. There were no outbursts. Audra adores Jamie, so that's the only reason she came. Come to think of it, that was the last time I spoke with her. Sometimes we talk on the phone."

"Is she close with anyone else in the family? Does she talk on the phone regularly with her mother or her siblings? And I've noticed you've mentioned the word 'difficult' a few times now. What do you mean by this? Difficult, as in . . ."

"Just personality differences with her other siblings and her mother. So no, I doubt she talks with them at all unless she has to. Well, Jamie, yes, but the rest, no. Ruby, our nanny, or nanny when the kids were young, still lives with us. She may have heard from her. All the kids adore Ruby. And I mean difficult, as she has a habit of starting arguments about how pretentious Charlotte and Abby are. Abby's her twin sister. Audra is not one for showboating. In fact, she is quite the opposite, so she sees her mother's and sister's behaviors as gluttonous and shallow. She has a sharp tongue with them, especially with her mother and, well, actually her brother Richmond as well, but she leaves him alone for the most part. Get-togethers can become heated and sometimes explosive. She's not into money and hates what it does to people, what it turns people into. She gets along well with Jamie and his wife because they are more like her. They lead simple lives and follow their passions instead of caring about what other people think. Audra is more into helping those less fortunate, especially animals. She's passionate about animals. And I'm not saying the fights are all her fault. Her mother and siblings are shallow and pretentious."

"How is your relationship with Audra?"

"I like to think it's good, but she's never really been one to open up to me. We meet sometimes for lunch or dinner, just her and me. I try to see her as often as she will allow, but I'm caught in the middle."

"Who initiates the phone calls?" Beau asked.

"I do, mostly."

"I see," Beau said. "You mentioned her car is missing. What is the make and model?"

"It is a 1991 four-door Mercedes-Benz S-Class sedan. I bought one for each of the girls when they graduated from college."

"If she's not into material things, did she not balk at you giving this to her?" Beau questioned.

"I think she had a better time accepting it because it came from me. I told her it would make me happy if she just accepted it graciously and that when she was ready to replace it, she could just donate it."

"That's an expensive car, the kind that makes a statement. Do you know whether anyone gave her a hard time about that?"

"What do you mean? Why would anyone give her a hard time about a car?" Oliver remarked.

"Well, most kids coming out of college don't drive Mercedes-Benz S-Class sedans or have a high-priced family name. People have been known to be jealous for less."

"Jealous? Enough to hurt my daughter? What the hell are you insinuating? That someone would take her because she drives a Mercedes? There are plenty of Mercedes in this town, if you hadn't noticed," Oliver said, rubbing his fingers across his forehead.

"We need to explore all options. We'll put out a statewide APB on the car. I'll need to get the tag number. Now let's move on to the next question. Does your daughter have any health concerns or allergies to anything?"

"Not that I'm aware of."

"Are you aware of any medication she may be taking?"

Turning his head away, Beau put his arm over his mouth to cough. "Pardon me. The air is dry in here."

"None that I am aware of."

"Now, this next question may stir you up a bit, Mr. Barrington, but I have to ask. Have you ever suspected that your daughter might take any kind of social drugs, or could she have a drinking problem?"

"I've seen her drink the occasional cocktail or two, but I can't say I have ever seen her drunk or suspected her of being involved in drugs. I never just drop in at her apartment, so I've not caught her off guard, but certainly any time we have met up, she never appeared intoxicated. This was never an issue when she was a teenager or a young adult. She was always a studious child and did not cause her mother or me any grief by partying or getting into trouble that way. And as a psychiatrist, she can write prescriptions. I'm not sure whether that is relevant to you or not."

"It's all relevant, Mr. Barrington. Have you noticed any recent changes in her behavior?"

"No, she's not a basket case, and if that's the impression I have given you, then it's incorrect. She just speaks her mind is all. And my wife can be, well she can be . . . a bitch at times."

"Any idea about her finances? Would you have any reason to suspect she was having financial issues? Any kind of expensive addictions? People she owed money to?"

"I have no reason to believe any of that. She makes good money at her job. I take care of her car maintenance. Well, that and her car insurance. It's just easier, as I have a service contract at the dealership, so I have both of my daughters take their cars there, and then the dealership just sends me the bill. As for the insurance, I have a group plan. It's the least I can do. Do you think this is about money? I think I would have some clue if she had an addiction of some sort. The gossip in this town spreads like wildfire, and if Charlotte heard even a hint of anything, she would shut it down in a heartbeat.

Staying on top is what Charlotte lives for. Plus, all my kids have stock portfolios that are quite substantial. I started buying from the time they were infants, so I can't see this being about money. She could tap into this at any time. It's in her own name."

"What about her job? Have you met any of her coworkers?"

Oliver's eyes suddenly shifted to the wall clock above the door in the interview room. This was crooked as well, same as the lobby.. *What is it about this place that they can't have anything straight,* he thought, then looked back toward Beau before speaking.

"No. She keeps things to herself about her work, and since doctor-patient confidentiality is critical, I tend not to ask her much. I have met a couple of coworkers in passing but just to say hi."

"You said Audra works at Newhaven Medical Center, correct? This is the one on Lancaster Street?"

"That's the one."

"I'll contact them for more information," Beau said reaching over and taking a sip of coffee. He shifted in his chair as he set the cup back down.

Beau took down more notes before continuing: "I know you said you don't talk with Audra much about her job, but do you recall her even casually mentioning that she was bothered by any of her patients or felt threatened in any way?"

"I don't recall her ever saying anything like that."

"Has there been any type of upset in your family life recently? The death of a grandparent or close friend?"

"Is this really necessary? Asking these types of questions? We are wasting time here. Who cares whether anyone died recently in our family? I mean, seriously. What in the hell does that have to do with Audra being missing? Shouldn't you get started looking for her?"

"We will, we will. Has she ever gone missing before?"

"No. She would go silent for days at a time by not answering the phone, but I am not aware of her missing work. This seemed to be the one area where she was thriving. Where are we going with this line of questioning?" Oliver asked.

"The more we know, the more we know where to look," Beau said.

"I don't feel like this is getting us anywhere," Oliver said.

"Could anyone want to hurt you or your family? Have you ever had any kidnapping attempts or threats made against you or your family? Could this be related to your business in any way?"

"No. Never. I can't think of any enemies we have. I am a home builder and employ many people. We pay them well, and I make sure they have plenty of time off to enjoy their lives. As far as I'm aware, we have an excellent reputation in the industry. That's always been important to me, to treat people well. I know Audra can be a little terse, but I certainly don't think it enough to be harmed by anyone, and she has nothing to do with my business. She never had a keen sense of business or an interest in home building. Oh my God! Do you think this is what happened? Do you think someone kidnapped her or harmed her because of me? No one's contacted me. Right now, I'm very confused. I'm having a hard time even formulating a thought. I'm sorry. This is all too much to take in. Can I get a glass of water?"

"Of course. I'll be right back," Beau said.

Beau picked up his notepad, got up, and headed to the staff kitchen area, all the while thinking about the family. Everyone in town knew who Charlotte Barrington was. She pranced around as if she were the queen of the city, and everyone should be grateful to be in her presence. Beau knew more about Abby, Audra's twin sister since she was a defense attorney. He had been in the courtroom a time or two when she was defending a client. Beau did not want to rule out kidnapping or even some kind of blackmail, but what kind?

Beau returned to the interview room and set the glass of water in front of Oliver.

"Here you go, Oliver."

"Thank you, Beau."

"Okay, so let's return to what we were last talking about. We can't rule out anything at this early stage, but in my experience, most kidnappers would have called by now with ransom demands."

Beau leaned back in his chair, toothpick situated just so in his mouth, put his two hands behind his head, and let his mind sort through his mental dictionary, deciding on the best words to use.

"How is your business doing? Is it suffering in any way? Any colorful characters you're involved with? Do you owe them money? Could this be used as a way of getting your attention?"

"I can't believe you would suggest that I would have anything to do with unscrupulous people. We aren't the mob, and we don't do business with mobsters. This is about my missing daughter, not my business practices."

"What about hobbies? We could check groups in the area that may know her and have seen her recently."

Before Oliver answered, he looked down at his hands again and suddenly realized the trauma his fingers were trying to do to this one lone piece of flesh. He immediately linked his hands together and placed them on the table. In plain view, the fingers would be better behaved.

"No, I am not aware of anything. She just never talks about her personal life. I've been such an absent father. I will do anything, absolutely anything, to see her again, to have another chance at being her father, and a good one this time."

"All right, you've given me plenty to work with, Mr. Barrington. Do you have a recent picture of her with you? Or I can get one tomorrow when I speak with your wife and children. I'll alert all officers to be on the lookout for a woman matching her description. I would like to interview your wife and other children in the morning, if that's possible."

"Of course. What time were you thinking so I can make sure their schedules are freed up?"

"Why don't we say tomorrow at 9 a.m.? I could meet them here at the station or come by your residence."

"I will see whether that works for them and get back to you. They will probably want to meet at the house, if it's not too much of an imposition for you."

"No imposition at all. So, Abby and Richmond still live at home?"

"For now. And Abby just until the wedding, and then she and Sterling will be moving into their new house."

With that, Beau stopped the tape, hit the rewind button, and looked up at Oliver with the same expression a father gives a child when telling him or her the family pet has passed away.

"Mr. Barrington, please understand that we will do everything we can to find your daughter. Many times, it turns out to be a false alarm, and there is a very simple explanation. Let's hope this is one of those times and she just needed to blow off some steam or that some wires got crossed about her days off."

At that, Beau got up from his chair, moved to the other side of the table where Oliver was sitting, put his hand on his shoulder, and said, "What we will do now is go around to her place of employment and her apartment. We will get the landlord to let us inside, since you filed a formal report, and interview anyone who knows her to determine where and when she was last seen. Contact me if you can think of anything else that may help our investigation. We'll stay in touch, and please let us know the minute she turns up. Here is my business card so you can get back to me about tomorrow. You can call me day or night. I'm here to help you get through this. Do you have any further questions?"

Oliver shook his head.

"I'll walk you out," Beau said. As he patted Oliver on his back, he uttered more reassuring words. "Truly, we will do everything we can to find your daughter. Have faith that she'll turn up soon. Oh, and one more thing. For tomorrow, I'd like to meet with Ruby as well."

"Of course."

The two men walked silently down the hallway to the front entrance of the precinct. Oliver turned and extended his hand to Beau, and as they shook hands, Oliver thanked Beau.

As Oliver headed to the front door, Beau turned around and returned to the interview room. Already his wheels were turning. Beau found it odd that he needed to book appointments with the rest of the family about a missing daughter and sibling.

He made a note of this. And where was Charlotte Barrington, anyway? Why was she not here with her husband? Oliver looked like a lost soul just going through the motions of life.

He took the cassette out of the recorder and stuck it into his suit pocket. He gathered the forms, getting them ready to walk over to Gerald so he could input the data into the computer and put out an APB on the car. Running his fingers through his hair, he slowly turned about, and as he made his way back to his desk, his mind began racing with a million thoughts. Nothing about this missing woman seemed logical to him, but then, crime was not logical.

Why did he just think crime? There was no proof the woman was in harm's way, just missing.

The chime sounded on the front door of the police station as Oliver Barrington exited the building. For a moment, Beau gazed in the sound's direction as he continued to gather his thoughts on his next move. Then he heard a loud, angry voice and ran toward the entrance. Grabbing open the door, there stood Larry confronting Oliver. Beau knew exactly who this person was.

Larry, who looked as if he were in his seventies but was probably in his fifties, was an overzealous woody character running lean on the mental aptitude scale. A sour, pungent odor emanated from his person, and his fermented breath was brazen and intolerable. This was a man who had not showered or changed his clothes for weeks, possibly months.

He had no teeth to speak of, or at least any white ones visible to the naked eye. If there were teeth in his mouth, they'd darken to a point of non-distinction similar to that of rotting fruit. To tell this person his presence was indescribably offensive was to no avail, as he felt no social responsibility to act in such a manner that others would find somewhat congruous.

Lacking the ability to pick up on social cues meant he moved forward in life, attached only to his world of victimization and not to any acceptance of choice or modification. Evolution to him dated back to dinosaurs and cavemen, to days where having a bath was not required just the odd splash of water here and there. To say he felt great disdain for mankind would be an understatement. Everyone dreaded and was incensed at the very idea of having to tolerate him. He took this as an opportunity to parade his garish ways to annoy people. He was the town drunk whom almost everyone knew, never talked about, and almost always avoided.

"Get outta my way, you no-good piece of shit," Larry said, lashing out at Oliver, who stood there dumbfounded. "Look at you in your high-class suit strutting around like you own the place. You nearly ran me over. Sorry bastard you are. Next time watch where you're going. Fuckin' asshole."

At that, Larry spit on Oliver's shoes.

"Hey, hey, hey!" Beau yelled out. "That'll be enough of that! Get the hell out of here, Larry, before I throw your ass in jail."

"You can fuck off, too, pig. Bunch of worthless assholes," Larry said barking the words as he stumbled away from the two men.

"God almighty. That's the first time I've seen him this riled. Are you okay?"

"Yes, I'm fine. He just ran up to me and started yelling obscenities. I know I've seen him around before but had no altercations with him. I thought he was just a harmless vagrant."

"Well, if you ask me, he's suffering from some PTSD, or all those years of drinking finally caught up with him. Are you sure you're okay?"

"Yes, I'm good. I'll talk to you tomorrow."

Oliver, still shaken, headed in the opposite direction from Larry. Beau stepped back inside to get started on his hunt for Audra. He took out his notebook and jotted down his next steps.

They would start at her apartment and then interview the people at her workplace. It was going to be a long night, but Beau didn't care and knew Kathleen wouldn't, either. She was used to his unusual work schedule. He remembered when she used to leave his dinner in the fridge; the plate would be wrapped neatly in cellophane, and there would be a note on top telling him how long to warm it up. There would also be a place setting for one at the dining room table, so all he had to do was reheat and enjoy. These days there wasn't so much as leftovers in a Tupperware dish. How strange that he couldn't recall when the shift occurred.

Time was of the essence now, as a missing person's first forty-eight hours are critical in generating awareness, following up on potential leads, and preserving any evidence that may be crucial to the investigation. Only the future held the answers to today's questions. The truth lay silent behind the veil, and with each passing second, the tightly woven story would begin to unravel.

## THURSDAY, MARCH 9, 1995

# THE SEARCH BEGINS

Beau walked out of his office and into the squad room. He looked around at who was available to ride with him, and his eyes landed on the new recruit. He decided the kid could use the experience and a break from the ever-growing pile of paperwork on his desk.

"Hey, Simon," Beau said. "You're coming with me to check out a missing person."

"Sure thing," Simon stammered back, grateful at the opportunity to get away from his desk.

Simon had graduated three months earlier, spending his time doing ride-alongs and paperwork with the other four classmates with whom he graduated. At 5 foot 8 inches and only 145 pounds, his skeletal frame made him prime pickings for constant teasing. This, along with his red hair, freckles, and a face that would turn as red as a tomato whenever he became even slightly emotional, meant he remained the brunt of their pranks and entertainment. He took it all in jest to try to fit in. It wasn't that he ever had his heart set on being a cop, but when the opportunity opened up that the police department was looking for new recruits, he decided it was worth exploring.

"Where you from, kid?" Beau asked on their drive to Audra's apartment.

"Detroit."

"How did you land here?"

"I was dating a woman, and she wanted out of Detroit, so she picked Charleston."

"A woman, huh? That'll get you every time."

"Well, she broke up with me not long after, but I decided to stay, anyway. I don't miss the winters."

"You're too young to have a ball and chain. Go have some fun. There'll be plenty of time for women. Do you know who the Barringtons are?"

"Should I?"

"Well, they have a lot of money and even more clout in this town. Oliver Barrington's a housebuilder and built himself this massive estate called Sutherland's Crossing. If you haven't seen it, you should take a drive by. It's quite the place. He's fairly down-to-earth, but I've heard his wife is a real piece of work. I don't know that personally, just what I've heard. Oliver has filed a missing person on his daughter Audra. Don't you think it's odd that the mother, Charlotte, didn't come with him to the station?"

"Sure, I guess."

"Well, I do. Anyway, we're gonna go check out Audra's apartment and talk with the landlord. Her car and she haven't been seen since Friday."

Simon shook his head in agreement. He knew he should be asking a million questions, but he didn't know the first thing about missing person cases, so he stayed quiet.

As they turned onto Kensington Avenue, they passed by magnificent Victorian homes whose landscaped grounds were works of art and nearly as stunning as the homes they surrounded, creating intimate and serene settings. Ornate wrought iron fences wrapped around the yards' boundaries and finished at the homes' entrances, where a more extravagantly ornamental iron gate completed the look—wrought iron, one of downtown Charleston's signature features, could be found everywhere and in every design pattern imaginable. Beau slowed the car to a crawl, looking for the address, which was at the end of the dead-end street, the rental property taking up most of the cul-de-sac. They turned left into the parking spaces and parked in the one marked Visitors.

The street was filled with character and history, but their destination was completely devoid of those qualities. This is where the enchantment ended. What was once a spectacular Victorian structure had been dissected, built on to, and degraded into multiple housing units. The landscaping was mediocre at best, and much of what was once grassed areas had been trampled over time, leaving blotches of bare dirt. Nothing stood out. The place was in dire need of a can of paint (or two), and it looked as if the handyman had given up caring long ago.

"Oliver said she drives a 1991 four-door Mercedes S-Class sedan. I'm not seeing it here. Are you, Simon?"

"No, sir, I'm not."

"There's the landlord's apartment. We'll start there."

It took quite a few knocks before Mrs. Woolenstock opened the door and stared at them for a few long moments. She was a woman appearing to be in her seventies, and from the tousled hair and groggy expression, it appeared they had woken her from a nap. Beau figured she must have been a stunner as a young woman, as even with her now aging skin, she was attractive with a captivating classiness. For a split second, Beau's curious mind wondered how this elegant creature ended up being a landlady, especially at her age. What travesty of life had diminished her to this?

"Ma'am, I'm Detective Beau Crenshaw, and this is police Constable Simon Miller." He held up his detective's badge for proper identification. "We are investigating a missing person—Audra Barrington. Do you have a key for her apartment?"

It took Mrs. Woolenstock a moment to take in what she had just heard and then spoke almost in a whisper. "Oh my. Audra? Missing?" She then reached for her glasses, which were on a chain around her neck. Putting them on, she leaned in and glided her index finger over Beau's credentials on his badge. Seemingly satisfied, she gazed away. Her brain calculated the last time she had seen Audra. Was it yesterday? The day before? Four days ago? Longer?

"Ma'am, can you please give us the key?" Beau said, pressing.

His voice brought Mrs. Woolenstock back to the present moment.

"Oh, my dear, yes," she said. "Of course, I will get you the key. This is all very shocking. Audra's missing. She is a delightful woman. Never a problem with her. If only all tenants could be like Audra. Hold on one moment. I'll be right back."

Mrs. Woolenstock shuffled off and returned after a short time, handing over a key with the number 1384 etched into it. As she placed it in Beau's hand, she said, "Just take a left from here, and it is the fifth apartment on the left. They all have their own entrance. I'll be here if you need anything more."

"Thank you, ma'am. We'll have it back to you soon. In the meantime, please don't mention this to anyone," Beau said.

# FOLLOWING THE BREADCRUMBS

As Beau and Simon walked over to Audra's apartment, Beau broke the silence by saying, "You know, Simon, the landlady was clearly surprised about the disappearance, which suggests she witnessed no commotion in the last few days. Remember that, remember to observe everyone you are talking to when investigating a case. Sometimes it's the outsiders who put the story together."

Simon looked at Beau intently, taking in his first lesson and nodding his head, acknowledging he understood.

"Now," Beau said as they continued walking, "what do you see, Simon?"

"Wh-what do I see, sir?"

"Yeah, what do you see? What does the place look like? If you had to describe it, what would you say? This is important. If you're going to be a good cop, even a detective someday, you need to hone your skills of observation."

"Oh, okay, sir," Simon said babbling. "Well, I see that all the apartments have the same features, three steps up to the front door, plain wrought iron handrails on either side of the steps, and plain shutters on all windows."

Pausing a moment, Simon looked around and then continued: "I see faded awnings over most of the doors, and it looks like some people have tried to spruce up the look with potted plants or a door wreath, but Audra's has none of these. This property looks plain and rather neglected compared with the homes we passed on the rest of the street. I wonder why she would choose to live here, given all her money."

"Good work, Simon. Yes, a neglected look indeed, but don't you think she lives here because she is fighting against her wealth?"

"I guess."

Before using the key for entry, they banged loudly on the door several times. After a few minutes, Beau put the key in the lock and opened the door wide.

"Charleston PD! Anyone here?" Beau yelled out.

There was no response, so they continued.

It didn't take long for them to suspect foul play from the scene before them.

From the front door, they could see nobody nor detect the odious stench of a decaying corpse, but perhaps it was too early in the putrefaction process for the odors to permeate the room.

The recruit was taken aback. His first three months were traffic violations and a few drunk-and-disorderly calls, but this was the real deal.

"Well, well, Simon. What do we have here?" Beau said, throwing a pair of latex gloves at Simon, and started putting on his own. "I would say this goes beyond being just a messy housekeeper, wouldn't you, kid?"

"You got that right, sir," Simon said as he gazed, dumbfounded, not quite registering the sight before him. "I've never seen anything like this, sir. Everything's been thrown around. Do you suspect someone kidnapped her? Is this why there's stuff everywhere?"

"That's what we're gonna find out, kid."

"Sir, yes, sir," Simon replied and almost immediately felt ridiculous saying it so sharp and forcefully as if he were a fresh recruit and Beau was his sergeant major. Thank goodness he had not given a salute. *Get a grip, Simon,* he thought.

"We need to check the apartment to see whether anyone is here first. Don't touch anything."

"Yes, sir."

Simon followed a few feet behind Beau.

"Nothing here on the main floor. Let's check upstairs. Don't touch the rail," Beau said as he surveyed the area.

"Yes, sir."

The upstairs was upended, similar to the downstairs, but no body was found.

"Kid, radio dispatch and have them send over a forensics team. Tell them to tape off the entire width of the apartment and out to the sidewalk until they clear the area. Got it?" Beau said authoritatively.

"Got it, sir," Simon said as he set about calling dispatch from his portable radio. His chest puffed up and his voice became more assertive as he spoke into the mike, saying, "Dispatch, Officer Simon Miller here with Detective Beau Crenshaw at 1384 Tradd Street. I repeat, 1384 Tradd Street. We are requesting a forensics team for possible foul play in a missing person investigation."

Simon was secretly hoping the other officers were also listening on the radio in awe of his being out on a real-deal detective case with Crude Crenshaw. Maybe then their ribbing of him might lighten up now. Then again, maybe not.

While Simon was handling the request, Beau got the tape recorder ready to start the preliminary investigation. He waited for Simon to finish before proceeding. He got a kick out of the kid repeating the address. He must have seen that on a cop show.

Beau looked directly into Simon's eyes and said, "You're about to receive your second lesson in investigative work, which is to treat everything as if it were a crime scene. Therefore, treat everything as evidence. Look for things that don't make sense. This means we will proceed cautiously so as not to destroy or contaminate anything that could be evidence. Don't touch anything unless you absolutely have to, do you understand? Oh, and do you have the camera ready to take pictures? I have some markers we can put around for anything we want forensics to focus on."

Simon looked wide-eyed at Beau and started to say, "Sir, yes, sir," but caught himself on the last "sir," making the reply more of a "sir yesses." Beau chuckled and thought to himself how the kid looked as if he were about to pass out. But he had to give him credit for his enthusiasm.

"Now," he said, "you must remember from the academy that we generally use one of the four specialized search patterns: strip, grid, spiral, and quadrant. Right? The specific pattern depends on the topography and size of the search area. Right? Now, for a house, what do we use?"

Simon was quick on his feet, remembering this well. "The quadrant or zone pattern is often used, meaning we will move from room to room together and cover an area before moving on to the next."

"Excellent, kid," Beau replied. "Let's go."

# THE SCENE INSIDE

The apartment was a two-story with two bedrooms and a full bathroom on the second floor, while on the first floor, there were a kitchen, living room, dining room, half bathroom, and a laundry/storage area in the rear. Almost immediately inside the front foyer were the stairs to the second floor, with an ornately designed, solid wood banister creating a masterpiece of intrinsic sculpted wood, and then a long, narrow hallway on the right led to the other main-floor rooms. Wood trim, crown molding, and high ceilings created texture and added character to the design. Once careful thought and pride had created the apartment's stylish existence before others later became determined to bastardize it, removing its glory and shaming it down, all for greed. Off the living room, a pair of French doors opened to a quaint patio and small grassed area. The completely fenced backyard had one gate opening, so the landscaper could have easy access to cut the grass.

"We will start upstairs and work our way back. Just keep taking pictures, kid. The more pictures, the better, and don't touch the handrail."

As their feet planted on the second-floor landing, Simon said sheepishly, "That poor woman. I hope she's all right. I hope she's not dead somewhere."

"Let's not jump to conclusions, now," Beau said, knowing he needed to rein in Simon's assumptions. "Good investigation means that you never assume anything. Let's start in the back bedroom and work our way forward."

The back bedroom was being used as an office. Simon started snapping photos of the desk drawers that had been opened, and of the papers strewn about. The bookshelf was knocked over, along with the desk chair and a pole light. What few items were on the bookshelf now lay scattered across the floor; the CD stereo with broken knobs and a cracked face lay innocently victimized, surrounded by a few CDs, some in and some out of their cases.

"Looks more like someone was looking for something than a tussle," Beau said.

Both men walked into the next room, which appeared to be Audra's bedroom.

"I agree, sir, someone was definitely looking for something. Every drawer is open, and all the clothes have been taken out. This just doesn't look like an argument with a boyfriend to me, sir. And is it me, or does there not appear to be a lot of clothes? I mean, she was a woman, after all. No disrespect, but most women I know have closets full of clothes. My last girlfriend sure did. Most of the U-Haul movin' here was her clothes."

"Good observation, Simon, but not all women are like that and she was living a minimalist lifestyle. I imagine this would have an effect on her wardrobe. But you're right, though, something like this would indicate that someone was looking for something. We don't want to rule out kidnapping even if no one has made a ransom demand yet. It's possible the kidnappers broke in, grabbed her, grabbed some of her clothes knowing they may have her for a few days, and scoured the place looking for money or jewelry, thinking that because she is a Barrington, she should have expensive items lying around. All things to consider."

"Seems reasonable, sir, but there was no forced entry."

"Good catch, Sherlock. You might actually make a decent detective someday, although we haven't checked the back door. Watch a few more cop shows and keep observing. Let's head to the bathroom next."

In the bathroom, Simon continued taking pictures. A toothbrush, toothpaste, makeup, and other personal-care items, such as shampoo and conditioner, remained in place.

"Look here, sir," Simon said. "There are two gold rings on the sink's ledge behind the electric toothbrush—one looks like a ruby, and the other has a pearl with diamonds around it. A burglar or kidnapper wouldn't leave these behind, would they?"

"No, they wouldn't. Look for any male products. We need to find out whether she was seeing anyone. And the garbage, Simon, is a great place to start. Never miss an opportunity to look through some trash."

A yell from downstairs announced the arrival of the forensics team. Beau walked to the top of the stairs.

"Hey, we're looking around upstairs, so why don't you guys start on the main floor."

A "Roger that" came from below, and he turned around, walking back into the bathroom.

Beau picked up the wastebasket and set it on the vanity counter.

Taking out his tweezers, he started sifting through the trash. There were a few tissues, a soap wrapper, and then he found it.

"An empty pregnancy-test package. No actual pregnancy test itself, but the box is enough to arouse suspicion. Well, well. Maybe she was seeing someone after all. What did I tell you, Simon? Trash cans are gold mines. Place a marker here, kid."

Simon smiled back at Beau, proud to be present during the "find." Boy, would he have some stories to tell the guys back at the station.

After finishing upstairs, they moved slowly back down the stairs, still careful not to touch the banister and steering clear of the forensics team as it scurried around dusting and gathering fibers.

Beau and Simon moved in unison to the living room. "You know, sir, the apartment is clean and organized, other than everything being tossed around."

"Oliver did say she was organized. Not everyone's into money, and according to her father, she wasn't much into material things, which would explain why there's not a lot of stuff, but you know what I find odd? I'm not seeing any personal photos of Audra, or anyone else, for that matter. And you know something else, Simon? I'm not seeing any mail, magazines, crossword puzzles, barely even a book. Given her profession, it seems odd that Audra would not have a library of books. Maybe she keeps them in her office? Maybe she stays there to read? And in all my years of detective work, one thing is usually present in a person's home, and that is a photo of someone. It might be in a fancy frame or stuck onto the fridge door with a magnet. It could be just a loose photo, but here? Nothing. Did you see a purse or phone anywhere?"

"No, sir. I haven't."

"Me, neither. That's odd, and kidnappers would have taken the car. They know they can't use her credit cards because those can be traced, so why take her purse? We need to check the back door to see whether there was any forced entry. If not, and they came in the front door, why lock the door behind you?"

As Simon and Beau moved from the living room to the dining room, the crunching of broken glass under their feet, they continued to look for clues, but as with the living room, other than the furniture's being upended, there was no other evidence present. Walking to the kitchen, Beau's eyes immediately fixated on the kitchen table, while Simon snapped pictures of the contents of the kitchen cupboards, opening every cupboard and drawer; even pulling the wastebasket out from under the sink to dissect its contents. He wanted to be the one to find the prize this time, if there was one.

"Sir, there isn't anything in the trash. Just an empty plastic bread bag, dried-up tea bags, and a rotting orange," Simon said, the disappointment clear in his voice.

"Roger that. Come over here, then," Beau mumbled. He was transfixed by the kitchen table. "See here? Looks like blood smeared on the tabletop. Question is, is this her blood?"

Beau raised his head to look over at the kitchen counter, then moved toward the sink. "Interesting. No knives or food on the counter or kitchen table to indicate she was chopping some food and cut herself. In fact, no food on the counter at all. Paper cut? Hang nail? Put a marker here."

"Now that you think about it, there are a lot of ways you could cut yourself, and maybe it's not her blood? Maybe she clawed at whoever was attacking her."

Beau looked back at the kitchen cupboards that barely had any food in them or dishes and opened the fridge door. It had a few essentials, such as eggs, milk, butter, pickles, and orange juice, but that was about it.

"Not much food here at all. Did she eat out a lot or at someone else's house? The guy that inspired the pregnancy test, perhaps?" Beau turned back to the contents of the table.

"Simon, bring a marker over here and put it beside this note. Check this out."

Beau had begun reading a folded-up newspaper that was open to the classified section. This was the only sign of a publication they had found. An ad read, "For Sale—Rare Richard Edwards Pair of Chippendale Side Chairs, Martin Jugiez, 1770-75. Will accept all reasonable offers over $18,000. Contact Audra today!" On top of the ad was a Post-it note with the name Joshua Sarkis, dealer; a phone number; and the comment "interested in chairs. Call between 10 and 2."

"Definitely someone of interest to have a chat with," Beau said.

Could this be the reason for her disappearance, he thought? Did someone call her about the chairs, knowing they were going to steal them from her, and then things went south? He walked back into the dining room and living room and then circled around back to the kitchen. No Richard Edwards chairs were visible anywhere. Maybe they were in storage? Did she have a storage unit, then? Did she meet the wrong person at her storage unit?

"Simon, when we get back to the office, find out whether Audra was renting a storage unit anywhere."

"Will do, sir."

This could be a crucial piece of evidence. Beau hadn't ruled out a kidnapping or a disgruntled patient, but now the expensive chairs needed to be added to the list. Beau was no antiques dealer, but he had lived in historic Charleston long enough to know a thing or two about the trade, and chairs like those could fetch well over $40,000.

The members of the forensics team continued to scurry about the apartment like squirrels gathering nuts, being sure not to overlook anything. They were forewarned that this was the daughter of Oliver and Charlotte Barrington, so everyone was put on high alert to do better than the best.

Before Beau and Simon headed back to talk to the landlady, they went out the French doors and into the fenced-in patio area.

"Simon, notice how the door was unlocked? Anyone could have easily come in through the back gate and entered the apartment from these doors, then. There's a service laneway running behind all the buildings, so no one would necessarily have noticed anything suspicious. So far, we have a possible theft of two expensive chairs or a kidnapping. It's a long shot, but let's check for any surveillance cameras in the back alley. Then we'll go back to Mrs. Woolenstock. Maybe she's woken up enough to give us some answers."

## THURSDAY, MARCH 9, 1995

# MRS. WOOLENSTOCK

Beau knocked loudly on the landlady's door, and it took about the same amount of time for her to answer the second time around. He suspected he was disturbing yet another attempt at a nap she was so desperately trying to get in. On the third knock, she answered, looking disheveled like before.

Before speaking, Beau removed his hat. "Ma'am, may we please come in and ask you a few questions?"

Running her hands through her hair to get all the loose strands back into a coiffed appearance, she replied, "Of course, come in." Mrs. Woolenstock gestured with her hand, leading them to the living room. "Please have a seat. Can I get you gentlemen something to drink? Some sweet tea, perhaps?" she offered.

"Yeah, I could use something to drink, and I bet Simon could, too. Thank you, ma'am."

Personalizing the situation as if a person were an invited guest allowed people to relax and talk more openly.

As Mrs. Woolenstock shuffled off to the kitchen, Beau looked about the room, noticing that his initial assessment of this woman was likely correct. He felt as if she came from money at some point, but that something happened to reduce her to a landlady. Death? Divorce? A falling-out with the family? The lighting, furnishings, and rugs looked antique and expensive, things Beau could never afford but could admire from afar in other people's homes. She definitely had a room filled with much to appreciate, especially the oil paintings, which looked to be from the early 1800s, with thick, ornate gold frames that gave them away as priceless antiques. The frames were designed to validate the importance of the artwork they enclosed, as such sophisticated frames declared their value. Beau hoped she had this treasure insured. Always thinking like a cop. He found her story intriguing and wondered whether he would ever get the chance to hear it.

Mrs. Woolenstock returned to the room, placing a silver serving tray on the coffee table that held two tall hand-cut crystal Baccarat glasses of sweet tea and a plate of Benne Wafers, a classic in Charleston.

Beau looked up and smiled.

"Please help yourself, gentlemen. I just made the wafers this morning and thought you might be feeling a bit peckish," Mrs. Woolenstock said as she sat down.

Simon was starved and wanted to jump right in, but he took his cue from Beau.

"Thank you, ma'am. We appreciate it." Beau reached over and took a wafer. Simon followed suit. "Now, for the record, I'm going to turn on my tape recorder while I ask you a few questions. I find this helps with my record-keeping, and then I can go back and listen to it again in case something jumps out at me later that didn't before. Are you okay with this, Mrs.?" Beau asked.

"Mrs. Woolenstock, but please call me Clara."

"Clara, excellent. You don't mind if I record this, do you?" Beau didn't wait for an answer, turning the tape recorder on record and setting it on the coffee table.

He took a sip of his sweet tea before returning to the task at hand. "Mrs. Woolen—Clara, when was the last time you saw Audra Barrington?"

"Well, you know, Detective," Clara said, "I was trying to think back to the last time I saw her, and I want to say it was about five days ago. My mind isn't as sharp as it once was, but I believe it was five days ago. She's a private person, so I see her only once in a while, a delightful woman and nothing like that wretched mother of hers. We do chat on rent day, which she always drops off a few days before, or sometimes I run into her in the parking lot. Audra is an excellent tenant, and I have never had any complaints about her. She's very quiet and works a lot or at least her car is gone all day, and she often doesn't return home until early evening. I notice these things, you know." Mrs. Woolenstock gazed away as she murmured, "Oh, I hope nothing terrible has happened to her."

"How long has Audra lived here?"

"Let's see. It's been about two years now, and I know she works Monday to Friday and sometimes on Saturday. I know this only because she told me once."

Beau then asked his next questions. "Have you seen anyone recently coming or going from her apartment? If there has been, did you notice any type of argument or yelling from her place?"

"No." Mrs. Woolenstock's face turned to one of bewilderment as she answered. "You know, come to think of it, I've never seen anyone visiting. I guess I never thought about it, or if I did, I assumed she went to her parents' home, since they have such a lavish estate. Who wouldn't want to go there as opposed to this place?" she said in a sour tone.

"Are you aware of anyone that Audra could be dating? Any men that you have seen coming or going from her place?" Beau asked. "No" was again the reply. "Have there been any handymen working here on the premises, or have you seen anyone suspicious in the neighborhood?"

"No handymen recently, just the regular lawn-maintenance folks. Oh, wait a minute, we had a roofer here to fix some shingles that had blown off during one of the last storms. No, never mind, that was over a month ago. You said she just went missing recently? Or when did you say she went missing?"

"Her father reported her missing this morning, so we don't have the exact day, but the last time anyone saw her was on Tuesday at her job," Beau replied.

"Oh, that poor man. He's such a wonderful man, you know? I see him every now and again, sitting in his car parked on the street. He's just checking on her to make sure she's okay. I've often wanted to knock on the window to tell him that he should just go and knock on her door, that she would enjoy the company, but I never did. Wait a minute. I take back what I said earlier. I do remember her sister visiting not too long ago—maybe in the last week or so. So hard to know who's who because they are identical twins. I only knew it was her sister because Audra met her outside. She didn't look happy. Audra, I mean. You know how family will often hug or smile when they greet each other, but Audra looked upset. The sister seemed insistent on talking to her, and they both went inside."

"This is helpful, thank you, Clara."

At that, Beau stood up and put his hat back on. Simon followed Beau's cue and sprang up from the sofa. He had been engrossed in not just the conversation, but also the sweet tea and Benne Wafers, all of which he now realized he had eaten. He felt embarrassed by what he had done.

"I may be going out on a limb here, but since you seem to be into antiques, do you know a Joshua Sarkis?"

"Joshua? Of course. Why, yes. Why do you ask?"

"His name and phone number were written on a note in her apartment."

"Well, of course it was. Silly me. There goes my mind again. I gave it to her."

"You? Why was that?"

"He's an antiques dealer, and she mentioned she was trying to sell some very exquisite chairs she had. I've known Joshua for quite a while now, as I used to work in antiques and thought he could help her sell them, or at least buy them from her. He's quite handsome, too. I figured she might enjoy the view."

"How well do you know this man?"

"Well, enough, I guess. I certainly wouldn't suspect him of hurting Audra. I've known his family for years. The antiques world is really quite small, everyone knows everyone, and I certainly haven't heard anything off-putting about them, and trust me, if there was gossip, it would be whirling around like a dervish."

"Is that why you got out of that world?"

"Detective, that is a story for another time and another plate of wafers."

Simon looked smug. She did notice the plate was empty.

"Any idea where his office is?"

"Certainly. His store's on King Street, Sarkis's Antiques. It was his father's business, but he passed away a few years back, and Joshua took it over."

"Why didn't you mention this earlier, Mrs. Woolenstock?" The moment the question left his lips, he was afraid he might have pushed things too far. He wanted her to keep talking and didn't want to think of sweet Clara Woolenstock as an accessory to kidnapping, but he found it interesting that she recommended Joshua and had an interest in the antiques world. People will do anything when they are desperate for money. He would do some investigating into Clara Woolenstock's finances. Maybe she was going to get a cut. Could this Joshua Sarkis be acting solo and just used Clara for information. Maybe . . .

"Detective Crenshaw, at my age you forget what you had for breakfast, let alone who comes and goes from other people's homes."

"Of course, ma'am. I had to ask. Anyway, we'll get out of your hair. Thank you for your time and the hospitality. Here's my business card. Call me if you think of anything else or notice anything suspicious, like Audra's car in the parking lot or anyone coming over to her apartment. Can you do that, Clara?"

"Of course, Detective."

"Oh, and one last thing. We will need to get a copy of the key made, so I will have someone drop off the original to you, likely tomorrow." Beau hesitated for a moment. He didn't want to frighten this elderly woman, so he wanted to select his words carefully. "We have some people in the apartment right now dusting for prints. We have to look at this from every angle. We would ask no one enter the apartment until we give you the say-so. As I'm sure you know, we can't rule anything out."

Mrs. Woolenstock gasped and brought a hand to her chest.

Beau decided he had better add some words to defuse the fear he was seeing, so he said, "I assure you, Mrs. Woolenstock, this is all part of our routine investigation. We hope this is all a misunderstanding, an isolated incident, but I need to say that until we have all the details of what's going on, please be aware of whom you are opening your door to and keep your house and car locked at all times. Good day, Mrs. Woolenstock, and thank you again for the tea and wafers."

"Good day, Detective. Officer," Mrs. Woolenstock uttered back quietly. She had her hand on her cheek as if to support her head. Suddenly Mary's death, the death that haunted him almost daily for the last twenty plus years, crossed Beau's mind, and he remembered using the same words, an isolated incident in a news conference about Mary years before. Haunting words that offered no guarantee.

As Beau turned away from Mrs. Woolenstock's door, he could hear the dead bolt close and the chain lock going across her door. Smart woman, he thought.

Beau's next move was to interview Audra's coworkers, Joshua Sarkis, the Barrington family, and their employees. Time had gotten away from him. He was being pulled in a different direction now and not one in which he really wanted to go.

"Let's get going, Simon. I've got an appointment I need to get to. I'll drop you back at the station. We'll pick this up again tomorrow morning at eight. You've got your list of things to start checking into and get some information on Mrs. Woolenstock's past life before living on Tradd Street. I'm interested in her finances, too."

"Sure thing, sir."

"I think you can start calling me by my first name now, son."

Simon smiled brightly and widely. He had achieved some level of greatness today. He got himself on a high-priced missing person investigation, and he was on a first-name basis with his superior. And by the sounds of it, he would work with Beau again tomorrow.

Beau didn't say another word to Simon the entire drive back to the station. His mind was going over the events of the day and kept coming back to why her sister visited. Oliver said they weren't close.

# 10

## EVENING OF THURSDAY, MARCH 9, 1995

# MARRIAGE COUNSELOR

"Look who decided to grace us with his presence," Kathleen said.

Beau's cheeks flushed out of both frustration and rushing to get to the appointment with the marriage counselor.

"Sweet Jesus, Kathleen, can you cut me some slack, just once in your life? We have a missing person we're dealing with, and traffic was a nightmare. I did my best."

"Funny how you do your best for everyone else except for the person who's supposed to matter the most," Kathleen said snarling.

"Beau, please sit down, and let's all take a big, deep breath in and relax. We will suspend all angry comments, as they create only more negativity. You're my last patients for the day, so we don't have to rush. We just started, Beau, so you haven't missed much. Please have a seat," Dr. Wesley said as he beckoned to the leather sofa.

Kathleen sat with arms folded and a sour look on her face.

"Now, let's pick up where we left off last week. Kathleen, you mentioned that you and Beau lost a child and that you both grieved differently, which is when your marriage divided, correct? Are you comfortable telling me how your child passed away?"

Kathleen, still maintaining a rigid posture, unfolded her arms and let out a sigh before answering. Her eyes looked past the doctor to the bookshelves behind him.

"I see it like it was yesterday. I see it every day. It was as if time stood still the day I found him. I had just stepped outside for fifteen minutes to bring in clothes from the clothesline—just fifteen minutes, maybe even less. Normally I would take the baby with me, but it was getting cool outside, and he was sleeping comfortably on a quilt on the floor. Back then, we didn't have much money to buy baby furniture, so we made do with what we had. I thought because he was on the floor, he would be okay. I mean, what could possibly happen, right? He was barely a toddler. The minute I stepped inside the kitchen, I saw his limp body in front of the sink with blood trickling away from his head and knew that something was terribly wrong. Why didn't I hear a noise? Surely, he must have cried out. I remember standing there in slow motion. My brain couldn't quite process everything fast enough."

Beau's head hung low, his fingers clasped together, each thumb rubbing the other, as if for comfort, as Kathleen recalled the day's events, words now mixed with sobs.

"I looked over at his lifeless body. He wasn't moving at all. His once big bright eyes were wide open and staring straight ahead, not at me. They had now turned a deep, ominous black as if his last breath had somehow sucked the color from his eyes, leaving only darkness. It was awful. His elbow must have been broken, as it was turned around in the opposite direction of where it should be. The pain this boy must have felt. There wasn't a stir from him. Not a sound. I screamed and ran to him, but it was too late, all too late. For being such a small soul, there was blood everywhere. Whether it was a mother's instinct or just the way he was lying there so crooked, I knew my boy was gone. I think about it every day. I picture what went wrong every day. It just goes around in my head constantly, like a giant loop, every day. Jacob must have woken up when he heard the back door close and crawled over to the kitchen sink. I had left a stepladder beside the sink because I was putting stuff away in the upper cupboards. The day before, we had been playing with bubbles in the kitchen sink, and I bet he crawled up there to play with the bubbles again."

Both hands were now on her head, and she was trying to catch her breath between sobs and words, her voice rattling in a higher pitch.

"My God, how could I have been so stupid."

Tears were now falling silently from Beau's face, his gaze still on the floor, his hands still tightly clasped, and he cleared his throat repeatedly.

"When he slipped off the stepladder, he must have caught his head on the corner of the counter before he hit the porcelain tile floor, because he had a fractured skull. Blood was trickling out of his head, and his arm became disjointed from the shoulder socket. I raced over to my Jacob, hesitating on whether I would hurt him more by touching him, his arm now like a rubber band dangling from his body. I picked him up carefully in my arms. I put my hand over the gash to stop the bleeding, but it wouldn't stop, and it kept running out of his nose.

I kept him in my arms while I dialed 911. I remember the stickiness of the blood. Blood was everywhere! He had beautiful fine baby hair, but it became sticky and heavy from the blood. I rocked him in my arms, waiting for the ambulance to arrive. I'll never forget the blood. I cried out to God. 'God, please don't take my baby boy today, please don't take him today. He's just a baby. Please don't take my sweet baby, not today, God, please not today.' But I knew he was gone. I knew he was already dead. I don't even know why I even bothered speaking to God. I just wanted him back again. Maybe some miracle. I wanted God to change his mind and give him back to me. I promised to be a better mother if only he'd give me back my sweet boy. I grabbed his cheeks with one hand, and I tried to blow life into his tiny mouth. Now his blood was on my face, on my lips. I'll never forget the taste. By now, his lips were turning blue, and his body was getting colder with each passing minute."

Kathleen leaned over and screamed into her hands. She brought her face up, wet, bloodshot eyes staring empty at the doctor.

"I was not a good Catholic woman, Dr. Wesley. I hadn't been going to church on a regular basis. I was so sleep deprived that on Sundays, when Beau was home, I tried to get any extra sleep I could. This was God's punishment, I'm sure of it. The ambulance finally arrived, and they took us to the hospital. The police followed us. They questioned me, questioned me about where I was when this happened. I wasn't some sort of neglectful parent. I was not neglectful. God was punishing me. I wasn't neglectful. I wasn't. How could I possibly think, in a million years, that anything like this could happen? I had only stepped outside for fifteen minutes. They only stopped badgering me because they found out I was Beau's wife."

"And where were you, Beau, when all this happened?" Dr. Wesley said.

"That's right, Doctor. Ask Beau where he was when all this was going on."

"I was at work."

"Of course, he was at work. That's his answer for everything, but we know that isn't true, is it, Beau?" Kathleen said.

"Where in hell would you expect me to be during the day, Kathleen? Somebody has to pay the bills, so yes, I was at work, at my job that gives me a paycheck each week to support us. Now drop it."

"But you weren't at work, were you? This all happened when you should have already been home from work, so do tell the good doctor where you were and why I had to take on this burden alone?"

"Kathleen, if Beau says he was at work, then we will have to believe he was at work. Why are you so angry at Beau?" Dr. Wesley asked.

"Because he wasn't sad. He didn't even act upset. Because he wasn't there but should have been. Do you want to know what he said?"

"What did he say, Kathleen?"

"He said, 'Things happen.' Can you believe that? 'Things happen.' Our sweet boy's dead body turning icy cold, and all he has to say is 'Things happen.' I saw him get more upset and cry over a case he was working on, but for his dead son, all he could say was that two-word bullshit."

"Kathleen, I don't think it is a good idea to hold on to the words he would have said at the time of a tragic accident. Everyone handles shock and grief differently. His pain is no less than your pain. He just expressed it differently."

"You're taking his side now?"

"There are no sides to be taken. I simply want you to see that during this period of intense shock, this is all he could formulate in his head. Would it make you feel better to know how upset he was? Beau, would you like to share how you felt?"

"Is this really necessary, Doc?" Beau asked.

"Your absolutely fucking right it's necessary," Kathleen said belting it out.

"Kathleen, let's try to keep the swearing at a minimum and not lash out at Beau. This is a safe space for both of you to express yourselves freely."

"Sorry, Doctor," Kathleen muttered, adjusting the hem of her skirt.

"It's Beau you need to apologize to, Kathleen, not me."

Kathleen didn't even look Beau's way when she snapped, "Sorry."

"Now, Beau, please help us to understand how you were feeling."

"How do you think I felt? I just lost my son. He was the very thing that helped me to get through my days, my days as a cop seeing all sorts of horrible shit. This world is a cesspool of degenerates. Cops get to deal with the worst of the worst, but he was this innocent little bundle of bliss that I got to come home to every night—him and Kathleen. They helped me keep going. With him dead, I wasn't sure how I was going to keep going. I was pissed at Kathleen, but I didn't want her to see this. She was a wonderful mother, and I knew that whatever had happened, it was an accident. She would never intentionally do anything to harm him - I knew that - but I knew if I said too much, she would see how pissed I was at her. I wanted to scream at her, but she was such a wreck, and it was like my brain had blown a gasket. All I could think of to say was 'Things happen.' Listen, I can't talk anymore about this. I'm not going to be dissected over every last word I said or didn't say from years ago. I'm doing the best I can."

"I knew you hated me for what happened."

"I don't hate you, Kathleen. It's just hard not to, well . . . blame you in some small way, that you should have been more careful. You were the one responsible for him. It's hard not to be angry with you, but I don't hate you. Please, I don't want to get into this."

"What has kept you two together since this happened?"

"Avoidance and our Catholic faith. Beau fell off the rails years before because he didn't solve a murder. You likely remember it from the news. It was the nurse found in the hospital parking lot."

"I remember it well. Beau, why don't you tell me about this case and how it affected you."

"This is worse than the interrogations we do at the shop," Beau said tersely, then paused.

"Sorry. I know we're here to talk. I had just passed my detective's test, and they threw me on this case. I had no actual experience being a detective, but the department was short-staffed. Listen, I think we have dredged up enough for one evening. I really can't talk about this now. Can we talk about Mary another time?"

"These sessions are meant to help you express yourself when you are ready to share your thoughts. They are meant to help you heal. It is not meant to make you uncomfortable. Let's pick this up next time, but I would like to send you home with some things to think about. When you are faced with unfortunate circumstances, it is often easier to blame the other person so that the blame we place on ourselves is not as painful. It is called transference. It is easier to blame the other person than to consider the part you played in the situation. I would like you to think about forgiveness. Forgiveness for yourself and forgiveness for each other. You both lost someone you loved dearly, and forgiving helps the healing process. Are you both willing to work on this?"

They each nodded their heads in agreement.

"Great. I will see you both next week at the same time. Now please try practicing kindness and forgiveness. Sometimes it's the little things that mean the most."

## FRIDAY, MARCH 10, 1995

# MORE THAN
# HE BARGAINED FOR

Just after roll call, Beau broke the news to Simon. He would stay back at the office so he could research the items Beau had given him to check out. He could tell from the look of disappointment on Simon's face that he thought he was coming with him for all the interviews.

"Listen, kid, this is important shit you're doing and way more interesting than what scalawags are doing." Beau tilted his head toward the other uniforms in the room who were processing paperwork for speeding tickets and no seat belts. "I'll take you to the lab with me this afternoon."

Simon's grin told Beau that's what he needed to hear to keep him motivated.

The interviews Beau could work alone. The first stop of the day was Sarkis Antiques.

The chime sounded as Beau opened the door at precisely 9:18 a.m. A man entered from the back of the store, mid-thirties with rugged good looks, of possibly Middle Eastern or Mediterranean descent with an olive skin tone and coffee-colored eyes. Beau suspected this was the man he was looking for.

"Joshua Sarkis?"

"That's me. What can I help you with today?"

"I'm Detective Beau Crenshaw, Charleston PD, and I'm investigating the disappearance of Audra Barrington."

Beau had flipped open his badge long enough for the visual of the police shield, but not long enough to read what it actually said.

"Audra? Missing? What the hell?"

The man looked genuinely surprised. But Beau knew this could just as easily be rehearsed as well.

"When was the last time you saw her?"

"Hmm, maybe a week ago, maybe less. How did you get my name?"

"It was written on a piece of paper in her apartment, along with your phone number. What was the nature of your visit? The last time you saw her, I mean."

"Listen, she called me about some chairs she wanted to get rid of, real rare, so I went over to have a look at them."

"So, you only met her one time?"

"Maybe a few times."

"Maybe a few times meeting her?"

"Hey, man, she's a smokeshow, and we kind of, well, took a liking to each other. So, we hooked up a few times."

"Just how many times are a few times?"

"I don't know. Maybe six, ten, dozen. I really wasn't keeping track."

Beau put his hands on his temples and kneaded his forehead.

"So, you just got together with her for sex? What a bargain for you. Sex and a commission."

"Well, it sounds bad when you say it like that. Trust me, it was a mutual hookup. I didn't take advantage of her, if that's what you're thinking. She wanted it as much as I did."

"I'm sure. So why don't you go back to when you first met her. When was that?"

"Ugh, I guess maybe two or three months ago?"

"And when was the last time you saw her?"

"Like I said earlier, maybe a week or so ago."

Beau grunted.

"Hey, we didn't have a falling-out or anything. It was purely pleasurable and consensual sex. Sometimes I'd go to her place, and sometimes she'd come to my place. She even said we couldn't be seen in public. Didn't break my heart. I'm not looking for a woman friend, but when Audra Barrington flirts with you, you jump all over that, you know what I mean? You're a guy. Wouldn't you tap that name?"

"So she flirted with you first, you being the prize you are?"

"I think it was a mutual go-around."

Beau shifted his weight from one side of his foot to the other and sighed.

"Did you two discuss birth control?"

"I'm a little old to be discussing that. I assume, given who she is, she'd have that covered, so no, the subject never came up."

"Lovely. What happened to the chairs?"

"I found someone to buy them from her. I took a commission

for lining the two of them up, and everyone was happy. I even got her way more than she was asking," Joshua said, grinning as if he were proud of himself for his find.

"Do you know where she got the chairs?"

"Said her grandmother. Told her to keep for a rainy day in case the witch of the east didn't die before her dad and cut her out of the will. Said she gave her other things, too, to make sure she would be taken care of."

"Interesting. How much did she get for the chairs, and how did they pay her?"

"A hundred thousand. They were pristine. I paid her cash. I took the money from the buyer so I could get my cut."

"Of course, you did. When did that happen?"

"Maybe a week or so ago."

"Seems to be a popular answer."

"What?"

"Nothing. Thank you for your time, Joshua. I may need to circle back, but this is good for now. And if she shows up, let me know before you have sex so her family can sleep at night."

"Hey, don't be telling others we were having sex. I wouldn't want that to get around."

An agitated nerve twitched on the left side of Beau's face.

"Do I look like the guardian of your reputation, Joshua?"

Joshua looked at him, dumbfounded.

Beau walked out of the store in disgust. He may be good looking, but what an arrogant son of a bitch. He had shown not even a hint of interest in her being missing.

*I wonder whether he knows he could be a father.*

**FRIDAY, MARCH 10, 1995**

# A VISIT TO SUTHERLAND'S CROSSING

A call from Oliver confirmed the Barrington family would be available to meet at 10:30 a.m. Beau sarcastically thought about how gracious they were to take time out of their busy schedules to meet him.

As he turned onto the driveway of the lavish estate, he was taken with the view in front of him. The driveway extended a quarter of a mile, and live oaks lined either side of the drive, all perfectly spaced apart. Spanish moss dripped from the limbs and danced in the gentle breeze. Birds took up residence in the trees of this perfect sanctuary. Black pasture fences surrounded each side of the tree-lined driveway, and horses gingerly grazed in the fresh emerald grass, their lives sheltered from harm. The dirt lane spilled into a circular drive. Sprawling gardens mimicked those found in England, shrubs trimmed with precision, purposefully and methodically placed.

An elaborate hand-carved stone water fountain sat in the center of the manicured roundabout, adding a touch of European elegance to the home's setting while manicured box hedges created beautiful art forms. The gentle sound of the fountain acted as a lure, hypnotically carving away any worries of the day. To the right were the stables and caretaker's cottage, perfectly organized and from the outside, anyway, looked cleaner than most homes.

Getting out of his car, he took a moment to just take in the beauty in front of him. The lavish postcard-perfect mansion, set on ten acres of lush pasture and farmland, acted as a backdrop of sprawling beauty and serenity. Its architecture mimicked Greek Revival with thick, masculine Roman pillars, a slate roof, bricked on three sides, while the front, white stucco with Charleston green shutters adorning all ten windows, made the house seem both stately and charming. The balustrade cordoned the front porch and created a tranquil setting, where rocking chairs lined up on both sides of the grand front door, a place where a person could come and sip a mint julep without a worry in the world. Ceiling fans strategically placed along the length of the porch delighted in extending its guests a level of comfort, the whirring of the blades twirling around madly, wrestling to oppose the heat from Mother Nature. The front entrance stood majestic with tall, oversize solid wood doors, adorned with beveled glass and sidelights of stained-glass shimmering from the sun and throwing off rays of intense color from its countless prisms.

Beau rang the bell, and after several minutes, Molly, the housekeeper greeted him with both a smile and a nod.

"Good morning, ma'am," Beau said as he lifted his hat from his head. "I'm here to see Oliver Barrington."

"Of course, sir," she said, "please come in. I will let Mr. Barrington know you have arrived."

Stepping inside the foyer, Beau took off his fedora and held on to it with both hands as he scanned the room, quite taken with its mass and grandeur. Inside the grand foyer his eyes fell first to the Italian black-and-white marble flooring before soon being drawn upward to the two magnificent stairways perfectly staged on both sides of the entrance, each outfitted with hand-carved stair railings in exotic walnut. Centered between the stairs, an opulent nineteenth-century Louis XVI chandelier, whose light danced jaggedly in every direction, proved to be the finishing touch to make this home an elegant masterpiece of embroidered design. From the baroque period, many enormous Italian seventeenth-century, giltwood, Roman-mirrored sconces lined each of the walls from top to bottom, while the hallway at the top of the stairs held the portraits of family members.

It did not take long for Oliver to enter the foyer from the left wing of the manor. As Oliver neared Beau, he extended his right hand as a polite gesture of greeting. Beau reciprocated.

"Beau, thank you for coming all this way. Let's head into my study," Oliver said as he released his hand and turned back in the direction from which he came.

Beau nodded and followed Oliver, both men silent as they walked into the study, with the housekeeper following suit. The study was lined with mahogany bookshelves, a large ornate wooden desk (mahogany, by the looks of it), heavy tapestries, and a burgundy leather sofa and chair to finish the room. Oil paintings protected by massive gold frames hung on every empty bit of wall space. A meeting table, set off in the corner with four ornate wooden chairs, had the same garish pattern as the desk. On it was a crystal bourbon decanter with four similarly patterned glasses. The lighting was masculine and strategically arranged throughout the room, and while the design held only a few elements, the room felt dense.

"Beau, please be seated," Oliver said as he gestured toward the furniture.

The housekeeper had followed both men into the study and dutifully stood by, waiting on instructions.

"Beau, would you care for something to eat or drink?"

"I would love some tea, black, if not too much trouble," Beau said, setting his hat next to him.

"No trouble at all. Molly, can you please bring in a pot of steeped tea and some biscuits, oh and please let Mrs. Barrington know that Mr. Crenshaw and I are here in the study."

"Right away, sir," Molly said before turning to head out of the room.

"Oliver, I checked out Audra's apartment yesterday, and it does appear some sort of scuffle took place. Stuff was tossed about, upstairs and down, but what was interesting was that she had placed an ad to sell a couple of antique chairs. Are you aware of these chairs? Did she collect antiques and store them somewhere else, because her apartment did not have any other antiques in it."

"Oh, my word, no. What do you mean it looks like there was a scuffle? Like she had a fight with someone?"

"Well, not necessarily. The entire apartment had been ransacked, more like someone looking for something."

"But Audra's never been into antiques, and I know nothing about these chairs. This doesn't sound like Audra."

Molly walked into the study carrying an ornate silver tray that accommodated a silver tea service set, teacups, and biscuits. She placed it on the table, keeping her eyes focused on her task. As she was exiting the room, Charlotte appeared, looking harsh and annoyed. Beau stood up to greet her.

"Mrs. Barrington, thank you for seeing me. I wish we were meeting under better circumstances."

"What did I just hear you say about antique chairs? Oliver, did that stupid woman steal our chairs and try to sell them?"

"No, Charlotte, sit down. And please don't call her stupid. He was mentioning that Audra's apartment had been rummaged through and that there was an ad offering two antique chairs for sale. It was Audra's phone number on the ad. No chairs were found in the apartment."

"Because she was likely foolish enough to have the person come to her home, and they stole the chairs. God only knows what they did to her."

"Charlotte, stop. I can't have you talking like that. I'm going to my office now. I can't hear any more of you bad-mouthing our daughter. *Your daughter.* Beau, don't hesitate to contact me for anything. Just let Molly know when you are ready to speak with Abby and Ruby."

"Thank you, Oliver. I'll be in touch."

Beau's eyes followed Oliver briefly, then turned back to Charlotte, who was now seated properly on the sofa.

"Mrs. Barrington, let me explain the purpose of my visit today. It is important for me to get a sense of who Audra is from different perspectives, so I will be speaking with anyone who knows her, and I also need to gather a timeline of her whereabouts."

"Did you start with her job, then? They are, after all, the people who saw her last. We haven't seen nor spoken with her for over a week, so I'm not sure what I can offer."

Beau, taken aback by this abrupt comment, continued: "I am

speaking with everyone. When precisely was the last time you saw or spoke with Audra, Mrs. Barrington?" Beau noticed she didn't tell him to call her Charlotte.

"Well, let's see, or like I just said, I suppose it was the dinner we had when Jamie was in town."

"And did you notice anything off with her then?"

"*Off* with her?" Charlotte said. "Audra is always *off*. That woman will do anything to antagonize me. I think she lives for it. I'm sure Oliver has filled you in that Audra can be a handful. I'm sure this is just another stunt for her to get attention and piss me off. She knows how much I hate gossip and scandal. She likely became perturbed at something at her work and decided to run off to show them a thing or two. Audra has always been trouble from day one, and Lord knows I tried with that woman."

"Why do you think that is?" Beau asked.

The clock on the wall struck twelve, its bell loud and menacing. Beau jolted back in his seat.

"Oh, pardon me, please continue," he said.

"From the day she was born, there were complications. I wasn't supposed to have any more children after Richmond, so the twins came as quite a surprise. I was bedridden for nearly a month, and when they were born, almost immediately Abby was sleeping through the night and was just the happiest baby, not a peep out of her. But Audra! Dear God, she was a nightmare. She was colicky and cried constantly. I understand how people can just simply place a pillow over someone to let them slip away. Of course, I would never do such a thing, but I can certainly empathize with how it could happen."

By now, Beau was both disgusted and shocked by what he was hearing. God almighty, what kind of monster was this woman! Having lost a child of his own, he was devastated by this kind of talk from a mother. He would have given anything to have seen his son grow up. This was one cold customer, he thought. The rumors were true.

"Yes, Audra came out a problem and has continued to be one, as you can attest to since you are here today. She gets along well with her father and her brother Jamie. They are the least ambitious of the family. I guess that's why they all stick together."

*The creature never stops,* Beau thought. He reached over to pick up the teacup and take a sip.

"Oliver mentioned a nanny. Did you have the nanny living here when you had the twins?"

"Oh, you mean Ruby. Well, yes, of course she was here. It's what we pay her for and why we keep her living in such grandeur as she does. Ruby did take Audra off my hands so I could get some sleep, but I still had to breastfeed her, so she would bring her around for that. Eventually Audra preferred the attention of Ruby over me. Imagine. That woman would run to Ruby for everything. It was always 'Ruby this' and 'Ruby that.' I am quite sick of hearing that name. Every time we had a disagreement, she would go running to her, as if that woman could help her with anything. Ruby is nothing more than a highly overpaid servant here. She's not part of the family, as Oliver would have you believe, but she's got Oliver by the balls. I would have tossed her out years ago had she not taken care of Audra. I simply did not have the time to deal with such nonsense. You are best talking with her about Audra. She likely knows where that sass-mouth has run off to. Likely whoring off with some degenerate. I'm sure this will all turn out to be an enormous embarrassment for the family. She would love that."

"As a young child or teenager, did you continue to have tension with her? Was there a reason you two didn't bond later?"

"Of course, I continued to have issues with her. She always felt as if I catered to her twin sister, Abby, more than I did to her. I can never win with that woman. If I say black, she says white. I have tried to talk with her, to reason with her, to be lenient or firm. Nothing has worked. She thinks I'm a tyrant, but I know what a tyrant is. That would be my father. Audra has an abstruse way of looking at life. She thinks it should be peace and love that we should be trying harder to help people and animals, that if all were equal, what a grand place this would be."

Charlotte threw up her hands, gesturing upward, then grabbed on to her face.

"She is lost in a sea of illusion. What she forgets is, because she was brought up with money, she can afford to play around in her mind with such stupidity. Animals are for eating or sport, and people, well, they can figure out their own lives. I had to. I've explained to her that this is hell, and that she needs to learn how to play the game if she wants to survive, that you can't run to Ruby forever. I used to say the old battle-ax won't be living that much longer, but yet she does. She keeps going on and on."

"What do you mean 'learn to play the game' if she wants to survive?" Beau asked.

Charlotte threw up her hands again as she rose from the sofa and crossed her arms in front of her. She began pacing back and forth. Beau, too, stood up and slowly wandered toward the window. He needed a diversion from this wretched woman.

"Listen, Mr. Crenshaw, I'm sure you didn't fall off the turnip truck yesterday. I'm also fairly sure you understand what a struggle life can be. Surely your job has opened up your eyes enough to see that."

Beau turned toward her, placing his hands in his pant pockets.

He started to jingle the coins. "I do understand that life can be tough sometimes, but what does that have to do with Audra surviving? It looks to me as if she went to school, got an education, and then landed a good job."

"Must you do that?" Charlotte snapped.

"Do what?" Beau looked dumbfounded.

"Rattle those coins around."

"Sorry."

"Are you married?"

"Ugh, yeah."

"God help your wife."

Beau wanted to defend Audra, and he knew he needed to rein it in, or she would likely continue to turn on him, too.

Charlotte pointed her index finger at him, as if she were scolding a child, then placed both hands on her hips. "My father taught me early on that in order to succeed in this world, you need to be ruthless. He showed me that every day, and it's important for her to learn this, too. If you don't stay on top, there is always some vulture waiting to take you down. I was not about to let my daughter act a fool and embarrass the family, so I had to stay on top of her, always. But when she moved out, I knew that it would be harder to control her. And poor Abby. Being her identical twin, people often mistake one for the other, and sometimes Abby was always left apologizing for her sister's poor behavior."

Beau nodded his head in acknowledgment.

"Would Audra have outbursts with people outside the family?"

"Lord have mercy. Sometimes I don't know where this child came from. Spawned by the devil himself, perhaps. She would protest at the state capital for animal welfare rights, for cleaner oceans or sex trafficking. Any underdog who she believes has been given a raw deal in life, she will side with and fight for. I told her so many times that what she needed to fight for was her reputation and namesake. Abby's a well-respected attorney, and the last thing she needs is to have a slanted identical twin ruining her status."

"But Audra is a clinical psychiatrist, correct? You don't think that is an admirable occupation?" Beau said, turning back to look out the window.

"Spare me, Detective. Where do you get your thoughts from? Anyone can sit and listen to people's problems all day long and scratch away at a notepad. What does it really accomplish? If you were crazy at the start of your appointment, you'll likely be crazy when you finish it. And who is Audra to tell people how to live their lives when hers is such a mess? What a joke. It's like the crazies are running the asylum. Have you seen where she lives? Let me just say it was a gross waste of valuable time and the money we spent putting that woman through school. Never did she bring a nice young man home to meet the family—'not interested in getting married,' she had said. Now Abby, she has her sights set on making a change, in working hard, and locking down the right man. She's headed for partnership at her law firm. Do you know Sterling Jackson? His family is quite well known in Charleston. They've been dating since high school, will marry, have children, and carry on the name with class and eloquence. Are you from here, Mr. Crenshaw? If you are, then you will surely know the name. Did your people farm? You have the body type of someone who looks like he came off a farm."

Beau spun around to face her, flabbergasted at the direction this conversation had taken. This was all about Charlotte Barrington and her social status and nothing about her flesh and blood being missing. She also had a sly way of demeaning a person without blinking an eye. It was as if she had no idea just how offensive she was behaving. Or perhaps she knew exactly how offensive she was being. A true narcissist in action. Beau thought back to his conversation with Oliver and now pitied the man. What an awful shrew of a woman. Somehow he knew she suffered at the hands of her father but instead of turning that around, she decided to become an even worse version of him. Needing to finish this, he continued. "Can you think of anyone that would want to hurt Audra, or can you think of any business associate that is seeking some sort of revenge?" Beau asked.

"After spending a night with Audra, they would surely dump her back to wherever they found her," Charlotte said snickering. "I don't have anything to do with my husband's business. I just put on the show whenever he needs to entertain important clients. This is how my upbringing has served its purpose. The outward appearance of a southern woman is that of grace and poise, sweetness, and timidity, while inside, a woman who is strong and steadfast knowing exactly what she wants and how she is going to get it. You know farmers are necessary. Someone needs to get their hands dirty, to fuel those of us that keep the country running."

Flicking her hair, and cocking her head to one side, she continued: "Charleston did not become what it is today by being weak, and the blood that pours through the veins of its early settlers, of which I can say proudly my ancestors were, and onto its descendants shows genuine passion and courage in continuing its legacy, in preserving its culture and customs. Surely you understand, Mr. Crenshaw. Didn't you say your people were farmers?"

"Uh, no, ma'am."

Beau wasn't expecting the history lesson but did want to learn a bit more about Charlotte's version of how Oliver and she met. He knew it didn't have anything to do with the case, but by now he was so intrigued by what would put these two people together, he had to ask. He had to see how calculating the upper echelon operated.

"How did you meet Oliver?"

Charlotte rolled her eyes.

"A debutante ball. My father had his eyes set on Oliver for quite some time once he started to see the fortune his family was acquiring. He wanted to make sure I married right. You likely don't know much about debutante balls, but it is a type of entrance to society for women in an effort for them to commingle with like-minded upper-crust society and available bachelors. You know even less attractive women can become Cinderella for the night with enough money, makeup, rhinestones, and satin. It takes months of planning and is a dressmaker's dream come true to be creating works of art for all high society's bachelorettes. The competition is fierce among them, as they know the best designs will be featured in all the magazines, which means their client base just tripled overnight along with their bank account. And having your design featured means you can name your price for future galas."

"Interesting," Beau said, "so, you purposely ran into Oliver at the ball."

Charlotte grimaced.

"Well, my father told me to flirt and bat my eyes a little, whatever it took to get his attention. And that I did. I guess you could say I beguiled him." Wincing as if in pain and then a gagging motion, she continued.

"Being a middle child to six other siblings means you have to compete for your parents' attention. Actually, you have to compete for anyone's attention—grandparents, aunts, uncles, cousins, even friends. I think because of that, I am not close with my siblings. Three women and three boys and all very driven by business, so that became their lifestyle, whereas I have more of a creative and imaginative mind. The differences in our personalities meant we really had nothing to talk about. I could never share my ideas with any of my siblings, as they would just scoff at me, hurling some sarcastic criticism about me wandering off in dreamland again and to get on board with reality."

Beau was shocked at her candor of selecting Oliver as a husband. But it shouldn't really have been a surprise. He'd seen a lot in his line of work, and at the end of the day, it always came down to money, never love. No wonder the man looked miserable. But he was most amazed at how she was more interested in talking about her past than in her missing daughter.

He was about to speak when she continued. "So, when my father made the comment about Oliver needing to be caught, I had to set my plan in motion. I needed to impress my father, that I had what it took to get Oliver. My passion was never as a wife or mother, no, no, no. I had my heart set on being a clothing designer, but my father would not hear of it. 'No respectful daughter of mine is going to become a seamstress,' he would say. 'We hire seamstresses, and I am not about to hire you. Find yourself a wealthy husband, be a good wife, mother, and lady of the house. That is your job,' he would say. And as much as I tried to explain to my father that a designer carries a far different role from that of a seamstress, once his iron fist was laid down, I knew I had to oblige him. The subject was dropped, and although the desire was still there, the dream of my actually becoming a clothes designer would be forever banished from my reality. You know, Mr. Crenshaw, the day my father laid down my path, a piece of me died. Our wedding was like a carnival show, and Oliver and I were the performers. We have been performing ever since. I decided that if I can't design clothes, I would bloody well buy whatever I wanted, and no daughter is going to shame me into thinking I shouldn't. You know the irony in all this, Mr. Crenshaw?"

"No, please enlighten me," Beau said in a perplexed tone.

"Within a few months after Oliver and I were married, both of my parents were killed in a car accident. Can you believe that? They were coming home from an event during one of Charleston's infamous downpours and were struck head-on by an elderly man who had suffered a burst aneurysm. The doctors said that while the leaking blood surrounded his brain and brain tissue, it caused a stroke. Can you imagine? There was nothing the man could do, and he died instantly. Both of my parents were alive during the crash, yet pinned in the car. After almost an hour of prying open the doors of the car with the Jaws of Life, my mother was pronounced dead, but my father still had a pulse, although weak. Of course he did! That was just like Father. They rushed him to the hospital, where he underwent extensive surgery to remove the fragments of the steering wheel that had impaled his chest cavity and to repair his collapsed lungs. He had a broken arm and a cracked kneecap. Doctors worked on him for a solid eighteen hours until this broken man finally gave up. Even in his last seconds, he would fight everyone to the end. I don't know whether that is just bad karma for me or not, but I often wonder . . . if only that man had had the stroke just months before with the same scenario, that maybe I wouldn't be standing here talking to you today, that I would be over in Paris frantically designing for the next fashion show. Well, enough of that. You didn't come here to listen to me babble on about how I got here, and these words I have shared with you I trust will remain confidential. If you have all that you need, Mr. Crenshaw, I must be getting back to my business, and I will show you out now. Oh well, actually I guess you need to speak with Abby. I'll go get her. But do make it quick. She has a very hectic work schedule that I'm sure she needs to get back to."

For a moment Beau felt taken by her words and that he was seeing a more fragile version of Charlotte, but the last comment snapped him back to reality, to the icy exterior she reserved for almost everyone. He noticed everything reverted to her being a victim.

"Thank you, Mrs. Barrington, for your hospitality. I must say you have a stunning home." It was all the obligatory politeness he could muster up.

"Designed it myself. It was a wedding present from Oliver's parents, Edward and Isabelle. It's named Sutherland's Crossing after Isabelle's maiden name. Oliver always was the sentimentalist. They built it, but I designed every square inch."

"That must have been quite the undertaking," Beau said with a forced smile, sweat now starting to bead on his brow, a reaction from his body wanting to get away from this woman.

"Indeed, but I was certainly up for the task. Better than running off on some dreary honeymoon with a man I barely knew." Her face puckered as if she were going to puke.

"And after all, this would become the home where Oliver and I raise their grandchildren and host our many parties for the company. Having outsiders in your home means you are fair game for criticism. It was important to Edward that our home could compete with the best of the homes in Charleston, even surpassing them. I think it was even more important to me, so I made sure to have the final say on how the house was being designed. To date, this is still my greatest work. Edward and I shared many of the same views with the house planning. Charleston is a place where material objects mean everything. Wealth is more important than sunshine, and everyone is on the fast track to climb the social-status ladder. Gossip is rampant, so you hold your head high but keep your scandals low. High society has a certain obscurity to it, a mysterious undertone of duplicity, so to speak, that is understood by only the people playing the game. Ultimately, wealth means power and control, and I set out to be wealthy."

"I think my wife even showed me a write-up in one of the local magazines," Beau said.

"Oh, honey, it has been in every home and social magazine you can think of. I have exquisite taste, an eye for quality, and am a master at organizing everything down to the last detail so there isn't much competition out there. The magazines are thrilled whenever I let one of their little shills come and interview me in my home."

Beau could only smile at that comment. By now, she had reached the door to the study.

"I'll send Molly in to refresh. Good day, Mr. Crenshaw."

"Good day, Mrs. Barrington."

Before closing the door, Charlotte turned back toward Beau and said, "Do keep Oliver abreast of any movement. I'm sure she will turn up someday soon," Charlotte said, then closed the door with a resounding thud.

Beau let out a heavy sigh and wiped the sweat from his face with his pocket handkerchief. He felt exhausted from being with her—mentally drained. Something was really off with this woman, he thought. He wondered how much of Audra becoming a psychiatrist was to learn how to handle her mother's off-putting personality. *If Audra did run, who could blame her?*

# ABBY BARRINGTON

Beau hoped the unbearable likeness to her mother was only in looks and not in personality. Every effort was placed in keeping his facial expressions monotone. The creaking of the hinges could be heard first, then the silhouette of a woman appeared as Abby Barrington stepped into the room. As she walked toward him, she extended her hand, similar to a business transaction.

"Detective Crenshaw, I'm Abby Barrington."

"Pleased to meet you, Ms. Barrington."

"That's my mother's name. Please call me Abby."

"Abby it is, as long as you call me Beau."

Abby smiled, but graciously didn't engage in the loose banter. "I am sick over my sister being missing. And poor Dad. He's a mess. What can I do to help?"

"When was the last time you saw her?"

"Well, I think as both Mom and Dad likely already told you, it was when Jamie was visiting from Virginia. She was here for dinner. Didn't stay long."

"Did you notice anything different about her?"

Beau, who had taken a drink of tea and was setting his cup back on the tray, hit the side of the teapot. The connection of the china against the silver gave Abby pause.

"Ugh, no, no different from any other time. Detective, that is very old and expensive china."

"Sorry, I'll be more careful. Abby, tell me a bit about your sister. I mean being twins, you must have a much stronger connection than regular siblings."

Beau decided to sit and clasp his hands together. The beads of sweat returned.

"You would think, but Audra and I have never been that close, even as young children. I tried to get close to her when we were kids, but she always pushed me away. I actually felt bad that people seemed to gravitate to me more than her—even my own mother— so I guess she felt left out and took it out on me. I love my sister, Detective, and I hope nothing terrible has happened to her."

At that, Abby started to sob and to wipe away the tears forming in her eyes. Beau could see that perhaps he was wrong about her. Maybe Abby was more like Oliver than he realized, but yet, there was something calculated about her actions and her answers.

"When we were kids, I used to tell Audra to just play the game, especially with Mother, but instead of just going along with her, Audra would stand up to her every time. They fight like cats and dogs, you know. She would get mad at me for not standing up for her, but honestly, I just didn't have the courage to, nor did I want to. I just gave in to Mother knowing it would be for the best. And many times, I agreed with Mother. We have a reputation to uphold.

I started to avoid Audra because whenever she wasn't around, life was more peaceful. I mean, Mother is Mother, and no one is going to change that. Audra soon pushed me away entirely, saying I was the 'evil' twin. It broke my heart. Dad, of course, did the best to keep us together, but even he couldn't get Audra to calm down most times. And something happened between her and Mother years ago. She would never say, though. It's very odd. I don't know whether it was something that Audra heard or saw, but by the age of twelve, Audra was completely nasty to her, always. The tension when the two of them were in the room was unbearable."

"So, who else was at the dinner when Jamie was in town?"

"Well, let's see. There was Sterling, my fiancé, Ruby, Richmond, Mom, and Dad. I was supposed to work late that day but wouldn't miss a visit with Jamie for anything. I miss him terribly, but I love that he is doing something he is passionate about. And I love that he and Audra are close. It gives me comfort knowing that she has Dad and Jamie to confide in. I wish it were me, too, but."

"How was she getting along with everyone that night? I know you said nothing was different."

"Her normal Audra self," Abby said laughing quietly. "I'll give the woman credit. When she has her heart set on something, she gives it all she has. Right now, she's all in when it comes to helping shelter dogs get adopted, so she attacked Mother and me pretty good on how pretentious and materialistic we are, that there is a special place in hell for people like us. She has never learned balance or to have a filter."

"Balance?" Beau said with a puzzled look.

"What I mean by that is you can help people while still living a productive life full of the things you work hard for. I do pro bono cases all the time and would love to share that with her. Maybe she and I could even do some good with my being an attorney, her causes, and her being a psychiatrist, but she wants nothing to do with me. And I don't know whom she loathes more, our mother or me. And she has this odd obsession with Sterling, my boyfriend. She can't quite figure him out. She doesn't go out of her way to talk with him, but she kind of just stares at him as if she's infatuated with him. Sure, he's nothing short of a looker, but it's kind of creepy. He says it's nothing that I should concern myself with."

"Does your mother ever talk with you about her, about how she could do things differently to maybe understand Audra better?"

"Ha! What? Our mother? Mr. Crenshaw, after speaking with my mother, I'm sure you figured out early on she is not someone who is interested in discussing touchy-feely things. It's Charlotte's way or the highway. Audra knows this, too, but I guess she thought she could somehow break her down in time."

"So, what do you think happened to her? Do you think she just up and left without telling anyone? Start a new life somewhere? Do you think your dad's business could have some rough characters that may have taken her? Her job? Do you think one of her patients could be dangerous?"

"Mr. Crenshaw, I really wish I could give you something, anything, but the truth is that I have no idea."

"In college, you must have crossed paths sometimes, right? Did you ever see her hanging out with anyone, or did she have a favorite professor?"

"No, my focus was law, and hers was science, so that meant we didn't share classes. Audra never brought friends home, and I don't recall her ever saying that she was going off to a friend's house, although she would never tell Mom, anyway. She just went where she wanted to, but mainly you could find her in the barn with the horses—even as an adult. That was her favorite place to be—the barn. Yuck! We've always had horses. Mother says they add a certain level of prestige, even though she doesn't ride. Me, I find them a gross waste of money. Detective, please try to understand that I did all I could to be friends with my sister. She would just not let it happen."

"I understand. I am just finding it odd that no one seems to have been friends with this young woman—well, other than the farm animals."

Abby chuckled, flicking her hair back as if the gesture added an effect.

"God knows I tried. I even called her once and asked whether we could meet for lunch. She picked me up at my office and drove to the bay. I thought we were going to have lunch at a nice restaurant on the water, but she just started lecturing me on how we're polluting our oceans, killing the sea creatures, and that instead of me defending criminals, why wasn't I using my power to make change."

Abby looked down at her nails, inspecting her manicure. Rolling her eyes, she continued: "She told me that our mother was a cult leader and had me brainwashed with all her materialistic socialite bullshit. I told her to take me back to my office, and that I had had enough of her crazy antics. We didn't talk the entire way back. Setting all that aside, I went to her apartment recently. I thought maybe she would be more comfortable on her own turf. Honestly, I was shocked she let me in. I told her I wanted her in my life and that I wanted us to be sisters, twin sisters, and what could I do to make that happen. I wanted to share joyful events with her. A funny thing happened. She grinned at me like a Cheshire cat but didn't say a word. It was really awkward. I didn't stay long because of it. I told her to give it some thought and let me know what I could do to help mend our relationship. She said she'd think about it."

Abby threw up her hands. "That was the last time I saw her. If that's everything, Detective, I'll send Ruby in."

At that, she stood up and headed to the door. *What happened to the first-name basis and warm greeting he got at the start of the conversation?* Beau thought.

The last comment came from nowhere. What an oddly interesting family. Sad, really, being so wealthy, yet so empty. Carrying on these types of charades must be exhausting. If only they could somehow release their miseries on one another, setting free the demons that seem to hang on so tightly to each of them. How has all this dysfunction played in Audra's disappearance?

*What am I missing?*

# RUBY RUTLEDGE

Abby's abrupt exit was the complete opposite of Ruby, who bustled through the door with a smile from ear to ear, holding out both hands so she could grab on and hold tight to Beau's.

"Aw, Mr. Crenshaw, I know you're here about our wee bairn. Do you have any idea where she could be?"

Beau, feeling the dampness on his fingers, suddenly realized that in her hands was a wet tissue she was using to dab the tears from her eyes. He was almost tempted to hug her.

"I'm sorry to say we don't, Mrs. Rutledge."

"Oh, let's not get too formal, shall we? Ruby, you must call me Ruby," she said, continuing to blot her eyes.

"So long as you call me Beau."

"Would you like a cup of tea, Beau?" Ruby said, pushing aside some wisps of stray hair from her face.

"No, thank you. I've had two cups already," Beau said, smiling.

He now didn't trust himself not to break one of the teacups and believed they were safer right where they were.

"Well, do you need to use the restroom, then? You've been here awhile."

"Now that you mention it, that would be great."

Beau stood up, feeling the stretch in his legs and the stiffness subsiding. It felt good.

"Let me show you where it tis."

Ruby walked over to a wall of books, with Beau in tow, and pulled a silk tassel suspended from the ceiling. At that, the door creaked and groaned as it opened on cue.

"Well, here you are. Tucked away like a mouse in a hole. It's one of Oliver's favorite places. I'll be here waiting."

"Thank you, Ruby."

Beau was grateful to step away for a moment to shake off the other two women. Their energy was heavy and unnerving. He splashed some cold water on his face hoping to wash away the ugliness, then took this opportunity to poke around a bit, opening the drawers or cupboards, looking for anything that might be of interest. He was always curious about what people had tucked away. He must have been gone for some time, as the knock on the door startled him.

"Beau, everytin all right in there?"

"Ugh, yes, be right out."

Ruby had moved to the window when Beau returned.

"That's a beautiful brogue you have, Ruby."

"All the way from Scotland, it tis."

He was drawn to her. She has a sense of warmth, and he could see why Oliver would be so fond of her and want to keep her around. *The only breath of fresh air in this place,* he thought. Imagine the sweet little grandmother type in any children's book, and this would be the mirror image of Ruby, upswept hair in a bun with wisps of gray springing out here and there. Her once thick Scottish accent was now watered down from living abroad. She had on a gray dress, a white apron, stockings, and black leather lace-up shoes. Beau guessed it was a uniform she found so familiar she was not ready to give it up. She had a jolly face with chubby, rosy cheeks, faded blue-gray eyes, and a smile that could light up a room.

"How long have you been here? With the family?"

"I came over from Wick, Scotland, by me lonesome on a cattle boat, when I was sixteen with only a suitcase and fifteen dollars in my wallet a very long time ago. You know, back then, the choices were few and far between, and each choice a bit much to bear, but I knew it was either leave Scotland and try to make a life in another country or starve to death."

"At that time, between the potato famine and wars, you couldn't just walk down to the shops for a packet of crisps, now could ya? I even knew of some who were forced to kill the family pet and eat them to survive. Others were forced into eating pieces of their dearly departed, may God bless their soul. Everyone was struggling. Graves were ravaged, and there were even reports of parents eating their wee ones and the wee ones eating their parents," Ruby's quavering voice paused a moment. She looked down at the floor and wiped a silent tear away, then lifting her head, and in a stronger voice she continued.

"It was harsh times indeed. Hard to think that's how it was then, especially when you're sitting in a place like this. There wasn't enough money for me entire family to move to America, and since I was one of the healthiest and at an age where I would be able to earn money, I was sent away whilst the others stayed behind. It was like a death sentence to me as I knew the chances of them surviving were slim."

"I remember asking me mum and pa not to see me off at the dock because I wanted to remember them all sitting around the kitchen table singing and talking about what we would do once we could get on our feet again. This way, with them not there, I could pretend I was just off on an afternoon journey, soon to return to them. I promised them that when I got to the United States, I would make enough money and send for them. Somehow, they all knew this would never happen. I did not want my last vision of my mother to be of her crying and upset at the boat dock knowing this was likely the last time we would ever see each other."

"When I landed at the dock, I set out right away to get work and found this job, to be a nanny to Oliver. He was such a sweet little lad. You can imagine back then, those big blue eyes looking atcha so innocently."

"You're a merry soul, just like Oliver. I'm sure ya didn't want to hear all that, now did ya, Beau?"

"I sure did, and I also want to hear what life was like for Audra living here and whether you talked with her recently?"

"If you ask me, she did this. She knows more than she's saying."

"Who do you mean by 'she,' and did what exactly?"

Ruby's voice got low, and she moved her chair in to get closer to Beau.

"That mother of hers. If you can call her that. But you didn't hear it from me. I raised those bairns, each and every one of 'em. I think she did something to get rid of her. When Oliver said Audra was missing, I was gobsmacked and started crying like a fool, but Charlotte, she stood there stone-faced. She's a viper, always has been."

"But how do you think she would do that?"

"She struts around like a proud peacock, but she's an awful nasty little thing, Beau. She treats Oliver and those kids horribly. Well, not Abby and Richmond, because they just do whatever she says, but the others? Forget it. If you ask me, I think she had someone take her. Audra hated her mother with a passion, and she so much as told me so. No, I think she has something to do with it. You mark my words."

"When you say she had someone take her, what do you suppose they did with her?"

"Well, that I don't know. It would be hard to imagine a mother killing her own wee bairn, so I don't know, Beau. I just don't know."

"You were at dinner when Jamie was here, correct? Did you notice anything unusual then? Did you pick up on any of the conversation Audra and her mother may have had?"

"Yes, I was there, but with everyone talking, I couldn't tell you what was said. My hearing's not the best these days, ya know."

"I do know that something happened between Audra and her mother awhile ago. A big secret. Audra said she had uncovered something about her mother that no one was ever supposed to know and that she stumbled upon it by accident."

"Did she tell you what it was?"

"No, I asked, but she said she wanted it to be a surprise for everyone and that she hadn't thought through all the details yet. I'll bet Charlotte found out. Oh, my poor sweet Audra. She's a good woman, ya know. I told her long ago to just move on, forget about her mother and start a new life. Has anyone called looking for ransom money?"

"No, which is what is making this all seem so odd. A rich woman vanishes, with no trace and no real reason to. Do you know any of Audra's friends, or groups she belonged to?"

"I don't know of any friends, Beau. She's probably closest to the people she works with. Charlotte never encouraged her to have any friends growing up. She was so cruel to that woman, so she never brought any home to meet us, and as for groups, I know she loves animals and had talked about helping at the animal shelter, but I don't know for sure. You might try there and ask them. I don't get to see her as often as I would like, since she doesn't come by here much at all and I don't drive anymore."

"How does Charlotte treat you?"

"She tolerates me because Oliver would give her hell otherwise. I'm the one person Oliver will actually stand up to her over. I stay out of her way if I can. Plus, how would that look to the city folk throwing the old nanny out of the house with nowhere to go. You know, Beau, I am a loving, God-fearing woman, and God forgive me for saying this, but that woman is Satan in designer clothes. Please help the wee bairn, Beau. Please find our darling Audra."

"I will do everything in my power to find her. Here's my card. If you think of anything, don't hesitate to call me. And Ruby, it was a pleasure meeting you."

"The pleasure was all mine. Now please bring Audra home," Ruby said as she grabbed on to both of Beau's hands again, her weathered fingers tightening their grip.

"I'll do my best," Beau said, being clear not to make promises he could not keep.

As Beau drove down the driveway of Sutherland's Crossing, he thought about what a dismal place it turned out to be. When he walked in the door earlier, it shone like a new penny, but now the light was gone, and only a dark-gray heaviness was left.

He headed back to the station to pick up Simon, and then they would head to Newhaven Medical Clinic. By now, Simon should have answers to what he was researching and could fill Beau in on the drive there.

## FRIDAY, MARCH 10, 1995

# NEWHAVEN MEDICAL CLINIC

Beau and Simon stepped inside the front doors of the Newhaven Medical Clinic's lobby, and the scent changed immediately from the fresh outdoor air to that of a sterile, bleached environment. How is it that all medical facilities smelled the same? *Hardly a place you are comfortable and at home in,* Beau thought. As he approached the front desk, the receptionist was as sterile looking as the rest of the place, with her hair pulled tightly back in a stiff bun and an expressionless face.

"May I help you?" the woman asked.

"Yes, my name is Detective Beau Crenshaw, and this is police Constable Simon Miller. We're here to see Lana Montgomery."

116

"One moment, please," she said without so much as moving a face muscle.

With precise robotics, she picked up the phone and dialed.

"Ms. Montgomery, Detective Beau Crenshaw and police Constable Simon Miller are here to see you. Of course."

There was a pause as the thin-faced woman put the phone back in the cradle and, raising her eyes to meet the men, said, "Ms. Montgomery will be with you shortly."

"Thanks."

Forgetting he still had that morning's toothpick in his mouth, he quickly tucked it away in his shirt pocket for later just as a woman approached from the left, this one far more inviting, as she extended her hand along with a wide, warm smile.

"Mr. Crenshaw. I'm Lana Montgomery. How can I help you today?"

For an HR person, she had an oddly pained expression.

"Thank you for seeing us." Beau turned slightly to his left and made a hand gesture. "This is Constable Simon Miller, and we're here to talk about Audra Barrington. Do you have some place we could talk in private?"

"Of course, please follow me."

The sounds of her clicking heels on the tile floor were dulled by the suctioning of the men's leather loafers as they moved along in pack formation. An eerily daunting and agitating sound for a place that was supposed to bring people out of their misery.

They walked without saying a word to a boardroom, sound-proofed by a wall of windows for privacy. Everyone sat down; Beau set out his tape recorder. Simon sat up tall next to Beau. Lana sat opposite, legs crossed, and hands folded in her lap.

"I'm going to tape our conversation, if you don't mind."

"Not at all."

"I spoke with Oliver Barrington, and he said you were the one that called him saying Audra was missing."

"Yes, that is correct. We had him as her emergency contact, and when she didn't show up for work by the second day, we felt something was wrong. Audra never misses work. She is always the first one here and the last to leave."

"Do you know her well?"

"I don't know whether you could say 'well.' I mean, we don't go out after work or anything, because I have a husband and kids to get home to, but I will say that at work we are close. We all love Audra here, and she has been a godsend for the patients. She has a wicked sense of humor but a unique way of putting people at ease, so the patients warm up to her easily."

"Do you know whether she is dating anyone?"

"No one she talks about. I don't even know how she would have time. Truly, the woman is here constantly—even on the weekends to accommodate those with full-time jobs during the week. She offers to see patients for any of the other doctors on vacation or if someone calls in sick. She knows how important it is for the patient's well-being to not have their appointment rescheduled, which is why her absence raised eyebrows."

"She sounds like a saint."

"She truly is, and we are all distraught that she is missing."

"Was anyone here friendlier with her, maybe someone that would go out for drinks after work, dinner, a movie?"

"Yes, speak with Rebecca Latham, but she's off today. She'll be back in the office on Monday. I can give you her phone number."

"Her number would be great. If I can't reach her, I'll stop by on Monday. Is she another psychiatrist?"

"Yes."

"Do you know of any patients Audra may have had a run-in with, maybe someone not pleased with her, stalking her? Can we get her patient list?"

"Not that I'm aware of, but I think for that information, you would need to talk with the director, Albert Lancing. Patient-doctor confidentiality, you know."

"We have a court order on its way to the judge as we speak."

"Don't you think that's a bit premature?" Lana said, her expression laced with concern.

"In my line of work, I've found doctors don't like saying too much for fear the crazies will get offended, so-"

Lana cut him off in mid sentence. "I don't think it's appropriate to call everyone who visits a psychiatrist crazy."

"True that, but commingled in among the semi-sane is a crazy, and that is the one we may need to weed out."

"Is there anything else you can tell us about her habits, places she may eat at lunch, hobbies she may have, clubs she belonged to?"

"I wish I could offer more, Detective, but I didn't get that deep into her personal life. I do think Rebecca will have more insight into those areas."

Beau shut the tape recorder off and tucked it back in his pocket while rising from the table.

"Well, thank you for your time." Beau handed her his business card. "If you think of anything, you can reach me day or night."

"Good to know you'll do everything you can to find her."

"Of course. Oh, and one last question, has she ever talked to you about her family?"

"Nothing out of the ordinary. The only one that I recall is Rita, Rosie, no, Ruby. She often talks about what a sweet woman Ruby is and how grateful she is that Ruby was always there for her growing up. I don't know what relation Ruby is to her, though."

"Interesting. We'll see ourselves out," Beau said as he got up to leave. Simon followed suit.

Back in the car, he thought about the vastly different picture he was getting of Audra depending on whom he was talking with.

"I wonder who you really are, but I think I know," Beau said aloud.

"What was that, sir?" Simon asked.

"Just that depending on who you talk with, people make Audra out to be this kind, caring person, while her mother and sister believe her to be a monster. Having met the mother and sister, if I were a betting man, Simon, and I am, I'm betting on everyone else. And don't you find it odd that this woman claimed to know nothing about her but yet could remember the nanny's name? I find that odd. Radio the station and see whether there is an an answer back from the judge. I want to see her patient files. If so, we'll swing back there, and if not, we're off to the forensics lab."

Beau could easily have done the task himself, but he kind of liked the kid, and he overheard some of his peers giving him a hard time about his scrawny body not being able to chase down a ten-year-old and how did he ever pass the physical. Beau hated arrogant jocks, so decided he might just take him under his wing. Maybe.

"Dispatch, this is Simon Miller, here with Beau Crenshaw. Has the judge signed the court order to review Audra Barrington's patients' medical records at New Haven?"

"Simon, hold while I check on that," dispatch said.

Less than five minutes passed before dispatch advised that the judge declined the court order, saying he couldn't sign it without probable cause.

"Well, ain't that a kick in the pants," Beau said.

"Why wouldn't the judge sign the court order?" Simon asked.

"It's typical in a situation like this. No body, no crime, no viable threats. There is just one missing person. Looks like we're off to the forensics lab. Let's see whether they have anything useful for us."

## FRIDAY, MARCH 10, 1995

# DUE DILIGENCE

Cecil, the crime-lab assistant, was drenched in sweat as Beau and Simon entered the lab.

"Cecil, what the hell, man? It has to be a hundred degrees in here," Beau said.

"No shit, man. I'm ready to pass out," Cecil said with a hardy laugh. "Heating system malfunction, so we all get to clean out our pores."

Cecil's thick Jamaican accent always made things sound less serious than they were.

"I trust you won't be working in this environment for long?"

"They are working on it as we speak, and don't even say it, Crenshaw. I know you want to."

"Say what?"

"That I should be used to the heat, comin' from Jamaica and all."

"I never said a word." Beau snickered. "I hope this hasn't messed up any of the evidence. What do you have for us?"

"What evidence? I wish I had something to give you, but I don't. There are no matches in ARBIS for the blood found in the kitchen. We got a set of her fingerprints from when she became licensed to practice medicine, so we isolated the prints found in the apartment that match Audra's. We ran the other two prints, but no matches came up."

"Cecil, I was hoping you'd be able to point me in the right direction."

"I can tell you where to go, man, but it's not going to help your case," Cecil jibed.

Beau slapped him on the back as he turned to leave.

"Always trying to be the funny man. Don't quit your day job, you've got mouths to feed. See you around, Cecil."

Simon scampered off behind Beau.

"Whoa, sure am glad to be out of that heat," Simon said. "Where to now?"

"Now we call the friend, what was her name, Rebecca? Let's see whether she can shed some light."

On the drive back to the station, Beau glanced over at Simon, who was sitting rigidly in the passenger seat.

"Any siblings back home?" Beau asked.

Simon looked grateful for the questions.

"Yup, three sisters, and I'm the middle kid."

"Mom? Dad?"

"Yeah, Dad works at the car plant on the assembly line, and Mom's a waitress at a diner near our house. I would have been on the assembly line, too had I not moved away."

"Your family must miss you, now that you're here."

"They do, but living there is a tough life, and my mom thinks I'll have a better future here. She's itching to get down here to visit me. I've been saving for a plane ticket for her," Simon said, beaming.

"You're a good kid. Keep up the good work, and you'll do all right," Beau said, reaching into his pocket for his toothpick, then pulled the sun visor down. "Sun's intense today!"

"What about you? Is your family from here?"

"Nope, and it's just me and my wife, Kathleen," Beau said while Simon nodded his head.

"Do you have kids?"

"No."

Seeing that Beau was not offering anything more, Simon decided not to ask any further questions.

They reached the police station, and Beau turned the car into the back alley, wheeled into the parking lot, and parked at the rear of the building with the rest of the police vehicles. Simon hopped out of the car while Beau grunted quietly, raising himself from the driver's seat. *Might wanna check into getting some more exercise,* Beau thought. As they entered the building, Beau turned to Simon and said, "Meet you in the conference in, let's say, fifteen minutes?"

"Good with me. See you then."

—

Simon sat across from Beau as he dialed up Rebecca Latham's phone number.

"Hello."

"Ms. Latham? Ms. Rebecca Latham?"

"Yes, who am I speaking with?"

"This is Detective Beau Crenshaw from the Charleston Police Department. I have you on speakerphone with police Constable Simon Miller. We're investigating the disappearance of Audra Barrington. Do you have a moment to clarify a few things for me?"

"Oh, Mr. Crenshaw. Yes, I'm so happy you called. I've been so worried about her. Have you found anything?"

"Not much I can share as of yet. I was hoping to ask you a few questions. I understand you both work together and that you may also socialize after hours."

"We are friends. I wouldn't say best friends, but we do hang out now and then."

"When was the last time you saw Audra?"

"At work on Monday. I was the one that said we should call her dad, because Audra is never late."

"You saw her Monday, then, and did you talk at all throughout the day? Did you go out after work?"

"I saw her at work, and we went out for lunch over at The Punchbowl Lounge. I know it sounds odd to go there for lunch, since neither of us had any alcohol, but on Mondays they have a two-for-one special, and their appetizers are literally to die for. Have you been there? If so, you'll know what I'm talking about."

"I'll be sure to check it out sometime."

"Audra loves the cheese-and-spinach-stuffed mushrooms and the atmosphere. She says nostalgia nourishes her old soul. Audra has a great sense of humor, and I love being around her. It's so easy. You know how with some friends, it's all about them, while others are boring, or narcissistic, but Audra, she's different. She's kind and caring, almost to a fault, but don't cross her. If she's standing up for something she believes in, she can whip that tongue around so fast they don't even see it coming. I've seen her do that on only a couple of occasions."

"Sounds like you two were close."

"We are somewhat close, because I don't know whether anyone can really get close to Audra. She's a private person, so she lets out only what she wants you to know. A wonderful friend and would do anything for you. God, I hope she's okay."

"Have you known her to do anything like this before?"

"No, never."

"Do you know whether she was seeing anyone?"

"Seeing as in seeing someone serious or just seeing someone, if you know what I mean?"

Beau shrugged. "Either or. Just throw them all at us."

There was a slight pause before she added, "Well, she did meet this guy that she would hook up with every now and then. Said he was pretty amazing in bed but had the personality of a block of concrete. And she said he was so full of himself that she could stand him only long enough to have sex, and then she would ask him to leave."

"Do you happen to remember his name?"

"No . . . Joe? John, maybe."

"Could it be Joshua?"

"Oh yeah, how did you know?"

"I've already talked with him, and I would say her assessment of him was pretty accurate."

Both Beau and Rebecca started laughing.

"That's Audra. She knew one when she saw one. She would even tell him that he couldn't say anything, or her dad would have his business shut down. Can you believe that? She's a pistol!"

"Did she ever mention that he had a violent streak or threatened her in any way?"

"No, I never got that he was that type."

"Did she ever mention a patient that she was having issues with? Stalker or violent type?"

"No, and I'm not supposed to divulge patient information, but if I knew of someone that I thought was going to hurt her, I would tell you, even if I did get into trouble."

"Anything else you can share with me that might help? Even if it seems unimportant, it could be. Hobbies? Did she belong to any clubs?"

"No, and honestly, I don't know when she would have had time. She was always working."

"Did she ever talk about her family?"

"She didn't seem all that close to her family, so I never asked about them. Figured that was her business, especially considering who they are. She knew I would listen if she needed to vent, but she never did. She was in great spirits on Monday. I think Casanova had visited her Sunday. She didn't seem upset by anything. She didn't talk about going away anywhere. I think I would have known if something was off, but I just didn't get any strange vibes, you know."

"Okay. If you think of anything, you have my number. Call me any time, day or night."

"Please find my friend, Mr. Crenshaw," Rebecca said with a cracked voice, emotions now starting to take hold.

"I'll do my best."

# THURSDAY, JUNE 1, 1995

# A BLANK CANVAS

Hours fell into days and days morphed into weeks, but Beau was still no further along from that first day when Oliver filed the missing person information report. He had checked her bank records. Nothing suspicious there. No movement of money in or out. He had checked all her credit cards, but any purchases ended the week she disappeared. He reviewed her phone records, but there was nothing out of the ordinary. It seemed the last call had been to Joshua on the Sunday before she went missing, which matched Rebecca's comment that she thought Audra had been with Joshua on that Sunday.

Beau had learned about some of Audra's favorite restaurants from Rebecca and visited all of them where employees confirmed they had not seen her after she went missing and never noticed anything suspicious or unusual about her behavior. They said she either dined alone, with a woman around her age, or got takeout. When shown a picture of Rebecca Latham, they all confirmed she was Audra's dining partner, and most made a point to add what a great tipper Audra was.

Beau sat in his office, pictures of her apartment strewn out in front of him. Simon sat across from him, quietly observing Beau's facial expression.

"Her mother confirmed the jewelry in her apartment as gifts she and her father had given her as Christmas presents over the years. The store clerk at Wallabee's Grocery seemed to be the last person to see her. She described what she bought that day, but the pictures we took of her apartment don't show any of the food the clerk said she bought, but then maybe she donated it to a food kitchen. She was, after all, into helping others. It just doesn't add up, Simon. It's as if she vanished into thin air. I imagine this is what an artist feels like when they don't know what to paint and are staring at a blank canvas."

"Where do we go from here?" Simon asked.

"The family will be making a formal statement on TV and radio about offering a two-hundred-fifty-thousand-dollar reward for anyone knowing her whereabouts. And you know the sick thing, Simon?"

"What's that?"

"I don't think the mother has any interest in being there during the announcement, but she will, just to save face and look like a caring, grieving mother. Prepare yourself for the worst too as our phone lines are about to explode. Everyone will want to cash in on this, and we will get people calling in who don't even have a clue who she is, but they saw someone who looked like her eight years ago. I'm not for something like this, but then we've exhausted all other avenues.

We may as well go down this path. Oliver is chomping at the bit to have this televised. He thinks this will work. That the money will make someone rat on someone or break someone down. Money does talk, so we shall see. Just be prepared for a lot of whack jobs."

Beau looked up from his desk and glanced at the wall clock that had just struck 6 p.m.

"Crap, I need to get going. Simon, why don't you get going, too."

"Okay, I'll see you tomorrow," Simon said as he got up from the chair and left Beau's office.

*I'm headed for divorce if I'm late for our dinner reservation,* he thought. He pushed all the photos back into the manila envelope, grabbed his hat, and headed out of his office.

The restaurant wasn't far from the police station, so he told Kathleen he would meet her there. This had been their third dinner out in the last month and a half. He had to say it was nice reconnecting with his wife, although something was always just a bit off, as if he were walking on eggshells but didn't know why.

He turned onto Blanche Street and self-parked. He didn't want a valet to have access to a police car.

Even though he was a few minutes early, Kathleen was already inside and seated. *Of course,* he thought. He just couldn't catch a break being one step ahead of her. Story of his life.

She smiled at him warmly as the maître d' guided Beau to their table.

"I was beginning to wonder whether you would make it on time," she said.

Bam! There it was. Not "Hello, sweetheart, I'm so happy to see you." Not " How was your drive over?" It was always some cutting remark, as if he were this useless tool that was capable of being only inadequate and she was shocked he got it right for a change.

"Well, you look very nice tonight," Beau said, knowing he couldn't say what he was really thinking. "Have you been waiting long?"

"No, I just got here myself."

"Good," Beau said as he made himself comfortable in the chair. "Ah, there," he said, letting out a big breath. "I'm ready for some grub."

"Beau, seriously," Kathleen said snidely. "This is a four-star restaurant. You better not let them hear you call their food grub."

"It was just a figure of speech. Now, let's see what's looking good tonight," Beau said, stewing over her comment but making sure his tone didn't come across as defensive, because his mind had already gone to wanting to shred her with words.

"Would you like some wine?" Kathleen asked.

"I'd love some. Did you see something in particular, or would you like me to select it?"

"Why, Beau Crenshaw. I'm impressed. I think that's the first time you have ever asked me that."

"I guess our counseling sessions are making me want to turn over a whole new leaf," Beau said, eyes remaining focused on the menu. He no sooner said the last word when he realized the wait-person had slid up to their table.

"Hello, my name is Harold, and I will be your server this evening. Can I get you anything to drink, or would you like to start out with an appetizer?" he asked, looking toward Beau.

"Wine would be lovely," Kathleen said. "Let's go with this Riesling," she added, pointing to the menu.

"That's a wonderful choice," Harold commented and walked away gracefully.

Beau felt the slap in the face but let it go yet again and instead said, "Riesling it is!" throwing his hands in the air.

Harold returned to the table with a breadbasket and wineglasses. Behind him, another server handed him the bottle of wine, which Harold took hold of, and he wrestled the cork from the bottle until there was a tiny pop, pausing for a moment as he calculated which person should be the taste tester.

"I will let the Mrs. do the taste test to make sure all is to her liking," Beau said to Harold, intercepting the awkwardness. Harold gave Beau a gracious smile that translated to "I hear you, man," poured a small amount of wine into Kathleen's glass, and waited for her to give the thumbs-up.

"That is quite lovely, Harold," she said.

"Excellent," Harold said as he poured the wine for each. "Have we decided on an appetizer, or are you ready to order your main entrée?"

"I think we need just a few more minutes," Kathleen said piping up.

"Of course. I will be back to check on you in a few," Harold said.

As Harold walked away, Kathleen held up her glass and said, "Cheers!"

"Cheers," Beau replied, clinking his glass against hers, not sure exactly what they were cheering for and definitely was not going to ask.

"Any news on Audra?"

That was the first time Kathleen talked about his work.

"No, unfortunately we are at a dead end. The family is going to offer a reward for any information leading to her whereabouts."

"That should open the floodgates and not in a good way. If you ask me, I think she ran away and is living on some beach on a deserted island somewhere."

"Really? Why would you say that? What would be the point? Why not just move away?"

"I think she met someone, maybe even one of her patients, and knowing her life would be under a microscope here with the local gossip and that mother of hers, she just decided to disappear with her man and live happily ever after. Get out of the limelight. Hide some money in an offshore account. Love makes you do all sorts of strange things."

"Hmm. Interesting. I guess I never thought of her running away with someone."

# CURRENT DAY—WEDNESDAY, JUNE 21, 1995

# FORENSICS LAB

As Doc drove away from the crime scene and headed back to the morgue, his mind raced with all that he had just witnessed. Although it was never pleasant to unearth a dead body for the loved ones left behind, Doc's scientific mind lured him into a world of intrigue and curiosity over the cause of a corpse's final moments, which then set in motion a type of predicted enthusiasm to piece the puzzle together.

Arriving at the morgue now, Doc began the preliminary work before beginning the autopsy. This he did alongside his trusted assistant, Heather Vance.

"Heather, let's get her out of this body bag," Doc said as he un-zipped the white plastic bag used to transport the body back to the morgue. Evidence that could get jostled loose from the body while in transit is seen better in a white bag versus a black bag.

With Heather on one side of the table and Doc on the other, they rolled the body gently to one side then the other as Heather carefully removed the bag away from the body, in its entirety.

"I'll begin the registering and tagging if you want to scour the inside of the bag for evidence. This one is a doozy, Heather. I doubt you've come upon anything so awful. We could have a serial killer on the loose."

"Oh Lord," Heather said barely above a whisper.

Within the hour, Doc and Heather had finished the tasks and were now ready to begin the autopsy. They would identify the body lying in front of them as Jane Doe until a family member could positively identify her as Audra Barrington. Heather, armed with the digital SLR camera, positioned herself to where she could get shots of the entire body, zooming in for specific areas.

With Heather busy taking pictures, Doc began his collection of facts for the autopsy report.

"We have a Caucasian female, Jane Doe, late twenties to early thirties with brunette hair, measuring five feet six and three-fourths inches in height and weighing 143.8 pounds. She is wearing an orange-colored sundress covered with tiny flowers in the shape of daisies with sandals along with a bra and underwear. No other items are present on her person, such as jewelry or hair adornments. Both ears have been pierced, but no earrings are present. There are no distinguishable markings such as scars, tattoos, or additional piercings."

Doc walked around the body, examining every inch before proceeding. "Okay, you can begin cutting the clothing, Heather."

Heather cut away the dress and undergarments and removed the sandals slowly from her feet so as not to disturb any potential evidence. Once all pieces were tagged and bagged individually, she walked them next door for processing.

Doc continued recording his observations. "She was found with bloodstains on her skin and clothing. Between her clavicle and groin, she has deep lacerations, each approximately six inches in length and sewn together loosely with what appears to be fishing line. There are twelve lacerations in total. Each of the lacerations is circled in what appears to be red lipstick."

When Heather returned, Doc had the tools laid out in the order they would use to extract tissue samples.

"I'm going to start with drawing blood."

It was a long shot, but Doc wanted to see the potassium levels of the vitreous humor, which is extracted from the liver, to see whether this could prove useful in narrowing the time-of-death window.

"Why don't you collect the fingernail and toenail scrapings."

"Sure thing, Doc."

Both worked in silence but spoke aloud when they discovered something worth noting. A large recorder above the table recorded this conversation so they could refer to it later.

As Heather reviewed the fingers and toes, she remarked that both the hands and feet were well manicured and painted in a blue-toned red polish that was smudged. This seemed to match the color of the lipstick on the lacerations. Before head and pubic-hair strands were plucked and bagged for the lab, they investigated the cuts, which were carved randomly all over her front section. When they reached her vaginal area, they discovered the vagina had been sewn shut. Doc cut the fishing line so they could gather vaginal fluids.

"Oh, my sweet Jesus, there is something in her vagina. What kind of psychopath are we dealing with here, Doc?" Using tweezers, Doc pulled out a tube of lipstick that was the same color as the circles on the cuts.

"Once we cut her open, we can see whether the killer has planted anything else. Let's continue getting our samples," Doc said.

Bodily fluids were extracted to test for any toxic chemicals. The vaginal and anal swabs would indicate whether there were any signs of semen or sexual assault present. Cultures were taken of the bowels and kidneys to look for any signs of an infection or toxic chemicals.

Every orifice, the nose, ears, mouth, vagina, and anus, was swabbed. As Doc moved the head to swab the ears, he made a new discovery.

"This is interesting. Heather, come and look at this. See the areas on her head where the hair appears to have been roughly cut close to the scalp, leaving these jagged, fringed edges? These are small, not large areas. What do you make of this?"

"The hairs have definitely been cut, and it looks like either a knife cut or a dull pair of scissors," Heather said.

"Dull scissors maybe. If cut by a knife, there would be a much higher concentration of upward movement with regard to the lengths, but this has been cut close to the scalp. Interesting. Go ahead and get lots of pictures of this. Actually, given how precise the lacerations were, the knife used was extremely sharp, so it is possible that the hairs could have been cut with the knife. Perhaps it is the same knife that made the other lacerations. Let's get her wheeled into the X-ray room. See what story those pictures are going to tell us."

A full body X-ray was completed.

Doc started into the full postmortem exam.

"I see five puncture wounds on her left arm, hand and face from what appears to be from a snake. We'll get a sample of the venom found in each of the bites so we can determine the type of snake. We know a water moccasin was found in the car, so we need to see whether it matches the bites."

"But we don't have the snake to match it to."

"Ah, but we do. I managed to bag the head before Walter got his hands on it," Doc said, holding up a clear bag with the jaggedly chopped-off head of the snake from the car. "That man's a pistol. You should have seen him in action."

"Ugh! No thanks. I hate snakes, so I will let you handle that, if that's okay with you."

Doc let out a chuckle and said, "You can carve up dead bodies, but you're afraid of a little ole snake."

"Dead bodies don't bite you!"

They would have to wait until they could turn the body over to determine whether any bites were present on her back. If bites were present, that would indicate a lot of bites for someone to have, making it appear she was flailing her arms around to get the snake away from her. That would also indicate that she was awake or partially coherent. If that were true, then she was alive when the snake bit her and likely alive when she entered the water. That would not have been a pleasant way to die.

"I've extracted the venom. Can you run this next door?"

"Sure thing."

Doc knew he needed to arrive at an approximate time of death, but when a body has been submerged in water, it is difficult to measure. The time of death on a fresh corpse can best be ascertained through a measurement of core temperature using a rectal thermometer. There is a common formula used to calculate time of death that states that the body loses 1.5 degrees Fahrenheit per hour. Other factors are taken into consideration. Was the body found inside or outside? What is the ambient temperature of each? Was the body clothed or unclothed? The time of death is crucial, as it aids investigators when interviewing people about their alibis and witness statements. When submerged in water, the body temperature drops, so that formula is not a trusted measure.

When the heart stops beating, blood stops flowing throughout the body and now responds to gravity, pooling into the parts of the body closest to the ground, causing a marbleized discoloration of the body. About twenty to thirty minutes after the heart stops beating, livor mortis begins. Doc knew the woman had been found sitting up in the car seat, so he started to look for blanching by which the blood will leave the area of the body wherever pressure is applied. Once livor mortis has fully set in, blanching ends, so if he were to come across areas in which he could detect blanching, this could mean that she was killed somewhere else and placed in the car. He did not detect any such blanching, so his theory of her dying in the car was much more plausible.

Approximately three to six hours after death, rigor mortis begins making the muscles lock into place, starting with the small muscles in the head, the eyelids, and jaws, moving on to the fingertips, neck, and lastly the larger muscles. Rigor mortis dissipates from eighteen to thirty-six hours in. As the rigor mortis was not present, he knew she had died longer than eighteen hours, then.

Doc needed to conduct another test, which looked at the decomposition of the body and what insects were now feeding on the corpse. He knew this was a long shot, since the car was completely sealed. Anywhere from ten to fifty hours after death, determining time of death becomes a wild card. Since bodies begin to decompose after the first several hours, each body can decay at a different rate, and this is dependent on many different factors, including the person's age and the health of the victim. Certain bugs known as blowflies are the first bugs to be attracted to a dead body. As long as they have easy access to the body, they will arrive in minutes, colonize within the hours and begin laying tiny eggs in batches generally in orifices or wounds, and about fifteen to twenty-six hours later, the eggs will hatch into maggots that will feed on the corpse for days. By day four, the maggots migrate and become cocoon-like pupae in dry areas away from the body and may begin to attract other insects that want to now feed on the pupae. Again, because the body was submerged in water and concealed in the car, Doc was not able to get an accurate result from this test, so he proceeded to check the bloating of the body.

The insects change on a bloated body, which is a byproduct of bacterial activity in the organs leading to an accumulation of gases. There are several areas to test, but the most prevalent is the measurement of skin bacteria, and the other is the bacteria in the small intestine. This form of measurement Doc knew was still in its infancy stage of testing and that his best guess would be but a long shot, but he also knew that any narrowing of the time was important. He gathered plenty of samples and went back to the lab area to check his finds under the microscope. Based on the decomposition of the body and Doc's test, the results narrowed the path, but still not to an exact time. Doc could only estimate she had been dead for less than two weeks.

"Let's take a look inside you, Jane Doe," Doc said, starting with a Y-shaped incision that went from both shoulders that join over the sternum and ended at the pubic bone. The skin and underlying tissue were then separated to reveal the rib cage and abdominal cavity. From there he removed the front of the rib cage to expose the neck and chest organs. This opening also allowed him to review the trachea, thyroid gland, parathyroid glands, esophagus, heart, thoracic aorta, and lungs.

"Everything looks good here. Even your heart is in good

condition, so it would appear you did not have a heart attack when bitten by the snake. Lord knows I would have. You are a brave woman, Jane Doe."

"How are your other organs?" Doc cut free the abdominal organs, which also included the intestines, liver, gallbladder and bile duct system, pancreas, spleen, adrenal glands, kidneys, ureters, urinary bladder, abdominal aorta, and reproductive organs. "Hmm, looks like the organs of a thirty-something."

As he moved to the brain, Doc made an incision in the back of the skull. Once cut, he separated and peeled it forward. Using a vibrating saw, Doc removed the top of the skull and gently lifted the brain out the cranial cavity. Once all the pieces of the body were cut and separated, Doc noted any changes visible to his naked eye. Was there any artery disease, atherosclerosis, or cirrhosis of the liver? Were any tumors present? Any signs of malignant cell damage? He took small samples of each organ and prepared slides that he could then examine under a microscope. While he examined each of the samples noting any abnormalities, Heather went to work putting the organs back into the body. Doc needed to determine whether there was some other medical reason why she ended up where she did. Once all the organs were put back, the body was sewn shut.

"Heather, it's been a long day. Let's get out of here and get some shut-eye."

"Sounds good, Doc. See ya tomorrow," Heather said as she headed toward the women's locker room to clean up before she left the building for the night.

## THURSDAY, JUNE 22, 1995

# THE EXAMINATION RESUMES

There was no conclusive evidence to support that Jane Doe had died of natural causes, but Doc would need to wait on the test results to confirm this before ruling it out completely. He knew Beau would be chomping at the bit for an answer, and when everyone learned that this could be a Barrington, no stone would be left unturned. Charlotte Barrington had a lot of clout in Charleston and was known to be extremely difficult. If this was indeed her daughter, all hell was about to break loose. There were a number of items on the table that could have killed her. Was it the lacerations? Snakebites? Drowning? Something else?

Eager to continue the examination, Doc arrived at the lab promptly at 7 a.m. Today he would focus on the lab results from the contents of the car. While not much, there had been the wallet, hairbrush, comb, compact mirror, a couple of Band-Aids, and some chewing gum. If the purse did indeed belong to the woman in the car, then the driver's license and other ID cards all indicated this was Audra Barrington. There was also a potato sack found in the back seat and lying next to it some twine.

He would also meet with Coleman Niles, an excellent crime-scene investigator whose task was to examine the car. Coleman, a retired marine, believed as Doc did, that murders had been a little scarce in the last few years, so this kind of case pulsed through their veins and got the adrenaline pumping.

"Coleman, my man, glad to be working with you on this. I know this is Beau's department and he'll be over shortly, but I wanted to see what you found and most particularly whether you found any signs of chemicals," Doc said as the two men shook hands.

"Pleasure's all mine, Doc. Let me take you back to the garage," Coleman said as he led Doc to the garage area where the car now lay exposed in many areas as the doors had been removed, door panels taken off, and all carpets removed along with the car seats.

"For the most part, the car was clean. We found three sets of prints. One set belongs to Wayland Stewart, who is a mechanic at Hobbs's Mercedes dealership where the car is serviced. He had a DUI some years ago, which is how we were able to match up his prints. I presume one set will be the victim, and then we have the sister's print, Abigail Barrington, from when she started working at her current firm. Wayland said one of the sisters had been there within the month to have her car serviced. They both drive the same year, make, and model. Their father, Oliver Barrington, has an account at the dealership, so he pays for everything."

"Interesting," Doc said.

"This is where it does get interesting, Doc. Check out the

scratches on the front bumper. They are relatively new, as there is no rust present. Exposed metal will rust from the constant humidity. The oxidation process starts at the very second that metal is exposed and becomes visible, depending mainly on the rate of carbon in that particular steel. This could happen in days or up to a month. Now, consumer-grade steel and other iron-rich metals are capable of developing rust iron oxide after just four to five days of exposure. No rust means that these scratches have occurred in the last four to five days."

"Fantastic. This helps narrow the timeline down."

"And the winch found at the scene did indeed have a tow hook and line attached to it. This explains the scratches on the car grille. At some point, the tow hook had been attached to the car, but was it to try to get the car in or out of the water? We don't know. Based on where the winch was found and the fact that someone had to manually crank it, the winch was not in an ideal place to pull a car out of the water. How the winch was angled supports the conclusion the winch was used to pull the car into it."

"Fascinating," Doc said.

"And check this out. The other interesting observation is that all the car door lock knobs have been removed and a type of putty shoved in each of the holes. We tested the putty, and it is an epoxy putty consisting of resin and a hardener so when mixed together, it forms an extremely strong water-resistant bond. Even being submerged in water, it will not disintegrate."

"Why on earth would anyone do this?" Doc said. "Just removing the lock knobs renders them inoperable. This doesn't seem like a case, then, of someone accidentally stepping on the gas instead of the brakes and ending up in the swamp. Somebody went to great lengths to make sure this woman was not going to get out of that car. Coleman, thank you for everything. This information is crucial to Jane Doe's death. I'll be in touch. Beau's going to want to go over all this with you."

Driving back to his office, Doc didn't like where his mind was going. What Coleman just told him meant this was premeditated murder.

Beau had been anxiously awaiting Doc's call, so answered on the first ring. "Doc, what do you have for me?"

"What I can say is you better come on over for a visit so we can discuss the details. It looks like premeditated murder is in play."

"Son of a bitch. And Mary? Does what happened to Audra mimic Mary's death?"

"I'm afraid there are a number of similarities."

"Shit, I need to get Oliver and head your way. Is she put back together enough for him to make a formal identification?"

"She will be by the time you get here."

"We'll see you shortly."

They still needed to determine how Audra died, why someone would kill her, and who did it. And the most burning question on Beau's mind was why she suddenly turned up dead now after all this time. *Where have you been, Audra Barrington?*

## THURSDAY, JUNE 22, 1995

# AN IDENTIFICATION IS MADE

It took Beau a moment to get his words formulated. Letting people know they need to identify their loved ones lying stiff on a cold steel slab in a morgue was never easy. This was one of the hardest parts of this job. Until this point, people have hope. Hope that the person would miraculously appear, but this visit meant all hope was gone. The only ceremony they would be planning now is a funeral, to allow for closure. Beau's demeanor would need to shift from ruthless killer catcher to a compassionate detective guiding the bereaved family through the process.

Today, as he had in the past, Beau would update Oliver on the status of the case, only today would be different. Today Oliver would get dreadful news. News that concluded Audra's existence. News that closed the chapter on her whereabouts.

Arriving at Sutherland's Crossing, Beau wondered whether Charlotte would make an appearance, finally convinced this was not a silly prank and that her children's count had just gone down by one. Entering the driveway of Sutherland's Crossing, he noticed for the first time how dreary it actually looked. This larger-than-life monstrosity of a home was supposed to be the biggest and the best that Charleston had to offer but instead looked like a sad and lonely place in which to shrivel away. The energy was never warm and inviting, but cold and haunting. Pausing for a moment to take a deep breath, Beau knocked on the door. After several minutes, the housekeeper opened the door with the same sad, sallow face as the house. He thought Molly would answer the door, but this was a face he did not recognize.

"Good afternoon. I'm Detective Beau Crenshaw. Is Oliver available?"

"Please step inside, sir, and I will check for you."

If Oliver were not home, Beau made a snap decision not to ask for Charlotte. Oliver could deal with his wife in his own way. Minutes later, the housekeeper returned.

"Sorry, sir, Mr. Barrington is still at the office. Would you like to speak to Mrs. Barrington?"

"Uh, no, thank you," Beau said. "I'll visit Mr. Barrington at his office. Do you mind calling him to let him know that I'm on my way?"

"Of course, sir."

The drive felt long and blurred, but he kept thinking about a comment he read in one of the magazines at the marriage counselor's office and by whom, he had no clue. It kept looping around in his head like a song that can't be forgotten. *We cannot solve problems using the same kind of thinking we had when we created them.* He wasn't even sure why it kept repeating in his head, but he wished it would go away. The sky, which earlier was a vibrant, crisp, periwinkle blue with fluffy white clouds, suddenly turned an ominous gray. Angry thunder clapped hard in the background, and the sky lit up as lightning bolts danced about, seeming to be closer than he would have liked. Was the thunder following his mood? The rain came next, hard and furious, making it difficult to see. These types of afternoon storms were not uncommon in these parts of the South. And just as fast as they arrived, they would go away but, in their wake, they could produce such excessive rain it would take a long while for the ground to accept the intense dumping of rainwater. As Beau turned the corner onto the street where Oliver's office was he thought about the storm he was about to bring this poor man. This storm wasn't about to leave as quickly as the one in which he was driving.

Beau ran from the car to the front door of the office, but even he wasn't fast enough not to be drenched by the time he got there. As he brushed himself off and tried to pull himself together, he opened the door into a foyer that was elegantly designed. On a different day, he would have stopped to admire the exquisiteness, but not today. It held no meaning for him today.

The receptionist greeted Beau with a smile. "Good afternoon, sir. How may I help you?"

Beau hated her fake smile but knew it was the news he was about to deliver that put him in this mood. He needed to shake it off. He looked at her nameplate. Susie Rowlands. Of course her name is Susie.

"I'm here to see Mr. Barrington. Is he available?"

"Do you have an appointment?"

"His housekeeper should have called ahead to let him know I was on the way."

"Certainly, sir. Let me check."

"Mr. Barrington will be right down," Susie said, placing the phone back in the cradle.

"Much obliged."

"Can I get you anything to drink while you wait?"

"No, thank you. I'm good," Beau said, wishing she would shut up now and shove that fake smile up her ass. He wanted to tell her this was not a social visit and beverages were not fitting for the news he was about to give. As the thought was leaving his mind, his heart started picking up the pace. Beau moved away from Susie toward the waiting area. Surely distance would make her stop. He needed no more questions from Susie. He needed to get himself settled before Oliver arrived.

No sooner had he turned around and headed toward the chairs than he heard the elevator door and a familiar voice greet him.

"Beau," Oliver said with a hopeful smile on his face.

Beau felt as if he were moving in slow motion as he turned around to greet Oliver, all the while wondering whether he should put on a pretend smile, just like Susie so as not to alert Oliver. He decided to look stone-faced instead.

"Oliver," Beau said as he reached out his hand to shake Oliver's hand quickly and sharply. "Do you have someplace we can talk?"

"Of course. Please follow me. It's good to see you. I do hope you are here today because there is some news. We'll go to the conference room."

Beau nodded and followed behind Oliver. "I trust Susie offered you a beverage?"

"She did."

By now, they had entered the room, and both men sat down at the conference table.

Beau took a big breath, his heart thumping in his chest, and said with hesitation, "Oliver, there's, uh . . . been a break in the case. A body has been found matching Audra's description, along with her identification. I need you to come to the morgue with me to formally identify the body."

Oliver could only stare at Beau, his mouth agape. The silence was thick and uncomfortable. Oliver hung his head low, and Beau knew he needed time to process what he had just heard, but he continued slowly and methodically. "It looks as if she may have drowned, and that foul play was involved." Beau almost whispered the last comment. He did not want to get into the details just yet, and the medical examiner hadn't confirmed drowning as the cause of death, but he believed that was the safest scenario to use. Baby steps, he thought.

"I didn't want you driving alone, Oliver, so I came here to get you and take you to where you need to go."

Oliver continued staring down, hands on head, then lifted his head to mutter, "She's dead? Dead? Audra? I can't believe my baby girl is dead. Are you sure it's her? Are you absolutely certain it's her? She's dead. No. No. No. My Audra's dead. No. No. No. Oh my God, this can't be happening."

At that, he jumped up out of the chair and said, "I need to see her, Beau. Let's go." Oliver's voice remained low and monotonic. It was easy to see he was holding back and trying to remain as strong as he could, but his quivering bottom lip was desperately trying to let the emotion out.

The two men walked out past the reception area and headed toward where Beau had parked his car. Oliver did not stop to tell Susie he wouldn't be back, that he was leaving to go view his dead daughter's body. *That would have wiped the smile off her face*, Beau thought. *Why was he so obsessed with this woman's smile? Maybe because she could smile. She wasn't dead. Where they were going, the only smiles would be the ones that the funeral home forced into place.*

Devastating is having to tell a parent their child is dead and then driving with him in the car to prove that fact. Beau decided to keep quiet during the drive and let Oliver decide whether to talk. He chose not to. He just stared out the passenger window. After what seemed like an eternity, they arrived at the morgue and walked to the waiting room.

"Please have a seat, Oliver," Beau said. "I'll let Doc know we're here."

Similar to when the electricity goes out and all that can be heard is the second hand of the battery-operated clock, so, too, was the quietness of the waiting room. As Beau stepped back into the reception area, he found Oliver bent over heaving. As he looked up, the eyes staring back at Beau had just aged thirty years.

"We are ready for you to come back, Oliver," Beau said gently. They walked slowly, knowing this was it. This would be the shock of a lifetime for Oliver, and by now Beau saw Oliver as this sad, lonely, wealthy man whose money was not buying him the happiness that maybe he thought or hoped it would. They stopped in front of a window area, and, as they turned to look inside, Oliver gave out a gasp and put his hand over his month. There before him was a dead body covered completely by a sheet and Doc standing next to her. Beau gave the nod to Doc to pull down the sheet to reveal Audra's face. Beau looked over at Oliver, who now had tears streaming down his face. In a very low voice, Beau said, "Oliver, can you identify this as your daughter Audra Barrington?"

It was barely audible, but Oliver muttered, "Yes. That's my daughter." At that, he began to wail uncontrollably. His hands on the window frame and head hung low, he unleashed his pent-up emotions and sobbed violently. As quickly as his emotions erupted, they ended just like the storm earlier that day, and he regained his composure enough to say, "Can I go in and see her?" Oliver said, looking at Beau pleadingly.

"Of course you can, Oliver," Beau said. "Please come in this way."

By now, seeing the hurt on this man's face, Beau, too, had welled up with a few tears. He put his hand on Oliver's back and led him into the room.

"Doc, Oliver would like to have some time with his daughter."

Doc had previously put a weighted liner under the sheet to prevent the sheet from moving around, and he placed a cap on her head to hide the surgical cuts and cuts to her hair. He wanted to spare Oliver seeing what travesty had been done to her body.

"Of course," Doc said. "Please take all the time you need. We'll be right outside the door."

Doc and Beau kept an eye on Oliver for a few minutes, to make sure he did not pass out, and then tried to look away, giving Oliver some privacy for his last words. Last words—something we all know we will have, in our lifetime, for someone we love. We just never know when. It was one of the saddest times Beau could remember. The sorrow on this man's face as he tried to hug her face was excruciating to watch. Audra's limp form was not responding to his clutch; gravity was now in control of her movements. A body that was cut up and stitched back together.

The scene was awkward and difficult to witness. He mouthed words as he petted her head, all the while his tears dropping onto her lifeless face. He would tenderly wipe them off as quickly as they met her skin. And then he would smile as if he were telling her something silly. As Doc and Beau waited patiently, their conversation was now on having to explain how she died, when she died, and by whose hands. This was not going to be good. They had to tell this father that his daughter had been murdered, but they were both committed to leaving as much of the details out as possible, because telling Oliver that she died in a horrific way, suffering intensely, was not going to be easy nor necessary. No parent needs that image left in his memory or at least not today. It would all come out in court when Beau found the sick bastard that did this to her.

Almost an hour had passed when Doc and Beau observed Oliver kiss her forehead one last time, and as he was mouthing some words to her, he pulled the sheet over her face. He stood still for a moment, then cupped his hands over his eyes as he burst into tears. His body was heaving. Next, he pulled his hands down and formed fists as he let out a guttural scream. Unclasping his hands and taking a deep breath, he moved away from the body and toward the door. The next time he would see his daughter, she would be lying in a casket in a pretty church, in a designer dress with her hair done and makeup just perfect. The very thing she loathed. Even in death, Oliver couldn't help her from the clutches of what she hated, but he would try.

## EVENING OF THURSDAY, JUNE 22, 1995

# MARRIAGE COUNSELOR

By the time Beau dropped off Oliver at home, it was already 6:18 p.m. and he had just twelve minutes to make it to the marriage counselor's office; that was at least twenty minutes away on a good day.

With a heavy foot he weaved his way across the side streets knowing full well the outcome of his tardiness. Kathleen and Beau had continued the counseling sessions faithfully each week, Kathleen absorbed in the past, Beau seeking to escape it. But if it pleased her and kept his marriage intact, he would oblige her.

At 6:38 p.m., Beau charged through the office door, out of breath and bracing for the onslaught.

"You're late. Again," Kathleen said disgustedly, arms folded together tightly.

"Nice to see you, too, Kathleen. Dr. Wesley, I'm very sorry for being late," Beau said, rushing to take his place on the sofa.

"It is quite all right, Beau. We were just getting settled in, so take a minute to get your thoughts together."

"There's been a murder. It's a woman that's been missing."

"Are we here to talk about a dead woman or our marriage?" Kathleen said in an agitated tone.

"Oh, Kathleen, have a little respect for the dead."

"How about having some respect for the living!"

"Let's not start today's session in a negative way." Dr. Wesley's soft voice carried the words more like a sonata than an instruction.

"Beau, some months ago, when you and Kathleen first started coming here, you mentioned a case you had worked on that seemed to have a grave effect on you. I would like to revisit that, if that's okay with you."

"I guess I'm gonna have to get it out at some point, since it keeps coming back to haunt me."

"Well, clearly it's affecting our marriage, so let it out so we can put this behind us," Kathleen said.

"Maybe you can just turn things off, Kathleen, but it's just not that easy for me. Not after what I saw. Sorry, but the shitty husband has emotions, too."

"Let's allow Beau this time to share his thoughts and reserve all comments until the end, okay?" Dr. Wesley said calmly.

"Well, as you may or may not remember, I was green. I just passed my detective's test, but I think I was pushed through because they were so shorthanded. I think the department thought that by throwing me a bone, it would entice me to stay. I was a rookie. I'd barely written traffic violations when I got called to check out a dead body in the hospital parking lot. Turns out it was Mary, Walter's

Mary. The same Mary that wouldn't hurt a fly. I met Mary. Hell, everyone knew Mary and Walter. They were involved with the church and every town social function you could imagine."

"When I got there, it was the most gruesome sight I had ever seen, but then I was so green I hadn't seen anything gruesome, not even a traffic accident. This was horrific to me. Blood was dripping from the bottom of the back door. I'll never forget the sound. Not even sure there was a sound, but I thought there was. Drip. Drip. Drip. I wanted it to stop. Awful. Her body was twisted up all wrong, and it looked as if she had been tossed around like a rag doll. I remember standing there looking at her, frozen, not even sure what to do next.

Guys were looking at me to give them directions on what to do, but I just stood there like a statue until finally a veteran cop gave me a nudge and told me to get on with it. This was Mary. Show her some respect. I wasn't being disrespectful—I just couldn't believe what I was seeing. This savage had raped her in a real bad way. And if that wasn't enough, he made strategic six-inch cuts all over her body and then sewed the cuts up with fishing line, leaving the stitches just loose enough that the blood would continue to seep from her body. Mary would have been alive during the process."

A gasp from Kathleen startled the doctor, who was holding on to Beau's every word.

"It gets worse, too. He had sewn her eyes shut, and when the medical examiner studied the body, he said the eyes had been removed. We never found them. Tell me, who keeps eyes they've cut out of someone's head? The cuts he carved into her were like a road map. Once the body was at the lab, we discovered he had circled all the cuts with red lipstick. We were never able to determine whether this was some sort of religious ritual or just some sick fuck with a vivid imagination. Chunks of her hair had been cut off close to her scalp, in random places. Mary's bloodstained clothes and nurse's cap were neatly folded in the trunk with the pieces of her hair and the tube of lipstick. Not a print to be found. We found ether in her system, so hopefully she passed out during it all, but who knows. To this day, that sick bastard is still at large."

Kathleen could only look wide-eyed at Beau as he continued his story.

"And we never figured out whether the killer looked for a large vehicle where he would have room to move about in the car's interior, or if he targeted her. She drove a 1974 four-door Chevrolet Impala that her Walter had bought in 1977 and kept in immaculate condition. I'll never forget that car, because my dad and I ran into Walter at the grocery store one day. My parents were at our house for a barbecue and we ran out of hot dogs, so Dad and I decided to run over to the store. We were in the parking lot, all jabbering away about what great shape it was in, and he was telling us about all the cool features it had. I bet he wishes he had never bought the car now."

Beau put his head in his hands. The room was dead silent. The ticking of the clock was the only sound that dominated the room. Lifting his head and looking years older just from telling the story one more time, Beau said, "So now you know why I really don't enjoy talking about it or the loss of our son. That shit will get hold of your core and drive you mad."

Even the doctor was at a loss for elevated words of wisdom.

"Thank you for sharing, Beau. I think we've covered enough for this session."

As Beau and Kathleen left the office, she took his hand for the first time in a long time.

**MONDAY, JUNE 26, 1995**

# LAB RESULTS

The only thing harder on a homicide detective than telling a person a loved one has died is telling them how the death occurred, and trying to soften the gory details of their demise if the event has been tragic. Having a person go through identifying the body at the morgue is excruciating enough for them and a memory that will stay forever engraved in their minds, but the gripping reality of the torture of what their precious loved one may have endured is not something for which people are prepared. They want to know, though. They want to hear it because somehow, they believe it will bring closure. Then, the minute the details are revealed, they wish they could hit a rewind button and erase it all. The brain fighting this newfound knowledge, not really knowing yet how to comprehend such damaging trauma, fighting now to protect its own self, not wanting to let such atrocious details in. And it never leaves; this thought, this memory that will strike with such pungent force, at any hour of the day or night, at any day of the week.

Getting to know Oliver more, over the course of months, meant that Beau could see what a kind and simple man he was, and who always had this look—a look of despondency as if everything was out of his control and he was merely a performing puppet brought to life when the show was about to start. He appeared hollow, as if there were no substance of his own, as if his mere existence were a struggle for him to get through each day. Beau believed Charlotte caused this man's defeat and his becoming an empty shell of a human.

It made Beau drift into thoughts of his own wife, Kathleen. His mistress was his job. Surely, marriage counseling would help get them back on course. They needed a reboot. Stripped back to the beginning.

Beau's mind jolted back to the present at the sound of his phone ringing, an annoying ring that jerked him up, and every time he told himself he needed to change it to something less irritating.

"Hello."

"Beau, it's Doc. We have some of the lab results ready. Thought you would like to know."

"On my way."

Beau made the drive in record time, likely breaking a few speed limits along the way, but he was eager to know what killed Audra Barrington.

Beau entered the building and started down the hall to Doc's office just as Doc was stepping into the hallway.

"That was fast. Follow me."

"Good to see you, too, Doc. What do you have that will catch a killer?"

Doc stopped dead in his tracks. "Beau, this one's ugly. Brace yourself. You're not going to like what you see."

The remainder of the walk was in silence, Beau's heart racing a little faster now wondering whether what he and Doc talked about at the crime scene may no longer be speculation.

Beau had been grateful he had been called out that day when the car was pulled from the water. Physical evidence is the most valuable tool in a criminal investigation as long as it is collected and preserved correctly. It cannot be retracted, is not contingent to subjective analysis such as when experts render a subjective opinion, in court based on the same tests and evaluative measures. The jury would be asked to provide a judgment based on the testimony of these experts, it can often be linked to a particular person or event and its use is not precluded by the First Amendment protection against self-incrimination.

The United States Supreme Court has ruled in several cases, including Schmerber v. California, 384 U.S. 757 (1966), that physical evidence, which can be fingerprints, blood, urine, photographs, and handwriting analysis, are not protected by the Fifth Amendment's protection against the self-incrimination clause.

As long as the physical evidence is collected and preserved in a legally correct way, it can and likely will be used in a court of law. Scientific analysis is generally considered to be irrefutable, such as when analyzing blood or bullet example comparisons depending on the expertise of the person offering the statement. The case Beau was building did not include any search warrants or witnesses at this time, so he was relying solely on the analysis of what Doc was about to give him, which made it that much more important for the evidence to be spot-on.

Beau had learned a lot since Mary's death, and he knew even as a young detective, everything had been done by the book but there was nothing to go on. Now with some years' experience behind him, if the killer left evidence, Beau was going to nail him.

They walked to the back of the lab, where the refrigerators were. Doc opened door number 458379 and pulled out the body of Audra Barrington.

"This is like a *déjà vu*, only more grotesque."

Doc pulled the sheet completely back as Beau gasped and took a step back.

"Oh my God! What the hell!"

"Seeing the cleaned six-inch cuts all over her torso area sewn together with fishing line was hard to take. This time, it looks like the skin has been folded over and cleaned with alcohol. He circles the cuts with red lipstick. I don't think he wanted her to bleed out this time. I think he wanted to keep his work secret until her body was found. Notice her nipples. They've been cut off, but we didn't find them. Remember with Mary, it was her eyes, and with this one, nipples. Is it because of two? Are these hate crimes against women or mothers? Also, this time, the lacerations were cut wider, forming a type of flap that he then sewed shut. She was penetrated vaginally, harshly. The walls of her vagina are torn and bruised. No semen was found in her vagina, but we did find something—a tube of lipstick. Guess what color, Beau? Red. He's back, Beau. The son of a bitch is back, and this time he's added some new things. Mary didn't have anything left inside her vagina. With Audra, not only did he shove the tube of lipstick inside her vagina, but he sewed her vagina shut. This is one sick mother."

"He likely had on gloves, probably a heavier grade to make sure they didn't rip. There were no evident skin cells under her finger-nails, nor were there any other hair or other fibers present under her nails. We did, however, discover very slight abrasions and contusions around all sides of her wrists, which would appear she was bound with something, but no other bruising was present. Unfortunately, with her being in the water for a period, this muddies things, so to speak, as it makes it difficult to give a timeline of when it happened. This, then, begs the question: Did she have these abrasions and contusions long before her event, or did they happen the day of?"

"We examined the contents of her stomach. As you know, while the major thrust of this analysis is to determine what she had as her last meal, it is also possible to estimate the deceased's time of death, although it is the least reliable. The stomach usually empties in two to four hours. The small intestine usually empties in ten to twelve hours."

"There are several variables that affect food digestion, such as stress. Extreme stress will slow the digestive processes. Illness is another factor that may slow or speed up the digestive processes. Nausea may lead to vomiting, thus emptying of the stomach. The type of food can also be a factor. Soft foods and liquids will speed up the process. Solids such as meat or corn will slow down the process. Drinking large quantities of liquids will speed up the digestive process. Well-chewed food will digest faster than slightly chewed food, and we look for the presence or absence of gastric/digestive juices."

"Audra's stomach contents held only trace amounts, suggesting she had not had a meal of any great quantity for several hours. Lingering acid levels showed fruit had been the last food eaten. No alcohol was present in her blood. We air-dried her clothes by placing each item of clothing on a piece of clean paper while drying. Once all was dry, we tested the materials for any kind of seminal fluid, urine, perspiration, other body fluids, stains, or blood. And while not meant to be all-inclusive for evidence, they help to paint a picture."

Suddenly Doc paused for a moment, getting his thoughts together, and then said, "We'll come back to the results of the material testing, but first I want to go back to the timeline and an approximate time of death. We can use the cloudiness of the cornea of the eye to estimate the time of death. Cloudiness will appear in twelve to twenty-four hours. The cornea is completely opaque in forty-eight to seventy-two hours. Audra's corneas were completely opaque, putting her in the forty-eight-to-seventy-two-hour range. Now speaking of the water." Doc swallowed and carried on. "We tested for longevity in the water. My first unfounded observation was up to two weeks but once concluded it proved to be closer to seventy-two hours, give or take."

Beau was aggressively chewing on the toothpick in his mouth, absorbing Doc's explanation, word by word, syllable by syllable, outraged at the likelihood that Mary's killer was still walking among them and had now struck again all these years later.

"Remember I said we would come back to testing the materials. Well, the toxicology report showed that she had ingested ether, and there were traces around her lips and inside her mouth. It was present in her blood and in the linings of her lungs. We even found traces on her right hand, which indicates she tried to pull it away from her face. This would also explain why we found it on the front of her dress, too."

"By ingesting ether, she would have experienced distorted thinking, euphoria, visual or auditory hallucinations, and with enough, she would have eventually passed out temporarily. It has similar effects as alcohol. Ether lasts between twenty minutes to two hours, giving the killer plenty of time to stage their next scene. Other abrasions and scratches on her hands corroborate this theory. She didn't wear false nails, and while you could tell her nails were manicured along the cuticles, her nails were ripped and broken as though scratching at something. The red nail polish was smudged, too. Was all the scratching from trying to fight off someone who was coming up behind her covering her mouth, or were the broken nails from trying to wrestle her way out of the car or a mix of the two?"

"When we examined the car, we found scratch marks on the driver's-side door and dash, all indicating she was trying to frantically claw her way out. Fluids extracted from her lungs would indicate that she had not yet died when she entered the water, so the actual cause of death was from multiple snakebites and not from drowning. What a horrible way to die. It doesn't get much worse than that. The paralyzing fear of having this reptile repeatedly attack and you have no way of defending yourself or being able to escape. The pain from all the cuts would be excruciating. Like having surgery with no anesthetic. It is hard to even think about. Whoever did this has a sick and twisted mind." Doc shook his head back and forth before he continued.

"Originally it was thought that the car door locks had been removed, but when we took the mechanism apart, we found the locks had been jammed down and then a compound put in place, which hardened quickly, making it impossible for the door-lock release to function correctly. Compound putty is a common product found in any hardware store. Beau, are you all right?"

Beau looked almost startled, realizing that Doc had just asked him a question.

"Yeah, yeah. I'm fine."

"Clumps of her hair had been roughly cut, close to the scalp, just like Mary, but in this case, he left the clothes on, and the hair was nowhere to be found.

"My timeline theory is she was grabbed, drugged with ether, cut up, then put back in the car, seat belt put on, the putty put in the locks. I believe the snake was loosely tied up in the potato sack we found in the back seat of the car, and eventually the twine that was keeping the sack secure became loose as the snake fought its way out or the person untied the bag when they shut the door. The winch was then used to drag the car into the swamp. It would have taken a bit of time, but then the killer knew this. They had to orchestrate the timing just right. Whoever came up with the idea is one sick and sadistic human being. She would have been terrified and died a horrendous death with the agitated snake continually striking at her and her being locked in such a small space with nowhere to go and no way to get out. Awful, just awful," Doc said as he shook his head from side to side.

"My God, Doc. Mary was killed years ago. Could this really be the same guy? Do you think some psychopath read about it and decided to copycat?"

"I've put in a request to get the evidence from Mary's death. It'll take some time to get, but there may be something there that will help us. We have better testing now. I'll keep you posted on that."

Walter suddenly popped into Beau's head. Did Walter play a part in this somehow? Interesting that it was his wife that died and now suddenly he is the tow-truck driver for Audra's crime scene. Beau thought about people who are so grief-stricken that they go on rampages doing to others what was done to them. *Give your head a shake, Beau. Walter would never have anything to do with this. The man didn't have a mean bone in his body.* And then he thought again about how Walter had savagely attacked the snake. *No—come on, Beau. It's all just a coincidence.*

"This next bit of information could put a spin on things and take you in a different direction from what or who you are investigating. When we examined her blood, she was ten weeks pregnant."

# PUTTING THE PUZZLE TOGETHER

Confirmation of the pregnancy added another layer of perplexity, or was it the catalyst.

"My one theory, Beau, is that the person who killed her also made the 911 call, but why wait days later? To have any evidence wash away? There had been a thundershower just a few days before they found her. Why make the call at all? Why not just leave her in the swamp to rot? He wants us to find him, Beau. This has now become a game to him."

"This will definitely help me determine which direction I take from here. Doc, you've been a big help, as always."

Doc gave Beau a nod and said, "If I come upon anything else, you shall be the first to know."

Beau smiled and, as he headed toward the door, gave Doc a grin and a farewell hand gesture.

As Beau left the building and headed to his car, his mind was alert and firing on all cylinders. His desire to crucify the person that so malevolently disgraced the sanctity of Audra's soul was so strong he knew that to catch this killer, he had to think like him. He had to get inside the mind of this madman. Beau kept going back to Doc's comment, that he wanted to be found, that this had now become a game to him.

Who was the father of the baby? Joshua? No one seemed to know anything about Audra dating anyone other than this friend with benefits. Did Joshua know more than he was saying? Did Audra confront him with the pregnancy, and he went ballistic? That doesn't add up. Maybe he was married. Was Sarkis married? He didn't think to ask that on the first visit. He would be paying Mr. Sarkis another visit.

There are many reasons someone keeps a lover hidden. Maybe her lovers were married. Maybe she had more lovers that she didn't tell her friend about. In Audra's case, Beau felt like the scrutiny of her family would be enough of a reason to keep a romance quiet, but he needed to investigate this further. Was she attacked and too upset or humiliated to say anything to anyone? Was it one of her patients? Did the pregnancy have anything to do with her heinous murder?

These were all the thoughts going through his mind as he drove back to the police station. Doc had filled him in on some exhausting information, and today, he would review what he and Simon had found in her apartment.

Beau nearly tripped over Larry, the town drunk, as he burst up the steps to the police station.

"Jesus, Larry. What the hell are you doing lying on the steps like that? You're going to hurt someone, namely me."

"Piss off, pig. Got some spare change?"

"I thought you were a rich drunk."

"That's a rumor."

Beau reached inside his pants pocket and pulled out a bill. "Here's ten bucks. That'll get you something."

"Much obliged. Hey, anything interesting going on I should know about?"

"Nothing you'd be interested in, Larry. Now go find you a bottle and stay off these steps."

"I'll go, but can't guarantee I won't be back. It's the safest place in town to loiter."

Beau just shook his head as he entered the police station.

"Gerald, you havin' a good day?" Beau asked as he passed the desk sergeant.

"Can't complain."

"You?"

"Same here."

Beau walked into his office when he thought about something Abby had said earlier about Sterling Jackson, that Audra would often stare at him, spare him from her outbursts, and that he didn't seem to ruffle her feathers. He was going to have a talk with Mr. Jackson. He'd been a part of the family for years, so maybe he would see things from a different perspective. Richmond, Audra's other brother, had been a waste of time. It was like a repeat of Charlotte and Abby, but Sterling, he might be a different story. Looking through his notes, he found Abby's phone number.

"Abby, this is Detective Beau Crenshaw. I was wondering whether you could give me Sterling's phone number?"

"What do you need that for?"

"I need to speak with him."

"I hardly see what for, now that she's dead, but I'll give it to you."

"I'd appreciate it."

Minutes later, Beau was talking with Sterling on the phone.

"Sterling, Detective Beau Crenshaw. I was wondering whether you could stop by the station today."

"In an hour? That works out just fine. I'll see you then."

While Beau was waiting for Sterling to show up, he stopped by Simon's desk to see what he was working on.

"Looks like one of the neighbors remembers when her sister Abby visited, sir," Simon said. "She lives just two doors down and was reading the paper on her front stoop. She said Abby had been inside awhile, but it was at the door when things started heating up and where she could hear them talking. She said she could hear Audra's voice getting louder as she told her sister that she was happy for her and why shouldn't she be the one to have everything handed to her on a silver platter, that it had been that way since birth. I guess Abby called her a sniveling, nasty, hateful human and that she could go to hell, then stormed off. Audra slammed the door."

"Good work, Simon. That's not quite how Abby told the story. Like mother like daughter, Simon. Those two women are wretched. Don't ever get yourself tangled up with a woman like that. Listen, I've got Sterling Jackson stopping by. Why don't you listen in on the conversation. It's good training for you."

"You don't have to ask me twice, sir," Simon said with a smile from ear to ear.

"Oh, and sir, the judge turned down your request to subpoena the client records at Newhaven. They stated there was still no concrete evidence linking Audra's murder."

"Shit. How in the hell would we know whether there was evidence unless we review the records. That was the entire purpose of reviewing the records. This is what's messed up with the system, Simon. We're supposed to be magicians without magic wands."

# STERLING JACKSON

"Sterling, thanks for dropping by on such short notice."

"My pleasure. My office isn't far from here, and I was heading home soon anyway."

"Can I get you anything, water, coffee from the vending machine?"

"Some water would be great."

"Simon, can you get Mr. Jackson some water."

"Sure, I'll be right back." Simon left the room as Sterling continued, fidgeting in his chair and swiping his hair away from his eyes with a head flip.

"What can I do for you, Detective?"

"Well, I'd like to ask you what kind of relationship Abby and her sister had."

"Wow, you haven't figured that out by now?"

"I believe I have but would like your take on it."

"They were always at each other's throat. Abby and her mother would tend to gang up on Audra. Her father, and I mean no disrespect, would do nothing to stop it. When her mother wasn't around, I would tell Abby to leave her alone, and sometimes she would. I'd never say that around Charlotte, or I'd be excommunicated from the family."

"So, you got along with Audra?"

Simon walked back in and placed the cup of water in front of Sterling, who immediately took two big gulps, then set the Styrofoam cup on the corner of Beau's desk.

"Aw, I guess I needed that more than I thought. Sure, I didn't have a problem with Audra. I kind of liked what she stood for. She never really bothered me. In fact, she had the sweeter personality."

"If you liked her personality better, then why didn't you date her instead of Abby?"

"Are you kidding me? I'd never get anywhere in my career or this family if I was with Audra. I have big plans, Mr. Crenshaw, so I need to do everything right."

"And that includes marrying a woman that you don't really love?"

"Who says I don't love Abby? I do. I just said Audra had the sweeter, more loving personality."

Sterling picked up the Styrofoam cup to finish the water.

"Were you close with Audra, as in, were you ever intimate with her?"

Sterling choked on the water he had started to swallow and began coughing excessively.

"Detective, is this really important? Why are you asking me this?"

"Well, you know, the twin thing. Compare notes. A lot of men seem to be into that."

"Really," Sterling said with a smirk.

"Did you?" Beau asked directly.

"Listen, we may have had sex once."

"Twin thing, then? You wanted to see whether they were different."

"Yeah, maybe something like that?"

"Or was it more?"

"Okay, so maybe we had sex a few times. It was kind of a game at first, and then I kind of liked the danger in it."

"And Audra didn't want more?"

"No, she said relationships weren't in her cards, would slow her down. This was perfect since I needed to be with Abby. I think she got a kick out of it because she was secretly getting back at Abby. And they were so identical, if you know what I mean, that after a while, I couldn't tell one from the other. Amazing how even their movements are the same."

"When was the last time you saw her, as in having a sexual encounter with her?"

"Um, let's see, maybe a month or month and a half before she disappeared."

"That recent? So, the sex wasn't from years ago, then."

"No, we would just randomly hook up when she felt like it."

"She was the initiator?"

"Mostly."

"Where would you meet?"

"At her place. I'd park on the next street over and come in through the back door, so no one saw me."

"Did you know she was pregnant?"

Sterling dropped the cup on the floor and flew up off the chair to miss getting the last drops of water on him.

"Sorry about that, but holy shit. You've got to be kidding me. It can't be mine," he said as he placed the empty cup back on the desk.

"Interesting, isn't it? The rest of the family doesn't know, and I would appreciate it if you would keep it to yourself. If I hear it's been leaked, I'll know it came from you," Beau said.

"Are you kidding me? Like I'm going to talk about her being pregnant when Abby's already suspicious."

"She is?" Beau asked inquisitively.

"She questioned me a couple of times, but I could talk around it. I really don't think she would suspect us hooking up because of the feuds she and Audra would have. I don't think she thought Audra would have sex with someone like me or that I would do anything like that with Audra. I think she thought I despised Audra as much as she did."

"Why do you think Audra would have sex with someone like you?"

"Really? Why wouldn't she? Not many women would pass this by, not even Audra Barrington. And like I said, I think it was also a revenge thing."

"This has been enlightening, Sterling. I appreciate you coming by. I may need to ask you a few more questions later."

Beau was keeping the pregnancy quiet but wanted to see what kind of arousal this news would bring to Sterling. His hunch turned out to be right, which got his wheels turning. The moment that Sterling left the police station, Beau bagged the cup from which Sterling had been drinking and headed over to the lab.

## 25

**FRIDAY, JUNE 30, 1995**

# MARRIAGE COUNSELOR

Beau was learning to play the game. Go in, say some words, drum up some emotion, and get the hell out of there. He was tired of the intrusion into his soul, but his marriage was hanging on by a thread. Today he was on edge, moody, and with a short fuse. He paused briefly before opening the door, getting his game face in order. The last session got him a few days' reprieve before Kathleen was back to her hateful ways and their war of words.

"Beau, great to see, and you're on time. What a pleasant surprise."

"Well, overcoming tardiness is not why I'm coming here. You do know that, right? Am I at the wrong session?" Beau was annoyed at the counselor's comment.

"Of course, of course. Just wanted to start the session off on a positive note."

"That backfired, didn't it."

Beau was tired of playing nice with this guy. He should be spending his time solving a murder and not being psychoanalyzed.

"I see you're in fine form," Kathleen muttered.

"Nice to see you, Kathleen."

"Okay, well, how did you both do on your last homework assignment?"

"Since this isn't school, I didn't do any homework, but we've managed not to kill each other," Beau offered.

"Interesting. And Kathleen, what are your thoughts?"

"I guess I'm less angry at Beau, and when we argue now, I think it takes less time for us to recover."

Beau disagreed with this statement but chose to keep his mouth shut. *This couldn't be further from the truth*, he thought, *but the devout Catholic just said all is getting better, so who am I to argue.*

"Excellent. Seems like progress is being made."

Beau pasted a pretend smile on his face. Maybe if he just made facial expressions instead of talking, the visit would end sooner.

"Kathleen, let's go back to you being a housewife and feeling undervalued."

"I put a lot of effort into keeping the house clean. I make sure meals are always made and the laundry done. I manage our finances and make sure I shop around for things like insurance. I take care of the home, too, but I don't get any thanks for it."

"Beau, would you agree that you don't thank Kathleen for her efforts?"

Seething inside, Beau decided to take the high road. "Maybe I don't. My bad. I'll do better. Is there any particular time or day that is best? We could have praise night."

"See, there you go, mocking me."

"Sorry, you're right. It just slipped out."

"It slipped out because you were thinking it."

"Beau, it's difficult for those that stay at home to have a sense of worthiness. You get a paycheck and that is your reward for a job well done, but Kathleen doesn't get a paycheck yet says she works hard to maintain the house."

"Okay, that's where I'm going to stop you right there, Doc. Listen, you're right. I get a paycheck that I hand over to Kathleen to pay the bills. I don't care what she buys as long as everything's taken care of. I take care of the gardening, the car, and the repairs. My boss doesn't tell me every week that I'm doing a great job—hell, I don't think he ever has—so forgive me if I am not quite up to speed in this new way of doing things or understanding where we're going here. Is it too much to expect her to keep the house up? Isn't that part of sharing responsibilities?"

"Right, but I think what she is saying is a kind word now and then will go a long way."

"You know what. This is messed up. I have a woman who's been viciously murdered, possibly by a serial killer, and I'm in here talking about kind words. I need to find out who this bastard is, so he doesn't kill again. I appreciate you. I love that you take care of the house and laundry, and you name it, I do, and I will try to do better, but Kathleen, your words aren't always kind, either. Why don't you and Doc talk about that for the rest of the time. I've gotta go."

At that, Beau stood up, dusted himself off, and exited the room, leaving both Kathleen and Dr. Wesley dumbfounded.

# THE LAST TIME

Even death doesn't set us free. Free of our bodies, at least. The medical examiner wanted to hold on to Audra's body as long as possible in case there was anything more they needed for their investigation, and while a body can be preserved in a morgue for up to two weeks, Oliver insisted he get her body back as quickly as possible so he could put his daughter in her proper resting place, so she could forever be at peace.

Oliver was holed up in his office when Charlotte marched in.

"Oliver, I've begun making arrangements with the church and funeral director," Charlotte said as matter-of-factly as if she had just ordered a new sofa.

"You can stop right there and unmake them. I'll be the one making the decisions on Audra's funeral. This will not be a social circus, and there will be absolutely no one not related to the family allowed anywhere near the church or the grave site unless I invite them. That means no pictures, no media, no magazines, no busybody snobs. No one but family. Are you clear on that? And I will approve everything down to the last detail. I'll be making the appointments with the funeral director and clergy. If you care to join me, great, and if not, oh well."

To Oliver, this would be the last time he would ever do anything for his daughter. This would be the last time he would pay for anything, arrange anything, worry about her. This was the last time.

Charlotte stood in complete bewilderment, never having seen this side of Oliver or heard him talk to her in such a harsh manner. He never raised his voice, so this new behavior was completely foreign to her.

"Well, I see you've grown some balls, so have at it, Oliver. Just don't do anything to embarrass this family."

Charlotte saw a different pair of eyes looking back at her, a pair of puffy eyes so saddened they no longer were twinkling but overshadowed by grief like the darkness that envelops a night sky. A man who was always so put together and willing to please, Oliver now looked on edge, ragged, and sallow. He even walked robotically and without form.

"I'm heading to the funeral home in a few minutes, so you can join or not. It's totally up to you," Oliver said.

"Don't you think it would look odd if I wasn't there? My God, man, how can you not think of these things."

"Shut up. Do you hear me? I'm sick of your obnoxious attitude. I'm sick of what comes out of that twisted mouth of yours. Just shut the fuck up," Oliver said with a bark, but the outburst worked as she became sullen.

With Charlotte in tow, Oliver drove to the funeral home to complete the details of Audra's funeral. When they arrived, he told Charlotte to go in and that he would be there momentarily.

She obliged. Alone in the car, Oliver had to collect his thoughts, needing to bury his emotions. This was, after all, about Audra today, a day when he would select the casket, a headstone, her favorite flowers and music. As his mind repeated all those items in his head, he realized he didn't have a clue what she liked. He didn't know what her favorite flower was or what music she listened to. He didn't even know her favorite color. Even in death, he didn't know her, but he would try at what he could remember from her apartment and how she lived there. Slamming his hands on the steering wheel, he sobbed uncontrollably, the sob that grabs on to the stomach muscles, clenching and releasing as he wailed on. Oh, how his gut muscles ached from the intense contracting they had endured these last bunch of days from trying to keep his emotions bottled up tightly inside.

"I'm so sorry, Audra. I'm so sorry, Audra," he sputtered as he tried to get himself together. "I know I failed you miserably. We all failed you. I'll do the best I can in making your funeral as close to how you would like it as possible. Simple. I'm so sorry, baby girl. I miss you and wish that I had been a better father, that I had been there for you. I will always regret that. If only I could do it over again. I would never fail you."

Oliver wiped his eyes, then rubbed his hands over his entire face roughly and got out of the car. Taking a big breath, he headed toward the door of the funeral parlor, muttering to himself, *Let's get this shit over with.*

Inside his head, he thought about how ghastly this place was, filled with death and morbidity, heavy energy that seemed so suffocating, clinging the minute you step inside. As he opened the heavy wooden door preparing for that very energy to come at him, Charlotte was there with the funeral director, Armand Culpepper, who extended his hand gently and graciously to Oliver and said, "Mr. Barrington, please come in. If you follow me, we will head back to the office area."

Oliver obliged the handshake and nodded his acceptance of following Armand without giving as much as a single glance toward Charlotte. As they all stepped inside Armand's office, he gestured toward two high-backed leather chairs.

"Please have a seat," Armand said as he sat down across from them and commenced his script once he believed they were settled. "Mr. and Mrs. Barrington, we are here to help you through this tragic time and lay your daughter to rest. We understand you are grief-stricken, which often prevents a person from thinking clearly or making decisions, so we are here to help in any way we can. Would you like us to offer suggestions for the casket, flowers, or music, or do you already have these items selected?"

At that he looked toward Charlotte, who sat there like a deer in the headlights, knowing she had best not utter a word, but all the while knowing that Armand knew she was the queen of her castle and Charleston's designer extraordinaire. Armand was expecting this to be a full-blown, lavish event, filled with high-priced items, that was sure to pad his finances quite nicely, but he was soon in for a rude awakening.

Oliver immediately piped up and said, "Yes, I have the specifics of the funeral."

Armand, taken aback and looking quite astounded, cleared his throat as he opened up his notepad. Glancing toward Charlotte, who gave a forced grin, said, "Okay, Mr. Barrington, please proceed with your request."

As if rehearsed, Oliver listed the details. "First," Oliver stated firmly, "this will be a small family-only ceremony at both the church and grave site, and you need to be very clear on that. The coffin will be a silver-gray platinum lined with soft pink satin. I want her makeup to be simple and not overdone and with her hair being as natural as possible. I will bring a blue dress and shoes over later."

He remembered he had seen a blue dress hanging in her closet the last time he was at her apartment.

"I have a gold pendant of hers that we, her mother and I, gave her when she graduated from high school, so I would like that placed in her hands. Do not put it around her neck, only in her hands. And there is a stuffed bear I found in her apartment she had since she was a wee child. I want that in her casket as well. That and the necklace are all. Do you understand?"

Armand nodded his head in acknowledgment.

"We will bury her in our family plot. I would like a gray marble angel-winged headstone with the caption to say, 'Like a bird suffering in a cage, you have been set free to fly. Spread your wings, sweet bird, and fly. Fly far, far away.'"

At that, everyone jolted as Charlotte burst into tears, her heaving and sobbing loud and dramatic. Oliver, completely unsympathetic to his wife's outburst, said, "Get a grip on yourself, and if you can't, please leave the room. This is about your daughter today and not you."

Armand, shocked at Oliver's behavior, tried not to show his reaction to such a bitter remark. Charlotte regained her composure as Oliver carried on.

"We will have a short church ceremony. I will provide you with the music later from Sonny Granville. This will be the only music allowed."

Oliver did not share with them he had found Sonny Granville's CDs in Audra's apartment, and, in fact, there was one in the CD player, which led him to believe this was the last music she had listened to before she disappeared.

"There is a song called 'Farewell'. This you will play at the grave site. In the church, I want the song called 'When Will My Tale Begin.' I also want a harpist at the church. There will not be a viewing, but I want the casket open at the church on the day of the funeral so the family can pay its respects. I want security outside the church keeping the piranhas away, and I want it at the grave site, too. And when I say away, I mean away. The block needs to be completely closed off. I don't care what the cost is for that, I just want it done. Understood?"

Armand nodded, and then Oliver continued. "Audra loved horses, so I would like the casket transported to and from the church and grave site with a horse-drawn carriage. Make sure the horses are well taken care of, no abused horses are to be used. I want this verified by having someone go to the farm to make sure. This is very important to me and to Audra. Do you understand, Mr. Culpepper? Do you? If I find out anything different, and I will, there will be hell to pay. Do you have any questions?" Oliver asked, his voice heightened.

Armand looked directly at Oliver and, using every bit of professionalism, said, "Yes, Mr. Barrington. I understand your need for privacy and will ensure there is more than sufficient security present to give you the privacy you want. I will have the block cordoned off."

"Excellent. For the flowers, I would like a cascade of pink-and-white roses on the coffin, almost covering the top, and that is all for the flowers. Mr. Culpepper, there is something you should know about my daughter. She did not like gluttony, excess, and she definitely hated showboating."

At that, Oliver looked at Charlotte in disgust. "Therefore, we are keeping it small and private. You are very clear on my requests, right, Mr. Culpepper?"

"Yes, sir, I am," Armand stammered. "We have the date set for Wednesday, July 5th, at 10 a.m. I will contact you prior to confirming the final details. I will place the order today for the headstone."

"Thank you, Mr. Culpepper and good day," Oliver said as he rose from the chair. He didn't even glance at Charlotte as he headed toward the door. She was invisible to him at this point. They drove home in silence, when Charlotte suddenly realized what their life had been with each other—silent.

As they drove down the lane of Sutherland's Crossing, they could see Jamie's car in the driveway. *Thank goodness,* Oliver thought. He missed his son, and although they were getting together in such horrific circumstances, he needed to see him and knew that his son was going to need him, too. Oliver couldn't park the car fast enough to get inside to see him. Jamie must have seen the car pulling up the drive, as Oliver no sooner reached the top step than Jamie swung open the door and went running out to his dad, arms outstretched, and as the two men met in their embrace, each clung to the other while the tears flowed.

After what seemed like an eternity, Jamie pulled back from his dad and said, "Let's go inside, Dad. Where's Mom?" Both men looked back toward the car but no Charlotte.

She had gotten out of the car, and when she saw the two men locked in a hug, she just patted Jamie's back on the way by and continued inside the house. What was going on with her family and her? It was as though she were being shunned, as if Audra's death was her fault.

Soon Abby, Sterling, and Richmond would arrive, too. Oliver needed to make sure they all understood the rules of the funeral.

He wanted these instructions imprinted on everyone's mind. They would have dinner in honor of Audra, and this is where he would fill them in.

Oliver told Jamie what he knew about the murder, which, at this time, was very little, as the investigation was still underway. At some point, it seemed both men decided they were worn out from talking about Audra and decided to talk about Jamie's apprenticeship with the boat maker in Virginia.

"So, son, tell me all about what's going on in your life?"

"I'm loving every minute and learning so much from Bob, the owner of the shipyard. I'm still too new to be left on my own, so I am attached to his hip."

Suddenly, Jamie realized he had not seen Ruby. "Dad, is Ruby home? I just realized I haven't seen her and I got here just minutes before you."

"Yes, Ruby's home, and it would be nice if you would go up and see her. In fact, let's both go up and see her. She hasn't been taking any of this well and has been bedridden the last couple of days. You know you kids are her everything—especially you and Audra. I've told her to stay quiet, I'm handling everything, and that she just needs to rest as best she can. I know she's going to be thrilled at the sight of you. And just to forewarn, she may look a little different from the last time you saw her, so don't be taken aback. Do you think you'll be okay?"

Jamie looked perplexed. "Looks different? Different how?"

"Well, it just seems when Audra went missing and then you left, it was as if her world fell apart and her fight to live left her."

"Oh my God, Dad, why didn't you tell me? I would have come back more often or taken her to Virginia for a vacation. I love Ruby. She is the best person in the world, and I would do anything for her."

"I know, son. I should have said something. We're on a hamster wheel these days just trying to get by and really not thinking clearly. Oh, and you know your grandparents will be here tonight, too, so just be sure to share your time with all of them. I really don't need to be listening to them later rehashing how they were not given enough attention."

At that, Oliver looked directly at his son, placing a hand on each shoulder. With the biggest grin he could muster, considering the circumstances, he said, "I love you, Jamie. Please always remember that I am on your side and please, please, always do whatever makes you happy. This is so important. I regret not saying I love you enough to you kids—especially Audra now."

"I love you too, Dad. I regret not being in Audra's life more, too, and letting her know how much I cared. Let's go see Ruby. Let's put a smile on her face."

As they knocked gently on Ruby's door, they could hear some shuffling and then a small voice that said, "Come in." Jamie was truly not prepared for what he saw, even though his dad had prepared him; he hoped it was not written all over his face.

"Look who I found wandering the halls," Oliver said cheerfully. "Remember when you used to find him wandering the halls when he was supposed to be in bed?"

"Ruby, did you miss me?" Jamie said playfully as he poked out from behind his dad. "But of course, you did!"

"Oh, my wee bairn, you've come home," Ruby said as she reached out her hands for him to come closer so she could give him a big hug, holding on tightly and not wanting to let him go, Jamie feeling the frailty in her once plump body. Ruby finally pulled away and put her now arthritic hands on his face. "Oh, look at you handsome lad. I've missed you so, my wee bairn. Now sit and tell me all about the ships you are building. I want to hear all about Virginia. I've heard it's beautiful and that it is very much like my home in Scotland. Well, I only know this from the television shows I watch. I have always wanted to go there for a visit."

"Well, your wish is my command, then. I am going to make that happen, and maybe you can even drive back with me. I would love the company and would love to show you all over Virginia. It is really quite stunning. Dad, maybe you could come, too? That way, we can all experience it at the same time. And goodness knows, we could all use some time together, if nothing more than to honor Audra. She would have loved Virginia, Ruby. I had so hoped that one day she would visit me there."

At that, Jamie started to sob gently, and Ruby immediately reached out and pulled him close while saying, "I know, wee bairn, I know. We loved our sweet Audra, didn't we? She was a special one, and I know you are hurting so much. I miss her so much, too."

Jamie left his head on Ruby's shoulder as she rubbed his back ever so gently, just as she had done when he was a small child, but this time, she too, had tears quietly running down her cheeks. The pain of Audra's first going missing and then turning up dead brought back the agony of losing her family so many years before when she traveled alone on a sea vessel to begin a life in a new country. She became more and more depleted, as if she were allowing herself to wither away and die. This could be such a cruel world for some, and she had seen enough suffering for a couple of lifetimes.

Jamie left his head on Ruby's shoulder for some time and then gradually lifted his head and wiped the tears from his eyes. "I'm sorry, Ruby. I didn't mean to upset you."

"My boy," Ruby said as she rubbed his hand. "You could never upset me. What happened to your sister is so sad, and you deserve to grieve for her. Always remember that." At that, she smiled and then said, trying to lighten the mood. "Okay, now ask your dad whether he is going to go on that adventure with us?"

Oliver had been watching the two of them with such empathy; his own eyes filled with tears, but now he switched gears and forced a smile.

"I think it sounds like a great idea, but don't forget we have Abby's wedding coming up in the next couple of weeks."

Jamie now recalled that the wedding was still lingering. Everything had been such a blur. Looking at his dad, he said, "Are we really going to go through with the full-blown wedding, given all that's been going on? I mean, we are burying our sister just days before."

Oliver, with a disgusted look on his face, said, "Yes, I think we need to do it for Abby's sake. Goodness knows your mother will still want the same big hoopla, and if it weren't for her, I would say no, but because of Abby, I want her day to be as special as it can considering the circumstances. It's not her fault that the timing is bad, plus we could all use something to lift our spirits, if only slightly."

Jamie turned toward Ruby and said, "Ruby, it's you and me, then. You can drive home with me. I can show you around and then bring you back whenever you want to, or maybe never. You may want to just stay living with me. Does that sound good?"

"I would love that, Jamie. You make an old woman so happy. I've missed you so much. And it has all been so hard here losing Audra, that precious wee soul," Ruby said as her voice quivered, but not wanting to get emotional again, she took a breath and carried on. "Now let's get back to you telling me all about the ships you are building up there."

Oliver smiled, looking at two of his favorite people. Then he tried to offer a bit of humor by saying, "Hey, what's with this never coming back? Remember, she was my Ruby before she was yours." At that, he took his hand and ruffled Jamie's hair.

# LAID TO REST

Sterling and Abby followed the procession in their own stretch limousine. Abby twirled the 1920s six-carat diamond engagement ring around and around her left ring finger.

"You know I never did tell you that I went to visit her."

"You did? Why? Why didn't you tell me? When did you see her?"

"I went to her apartment. The bitch barely let me inside the front door."

"I hardly think calling her a bitch is appropriate, since she's going in the ground today."

"Whatever. You remember the last time we met for lunch, and we got into that pissing match. Well, I just wanted to share our news in the hopes that she would lighten up and be happy for us. I wanted her to just let go of everything and be excited for a change."

"I take it she wasn't?"

"Are you kidding? She freaked out and started yelling about how selfish I was, that of course I would go there making it all about me but what about her? She went on and on about how I never stood up for her around Mother. Can you believe she said she didn't give a shit about my happy news and why would she be happy when I've never even acted like a sister or cared anything about her. She completely turned everything around and made this about her."

"Do you think you could have been a little more inviting and maybe asked how she was first?"

"Maybe. Who knows. Can you believe that? My own twin sister saying such hateful things after I extended the olive branch. This is why I stopped trying in the first place."

"Really, Abby, I don't know why you would expect her to be happy for you. It's like rubbing salt in the wound. You've always been at odds with each other, so why would you think she would suddenly do a turnabout?"

"I guess you're right. What a waste. God, and so close to our wedding, too. Ugh! You know this is rocking Mother's world. All the vendors are acting so sad around her, and she is trying to put on a good front to get the job done. She said she wished they worked as hard when someone hasn't died in the family. And Dad, what the hell has gotten into him? I heard him snapping at Mother and thought, *Man, he'd better watch himself*, but she didn't freak out on him. Ruby's a mess. Mother would love to find an excuse to get rid of her. She never expected her to live this long. She said she's hoping this will put her over the edge."

"God, you two are evil. Ruby is the sweetest."

"Well, Mother has a point. At what age do you just become a money drain?"

"I'll keep that in mind."

The procession had now stopped, and everyone was exiting the vehicles and walking toward the grave site.

Abby grabbed Sterling's arm as they were getting out of the car.

"I'm sure Audra's rolling over in her grave at the sight of Mother and me at her funeral. I'm not sure whom she hated more—Mother or me, so we may both be dodging thunderbolts and daggers today."

"Oh, stop, Abby. Your sister wasn't that twisted."

———

Beau had offered to be part of the security detail for Audra's funeral by keeping photographers and just plain nosy people away. Since Oliver wanted only immediate family and no one else, Beau needed to be sure Oliver's wishes were followed through on, but there was another reason he needed to be attending Audra's funeral that he did not share with Oliver. Killers often end up at the grave site to watch the event. It's like closure to them or the last bit of torment from which they could get pleasure, so Beau needed to see whether any suspicious characters showed up at the cemetery. By having only immediate family, this made it easier to spot anyone who did not belong.

Standing respectfully back from the grave site, Beau watched first the female family members approach, making their way toward Audra's burial site while the pallbearers stayed back awaiting the carriage. Abby and her mother, both dressed in black designer outfits with long black veils, stood gaping at the open hole where Audra would soon be placed.

In a few short minutes the clip-clop, clip-clop of the horse-drawn carriage could be heard as it drew near and stopped on the road. The funeral attendant hopped down from the carriage and opened the door. As the pallbearers pulled the coffin out, Beau could see each man's shoulders moving as if in unison, knowing that behind each movement was a man sobbing at the loss of such a young, beautiful soul.

It was a very somber sight to see. Once the coffin was laid in position, Oliver placed the cascade of pink-and-white roses on top and then walked toward Ruby. Only Ruby stayed seated, not having the strength now to stand for a long period. In her feeble hand was a pink honeysuckle flower that Oliver took from her and laid on the casket. She had previously asked him whether he could put this flower on Audra's coffin, as it meant devotion and everlasting love. Oliver lovingly obliged his sweet Ruby. He knew she was one of the few people who truly adored and comforted Audra. As Oliver stepped back from the coffin, Reverend O'Dell began a quaint and simple sermon not about the person that she was, since he didn't really know her that well, but about the tragedy of such a young soul taken too early, how God has her now in heaven without pain, and how she will be forever remembered by the family that loved her.

As the last of the words were said by Reverend O'Dell, Beau, who had been carefully watching over the area, noticed a young man who seemed to be paying his respects to a loved one nearby, but who was also keen on what was going on at Audra's burial. Whether this was a photographer being coy about trying to get some unsolicited photo opportunities or someone of interest, Beau decided to pay him a visit while trying not to disturb the others. He beckoned to another police officer, who then put his attention on the young man and slowly came up from the rear. He was almost within arm's reach when the young man tried to bolt, but Beau, anticipating this, lunged forward and tackled him to the ground. The other police officer was there within seconds.

"Get up," Beau said firmly but quietly as he brushed himself off, all the while not wanting to make a scene. "You seem to have a big interest in what's going on at the funeral today. Is there a reason for that? Why did you run?"

At that, Beau noticed there was no camera present, so he ruled out photographer, this person now becoming of even more interest to him. "Start talking," Beau said with gritted teeth.

The young man burst into tears.

"My name is Callum." At that, he put his hands over his face and started weeping relentlessly.

That did not stop Beau from pummeling Callum with questions as he said, "I asked you a question. Why the interest in this funeral?"

"Because she helped me."

"What do you mean she *helped* you? Helped you how?" Beau was now very interested in what the next words would be.

"I was one of her patients," Callum said, now settling down from the earlier outburst. "I was one of her first patients. She helped me so much with my issues. She would spend so much time with me, way past what it was supposed to be. She would fit me in when I was having a bad day. She could help me get a grip on my demons that other doctors weren't able to. I knew the family wanted a private funeral, but I just wanted to come and pay my respects. I don't know what I am going to do without her. I know she was a doctor, but I considered her my friend, too. I would do anything for her."

At that, Callum put his hands over his face and started heaving and sobbing. "I miss her so much. It's been awful without her," he said. "I don't know what I am going to do. I don't know what to do."

"Okay, well, settle down and get yourself together. You don't want to make a scene for the family. Wait until they've gone, and then go pay your respects. I'll need to see your identification and take down your contact info."

Beau wrote down Callum's phone number, address, and license information, advising him he would be contacting him later to ask more questions. Beau didn't sense that Callum could be a killer but was going to keep a close eye on him and run a background check to eliminate him as a suspect.

Oliver was oblivious to the commotion going on between Beau and Callum. As he watched his daughter's body being lowered into the ground, inch by inch, a wave of panic came over him. He suddenly felt like a porcelain doll that had fallen to the floor. As the doll makes contact with the floor, a tiny piece of the porcelain cast breaks away and scatters across the floor, lost forever. That is how Oliver felt. He was still a person, a body for all intents and purposes, whole yet not, as there was a piece of him, too, that had fallen, broken away, and was lost forever.

**28**

## TUESDAY, JULY 11, 1995

# MARRIAGE COUNSELOR

Rushing out of the police station to make it to the counseling session, Beau nearly collided with Larry Wycliff, the town drunk.

"Damn, Larry, what the hell are you doing here again?"

"It's a public place. I can stand here if I want to."

"How about moving down a few feet next time?"

"Whatever. Hey, any bites on the missing woman?"

"What missing woman are you talking about, Larry?"

"How many fucking missing women are there today, cop? You know, the rich one."

"Nothing yet, Larry. Know anything?"

"If I knew something, then why would I be asking you whether you knew something, you stupid cocksucker?"

"Jesus, Larry, get the hell out of here."

Beau scurried on partly because he couldn't be late yet again and partly because the stench coming off Larry was unbearable.

On the drive to the clinic, Beau thought about how he was no closer to being "better" nor did he believe his marriage had taken a miraculous turnabout, and he was tiring of the charades he was playing, opening up his life to a complete stranger and to the woman he'd been married to for years. This was more of a violation than a healing. With only minutes to spare, Beau burst through the door of the doctor's office, winded after sprinting across the parking lot.

"Beau, good to see you again."

"Same here, Doc. I promise to be better this time."

"By the grace of God almighty, I can't believe you managed to make it on time."

"Nice to see you, too, Kathleen."

"I've hope you've both had a good week. Let's pick up where we left off," Doc said as he rustled through his notes. "I know we didn't have, perhaps, the best session the last time. Beau, you were telling us about Mary's murder and how this affected you. How do you think it changed you?"

"I'll tell you how it changed him." Kathleen was more than eager to share with the doctor.

"Kathleen, I think it would be best to let Beau tell us, in his words. We need to allow him space to share his thoughts."

"Fine."

Beau loosened his tie. "Man, where do I begin? I mean, I needed an outlet, a place where it would drown out the noise, drown out everything going on in my mind, so I did what most men do—I started drinking more, gambling more, staying out more. You get the picture."

"Did you ever try to talk with Kathleen about this?"

"As a rule, Doc, you know men don't talk about their emotions. I wasn't raised that way, but yeah, I guess I did try to bring it up a few times but got shut down, so I stopped talking about anything."

"Shut down? I hardly think so," Kathleen retorted.

"Okay, okay, I felt as if I were being shut down."

"As in?" Doc asked.

"Well, I was told to grow some balls and get over it. What's done is done, and you can't erase the past."

"Doc, seriously, I don't think it was said quite that way," Kathleen said, looking away.

"Then how do you think it was said?" Doc asked.

"I'm fairly sure I was trying to be positive and to say that perhaps it may be better for all if he were to just let it go and get back to the way things were before the incident."

"Hmm, not quite how I remember it, but okay."

"Beau, please continue with how you felt."

"How I felt? I felt crappy about everything, about life. I lost my son tragically, and then I'm lead detective on a murder case I never should have been lead on, never catching the killer. I paid a price for that. My coworkers, the town all saw me as the sad, grieving, incompetent cop who couldn't solve a crime. I drank and gambled away our life savings, and we nearly lost the house. Everything was on my shoulders, and I just wanted to run away to la-la land. When we got the foreclosure notice, I knew I needed to get my shit together. I knew I owed it to Kathleen not to make her homeless."

"How did you avoid the foreclosure?"

"We borrowed some money from her parents, which I paid back, and I took on some side security jobs."

"Do you still drink and gamble?"

"No, I stopped when Kathleen threatened divorce. I stopped

gambling, I meant. I still have the odd drink. I knew it had to be bad for a devout Catholic to threaten divorce."

"What is your outlet now?"

"What is my outlet? I don't know. I get up every day, go through the motions, pay the bills. I guess being the best cop I can be and well, of course, husband. I have the odd sip of bourbon and call it a day. There. Is that good?"

"Those things aren't really outlets, Beau. Do you have any hobbies? Golf? Things to get the frustrations out?"

"Birdhouses. I like to build birdhouses and putter in the yard. It's quiet back there. That good?"

"Great. For our next session I would like you to write down the five things that attracted you to each other and the five things you are most grateful for in your marriage. Do you think you can do that?"

"Sure," Kathleen and Beau said in unison. And while in Kathleen's mind she was convinced progress was being made, Beau's mind was taking a sharper turn and wondered whether divorce would be the better option. He wasn't sure how much more he could take of this probing. There was still the ball that could drop that would take things in a completely different direction.

## SATURDAY, JULY 29, 1995

# WEDDING DAY

Challenged with contradictory emotions, the Barrington family had to set aside their tears of grief and replace them with tears of joy on Abby and Sterling's wedding day, flip-flopping from foreboding and sadness to false smiles mixed with forced laughter. Had a member of the Barrington family not been laid to rest just days before the big day, one might say a more perfect day could not be had for two people tying the knot, pledging their love for each other till death do they part. The sun was shimmering overhead, songbirds were chirping their practiced melodies in the trees, and the periwinkle-blue sky was filled with soft, billowy clouds like overproduced cotton candy, all extending to the graciousness of the day this Saturday, July 29, 1995, when Abigail Barrington would wed Sterling Jackson.

The bride woke at Sutherland's Crossing having spent the night before her big day in the place that was her childhood home, her first home and the place where memories were made, the place that molded her into the woman she now was. The night before, she had celebrated with her family, a dinner in, but retired early, so she was well rested. Even Charlotte encouraged the idea, knowing she had many things to take care of before the big event, Charlotte acting meeker these days and less filled with exuberance to control everything. In fact, she looked rather downtrodden, as though her world were crumbling around her.

Hugs and kisses to the family now complete, Abby made her way up the stairs to her room. As she opened the door to her bedroom, there in the corner was her wedding dress, hanging in anticipation of the big reveal. Between the lace and the beads, all painstakingly sewn to perfection, the dress was a piece of art. She walked toward it and ran her hand over the bodice and then downward to the skirt. All her carefully laid plans were coming to fruition.

As she prepared for bed, she reminisced about all that was about to happen and all that had happened. The real reason she wanted to go to her room was just to have some quiet time, some time to reflect and gather her thoughts, which now kept going back to her sister. Maybe if she had tried a little harder to understand her, things would have been different between them. Why had they turned out so differently? Why did they not have the twin bond, as so many other twins talk about? Why was being in the same room with her such an insult to time versus a momentous experience? If she were still alive now, would things really be different? Would she have ever gotten through to her sister to have them mend their ways? The sad reality is likely not. They were just two very different people, or at least they projected themselves that way, so she had to stay the course. Maybe this would end the curse. As she crawled into bed, she positioned herself in the center, fluffed her pillows, and pulled the top sheet over her head, hoping this would keep the monsters out, a ritual she practiced since a small child.

The bride awoke abruptly after a night of turbulent dreams and at the sound of her alarm piercing her ears as it echoed through the hollowness of the enormous bedroom. Quickly hitting the snooze button, she drifted back into a state of subconsciousness, but all was short lived, as the alarm went off yet again ten minutes later. Immediately, her mind went to what was about to unfold. This was it. This was the big day. Giving her body time to get accustomed to just waking, she looked about and realized she was not sure what her mother had planned for the morning, but knew that if she stayed in bed, she would fall asleep again. Rising now, she went to the window to look out. A big blue sky encapsulated her view. A knock on the door took her attention away, and she yelled out.

"Come in."

As the door opened, there stood her brother Jamie. He was the last person she was expecting. Jamie had been rather put off with her because of her forging ahead with the wedding.

"Good morning, bride."

"Good morning, brother. You are a sight for sore eyes today."

Jamie walked into the room and then closed the door.

"Before things get crazy," he said, speaking as his eyes first gazed downward toward the floor and then up to meet hers, "I just wanted to tell you I know I have been acting annoyed at you lately, but I realized regardless of whether you get married today, next month, or next year, it still won't bring her back. I know you two weren't exactly the best of buddies, but you must still feel awful. She will not be at your wedding today, and you are probably going through things that I don't know, especially since you were twins and all. There has to be a strange connection we aren't even aware of, something even more than non-twin6 siblings have. I know I haven't been taking your emotions into consideration. First her disappearance, then finding her dead and in such a crazy way. My God, what kind of hell did she go through before she died, and where has she been all this time? I keep going over this in my mind night and day, day and night. I can't stand that we allowed her to keep up her secret little life because we thought that is what she wanted, but now I wished we had pushed our way inside—get to know her, get to know her job and her life. I really regret that. I miss her so much. I know you always had an issue with her simplicity, but that is what I loved most about her."

At that, the bride-to-be started to cry and ran over to hug Jamie.

"Oh Jamie, I have missed you so, and I am so glad you are here with me now. I needed you to say this because it has been awful for me," she said between sobs.

They stayed embraced in each other's arms, and after some time, Jamie broke the ice by saying, "Okay, we have a big day ahead—well, you, actually—so you'd better let go, or you are going to be late for your own party, and you don't want puffy, bloodshot eyes for the photos. Mother wouldn't have that. Can you imagine? Now let's take a look at that dress. You know, Mother is going to have it framed like a museum piece after this eventful day."

The bride chuckled. "Oh, Jamie, you always did have a way of making me laugh. Now get out of here, you rascal, so I can get ready. I'm not sure what Mother has planned for this morning, but I know I'm starving."

"Well, first things first, then, sis. Let's go downstairs and have some breakfast. Let's see whether Ruby can join us."

Just as Jamie was about to put his hand on the doorknob to leave, there was a slight knock, and then Charlotte cracked the door enough to peek inside.

"Rise and shine, sleepyhead. You are about to become Mrs. Sterling Jackson."

Seeing Jamie standing there, she moved toward him and said as she put her hands on his face, "Good morning, son. I see you have beaten me to getting your sister up and going. You know I so adore having you home with us. I've missed you."

Jamie was taken aback by her kind gestures but made sure his face did not express his surprise. Instead, he smiled and looked back at her affectionately.

"Me, too," he said.

"Jamie and I are about to have some breakfast and check in on Ruby to see whether she may want some, too. And Mother, remind me again. What's on the agenda for this morning?"

"Well," Charlotte said. "After breakfast you can shower, and by then the manicurist and makeup team will arrive to get us glammed up for this most memorable day. Oh, and we will have pedicures, too. Jamie, would you like a manicure?"

Laughingly, Jamie said, "Yeah, I don't think so. I will leave that bit of fun for you ladies, and at that, I will see you downstairs for breakfast in case I get coerced into doing something that goes against my manhood."

As Jamie closed the door, Charlotte walked toward Abby and gave her a big hug.

"This is it, sweetheart. This is the day you've been waiting for."

"Well, I am not sure it is the day I've been waiting for, but more the day you've been waiting for."

"You might have something there. I just wish all this other

stuff wasn't lingering like a rotten-egg smell. I'm on the edge of a precipice."

"Oh, Mother. That's dramatic."

"Don't 'Mother' me. You know exactly what I'm talking about. Now get yourself ready, and I will see you downstairs."

—

The ceremony was set for 4:00 p.m. at Saint Philip's Anglican Church, which was often referred to as the Westminster Abbey of South Carolina. The church had been chicly styled with ornate French candelabras and oversize bouquets of roses and burgundy calla lilies, while sheer gold organza was contorted and conformed into delicate forms. Three photographers from three magazines were allowed to attend both the church ceremony and the reception with a disclaimer that Charlotte would have to approve all pictures and they would give her all proofs. There would be only one magazine allowed to write a story on the wedding, and Charlotte would be the one to select the magazine based on the photos she liked the best. The magazines were more than happy with this arrangement, as each believed they were superior to their rivals.

As guests arrived, they were escorted to their seats to wait for the bridal party to start the show. A harp played angelic music that was both inviting and mystical. As the church's bell struck four, the groom and his groomsmen emerged from a side door at the front of the church and made their way in formation to stand just beside Reverend O'Dell, the very reverend who had, just a couple of weeks earlier, given a eulogy for one Barrington daughter, and was now set to give a blessing of marriage today to the other. Sterling looked every bit as dashing as always, but there was a definite nervousness to his usual confident self. Looking out into the crowd, he felt both excitement and relief this day had finally arrived. As his eyes turned toward Charlotte sitting tall and proud as a peacock, he briefly thought that Abby would finally be set free of her mother's clutches, but that hopeful thought soon vanished like a puff of smoke as his waking, realistic mind knew that Charlotte would not relax her clutches, and somehow, he knew the next thing she would harass them for would be grandchildren, miniature show ponies. He then looked over at Jamie seated next to Ruby, and on her other side was Richmond. How opposite these brothers were, just like the sisters.

Trumpets sounded in the church's rear, announcing the ceremony was about to begin. In unison, the guests all turned their heads toward the back of the church while the music shifted from the harp's soothing melody to the cellist and flautist harmonizing to ignite a more spirited blend of tones. First the flower girl, Sterling's five-year-old niece, threw burgundy rose petals from a white wicker basket as everyone oohed and aahed, whispering to his or her neighbor at all the cuteness. Next, the three bridesmaids slowly made their way to the front of the church and took their places in the lineup.

After a pause, the music transformed yet again into a more serious and rich melody so all attention could be focused on the bride. At that, everyone stood as the bride and her father appeared in the doorway; his handsome frame paled compared with the vision of beauty that stood beside him, her arm placed gently through his, the lace veil offering only a hint of her facial outline while the rest of the veil draped downward exposing a scene of unrefined beauty.

Crystals and pearls had been painstakingly sewn together so delicately, etched into the fabric to create a muted pattern of breathtaking proportion. As the father-and-daughter duo stepped forward, women put their hands to their chests as the men smiled respectfully.

When father and daughter had completed the last of the journey, Oliver stopped, lifted the veil, and gave his daughter a kiss, the send-off kiss that would memorialize his blessing of her marrying Sterling Jackson. He mouthed the words *I love you* before turning away and taking a seat next to his wife, who was grinning from ear to ear.

The bouquet was handed to the maid of honor so the bride and groom could take each other's hand as Reverend O'Dell began his well-rehearsed wedding-vow speech, a speech long in both time and reverence. Finally, as each said, "I do," the reverend asked the bride and groom to repeat the wedding-vow poem together: "If the stars were aligned, if only a short time, but no matter where, whether we were or were not there but no matter the length, we will pretend it is now as we will weather it together even though we are only together a short time."

Reverend O'Dell, smiling brightly at the happy couple, uttered the words "I now pronounce you husband and wife. Sterling, you may kiss your bride."

It did not take long for Sterling to lean in and kiss his now wife. The bride reciprocated, then graciously turned around to face the guests, and while looking at Sterling with adoration, she placed her arm through his as they began their first steps down the aisle to the door as Mr. and Mrs. Sterling Jackson. Charlotte had been welling up with tears throughout the ceremony, and as Abby and Sterling stepped away, she broke down into silent sobs, not wanting to draw attention to herself and take away from her beautiful daughter.

The horse and carriage were waiting for the bride and groom as they walked outside the church, people throwing rice and confetti, wishing them well and clapping their hands in celebration of their marriage. Flashbulbs went off here and there as photographers grabbed on to this opportune moment to get a glimpse of the bride and her couture while at her handsome husband's side. The carriage would take them for a carriage ride through town before settling them back at Sutherland's Crossing for the reception.

While the bride and groom rode through town, the wedding ensemble and guests all headed to Sutherland's Crossing to carry out the night's festivities. The vastness of the grounds created a backdrop of lush splendor while the white tents offered an inviting canopy of friendly spirit and entertainment. There were flowers everywhere, acting both as directional markers, enticing visitors to follow the passageway to a night of gaiety and excess, and serving as extensions of the elaborate decadence creating a wonderland of beauty.

The view was breathtaking shades of whites, burgundies, purples, and crimson, all marrying together to form a masterpiece of dimensional colors and patterns. This would be a night like no other, this being the first marriage of the Barrington children, and the stage was about to be set for future generations. When the newlyweds arrived at Sutherland's Crossing and entered the reception area, cheers rang out, which signaled the party was about to begin.

A trio of musicians played a welcoming symphonic melody that added to the ambience. By now, everyone was seated in assigned places at the tables, tables that were showpieces of grandeur. The chairs were covered in soft burgundy velvet and tied with large gold satin bows. In the center of each table was an antique French rococo gold bronze candelabra signed "Henry Dasson, 1889." Surrounding this was a mixture of burgundy and soft-pink-hued flowers. Dinner was served on Duke of Hamilton porcelain service by Derby and Duesbury, George Adams antique English sterling-silver flatware, and nineteenth-century Baccarat stemware. Above each table hung nineteenth-century French Baccarat-style crystal and bronze chandeliers. It was as though the setting had been plucked from a French castle.

The bride and groom graciously acknowledged their guests with waves and smiles as they made their way to the bride and groom's table. Occasionally, throughout the five-course meal, someone would clang a knife or fork, which meant the bride and groom were to kiss. They obliged in kind. After dinner, it was time to cut the cake that Charlotte had designed, a six-tiered cake, each layer wrapped in white fondant, and inlaid were strands of pearls and crystals forming both argyle and flowered pattern. As if suspended in air, tiny burgundy, lavender, and soft-pink rose clusters draped down the sides of each layer. It was a showstopper but was soon disfigured as the bride's and groom's hands, lying one on top of the other, took the knife and pierced the objet d'art. Everyone clapped as the newlyweds fed each other the cake to symbolize their union and the promise to forever provide for each other. This event also prompted a big band to begin playing, signifying the day of formalities was now over and it was time to move into the next phase of letting one's hair down and enjoying a night of dancing.

"We want to thank everyone for coming and being a part of our special day. Abby and I will leave for a short time to do an outfit change into something more practical for an evening of fun. Please start drinking, dancing, and having fun," Sterling said.

About an hour passed before they were back to join in the festivities. The bride immediately sought her father to have the father-and-daughter dance, the first dance before she would be turned over to her husband-in-waiting. This first dance was meant for only the two of them on the dance floor. Oliver looked at his daughter with such glowing love and gave her the biggest hug. They slowly rotated in unison around the dance floor as onlookers sat watching the duo holding each other tightly to the song "You Are So Beautiful" by Joe Cocker, but to them, at this moment, there was no music. To them, the room was empty without a hint of outside noise, because the moment they were now sharing was their own magical music. As their song faded away, Sterling approached the two to reclaim his bride. Oliver touched Sterling's arm softly, patted him on the back, and walked away listlessly. He needed some time to himself and decided to head outside to have a congratulatory cigar that he had been stashing away for this occasion.

As the tempo picked up, more people were now on the dance floor gyrating, turning, spinning with wide smiles and arms flailing. It was a time to let loose and have fun.

As the end of the night drew near, Charlotte approached her daughter with outreached arms to embrace her daughter with a warm hug. Charlotte knew that her beautiful daughter would soon leave with her new husband. First would be their honeymoon and then on to the beginning of their new life together. A life she was expecting to be a part of. She nestled her neck against her daughter's for one last embrace as the bride whispered in her ear.

"See, Mommy? You do love me as much. See how much fun we are going to have together? You can tell me all about Roger, too. I found your letters. I noticed you didn't invite him tonight. You used to invite him everywhere. Why not now? Where's Uncle Roger, Mommy?"

In an instant, Charlotte's body stiffened, and she pulled away. She stared wide-eyed into the eyes of the bride, who put up her hand to slowly move a hair away from her mother's eye, then reached down to take Charlotte's hand in hers. "What's the matter, Mommy? Cat got your tongue? Is my talking about Uncle Roger going to cause a scandal for you, Mommy?"

Charlotte yanked her hand away and clutched at her chest. No one seemed to be noticing what was going on between the two women. "You. What have you done?"

Trying to shriek, her vocal cords shut down from the shock. And at that, she collapsed to the ground, still clutching her chest. Suddenly, everyone turned to look at the fallen mother of the bride just as the bride yelled out, "Mommy, what is it? Are you okay? What is it? Someone call 911! Hurry!"

The bride leaned in closer, right next to Charlotte's ear, and hissed. "By the way, Mommy, you would have been a grandmother by now. I prevented that from happening since you are a nasty, fucking human, and we need no more like you. You know, this is the perfect ending to a hideous day. Look at you lying there all helpless on the floor. You look a mess. Goodness, Mommy. What will people be thinking?"

Charlotte looked deeply into her daughter's eyes and kept trying to repeat the words, "What have you done, what have you done?" but no words were coming out, only puffs of air. She took one last gasp, and then she was gone. Everyone looked around in awe and bewilderment at what had just happened, not knowing what to do. The bride lay on the floor with her mother's head in her lap, sobbing out loud.

"She's gone. She's gone. Mommy, don't leave me. Please don't leave me. I can't live my life without you. She's gone. Someone, anyone, help her."

Tears fell onto Charlotte's dress, and as they hit the fabric, the wetness spread. The bride rocked her mother's twisted body back and forth in her arms and was now performing an uncontrollable cry.

Oliver, who had been on the terrace smoking a cigar with a few of his friends, came running into the room. It took a minute for his brain to register the scene in front of him. His wife lay in a heap on the floor with her head in his daughter's lap. He started saying, "Oh my God, no. Oh my God, no. What on earth just happened? Oh my God, no. Not Charlotte. Not today. Please, God. Please help us. What happened?" he asked again as he got closer to the incident.

Looking up with swollen red eyes, the bride sputtered. "I don't know, Daddy. She just collapsed. I knew this wedding was too much for her. It's all my fault. I never should have done this to her."

Oliver took his daughter into his arms, rocking her back and forth ever so slowly, and spoke. "Oh, sweet child, this is not your fault. You know how your mother loved to overdo it and push herself. You were her pride and joy. She loved every minute of this wedding and in planning it. There's just been a lot lately."

It was an awkward and arduous sight. Only moments before, the room was lit up with laughter, dance, and drinks but was now reduced to murmurs and sober moods; this wedding anniversary was surely not one to remember.

The photographers were discreetly taking pictures of the dead, crumpled woman and the sobbing bride. A headliner like this would bring in the big bucks. Since she was dead and the contract of confidentiality was between her and the magazines, all thought the deal was off the table and they could do what they pleased with the pictures now. They would all have their opportunity to shine brightly and may the best man or magazine win.

Off in the distance, could be heard the faint sound of the ambulance siren, and each passing second it became louder and louder. In under twelve minutes, two paramedics came rushing inside with their medical equipment and started to check the vitals, along with administering CPR, but it was too late. They pronounced Charlotte Barrington dead at 9:42 p.m. on Saturday, July 29, 1995.

# 30

# BLURRED LINES

"Beau, I'm so sorry to wake you. I didn't know who else to call."

"Oliver?" Beau said as he got up from bed and left the bedroom, not wanting to wake Kathleen, his mind still trying to clear away the cobwebs.

"Beau, she's dead."

"Who's dead?"

"Charlotte."

"What? What happened?"

"She died tonight at the wedding reception. Just fell over and died."

"Oh my God. Oliver, where are you now? Are you at home?"

"Yes—I just don't know what to do. You were the only person I could think of calling. I'm so sorry to bother you this late."

"It's okay. I'll be right there."

Beau dressed quickly, left a note for Kathleen, and headed over to Sutherland's Crossing. The Barrington family seemed to have contracted the Kennedy curse with this now series of bad and unfortunate events, keeping the family forever in turmoil, much like churned-up, rapid waters. Getting caught in a hydraulic that swirls around in a circular motion holding its victims captive. It was all very surreal. Charlotte dead? She wasn't that old. Only a couple of weeks before, the family was laying one of its own to rest, and now, the matriarch would be buried just a few feet away from where they had all gathered such a short time before. *I wonder whether she had a premonition she would be back at the grave site in such a short time, but this time she wouldn't be leaving.* Sutherland's Crossing, once thought of as the glamourous sanctuary filled with priceless antiques and opulent materials, a treasure trove of luxury that outsiders could admire only from afar, now seemed more like a house plagued with malevolence.

Remnants of the ceremony from hours earlier still lingered about. The house loomed darker than ever. Beau rang the doorbell, and the massive door swung open almost immediately. Oliver stepped forward and embraced Beau tightly, clutching him like a child would to a favorite teddy bear as he sobbed uncontrollably. Beau lost his footing a few times as Oliver staggered this way and that, Beau supporting him to keep him upright.

"Beau, I can't believe this is happening. I can't believe she's gone, too, and on Abby's wedding day." Then Oliver started to chuckle nervously. "How ironic that the very woman who did everything in her power to avoid being talked about, well, she sure went out with a bang on this! She'll be talked about for years to come."

"Oliver, how much have you had to drink?"

A housekeeper stood behind Oliver looking wide-eyed and shaken.

"Probably too much, Beau."

Beau glanced over at the housekeeper, who was nodding.

"Did you take any pills?"

"No."

"Okay, let's get you upstairs and put you to bed. You need some sleep. Things will look different in the morning."

It took almost an hour for Beau to get Oliver upstairs to his bedroom and to pass out. He made sure he was on his side in case he vomited in the night, and he placed a wastebasket on the floor, next to him.

"Are you supposed to be working at this hour?" Beau asked the housekeeper, who was nervously standing by.

"Yes, because of the wedding, I was put on the night shift to help clean up. I've never seen him like this, never."

"Okay, well, can you just continue to keep an eye on him, then? I'll check on him in the morning. Is there anyone else here to help you?"

"Yes, Rosalie is here, too."

"Okay, good."

Leaving the bedroom, they both headed back downstairs.

"Don't be upset. Everything will work out," Beau said as he exited the front door.

He could have sworn he heard her say, "Upset? This is the best day ever. The witch is dead."

# NO STONE UNTURNED

Beau, still investigating Audra's murder, was coming up short of answers or suspects. Doc had revealed nothing in the autopsy that was helping to find the killer. The leading cause of death was drowning (although Doc first thought it could have been the snakebites), given the amount of water in her lungs. The snakebites, while venomous, would have only contributed to the woman's terror.

The only determination Beau made was that there was a killer. A devious, demented monster who maliciously put this woman through hell to kill her, not sparing any compassion at all. This was a hate crime. How was she chosen? Or did he choose her? Was it just random? Did he know her and hate her? But why?

The newspaper ad with the antique chairs led nowhere other than a few rendezvous for Audra. He learned Joshua wasn't married and had no apparent significant other, so that ruled out an angry spouse or girlfriend. Sterling didn't seem like a likely candidate for a killer. He seemed too soft and preppy to perform those grisly deeds.

He had no reason to kill her, because there would have been no reason for Audra ever to tell Abby about the affair. Who would believe it? And once Sterling and Abby were married, then he would be set for life. Or was he? He needed to check whether there was a prenup. Her workplace didn't uncover anything suspicious, and because the judge wouldn't issue the warrant to seize the medical records, there was no way to find out whether a patient was involved. He was still pushing Doc to find something that would force the judge into issuing the warrant. Her work colleagues all revered her like a patron saint, so no suspects there. There was no other evidence of a male presence in her apartment.

The lab results were inconclusive with any prints they managed to lift.

Only the substance found in the door locks had been properly identified as compound putty, a finely powdered calcium carbonate and boiled linseed oil found in any hardware store. Checks of all the local hardware stores turned up nothing. Purchases that had been made in the last year were not able to be identified as to who the buyer was. The only certainty was that it was a popular brand, making it even harder to isolate.

A woman and car matching the description had been seen getting gas locally, but without the license number, there was no proof it was Audra. The police also could not validate the exact date and time. Abby had confirmed that she often used that very gas station, so it could have been she. There had been no activity on her credit cards or bank account. Every turn led him nowhere.

While a long shot, Beau interviewed the attendees of the wedding to see whether they knew Audra and whether they had anything of interest they could disclose. Two of the guests had volunteered information that, while it may have seemed irrelevant in regard to Audra, they wanted to share that the mother and the bride were arguing about a man named Roger. This had seemed to be the triggering point when the heart attack happened. Beau did not know who Roger was but planned to find out.

# CONFESSION

On Monday, August 21, 1995, Larry Wycliff walked into the Charleston police station.

"I need to talk to the big guy."

"I presume you're talking about Beau Crenshaw. Have a seat, and I'll see whether he's here."

"I know he's here. I just saw him walk in."

Gerald, the desk sergeant snickered to himself as he walked back to Beau's office.

"You're gonna love this one. Stinky pants is here to see you."

"Oh, you've got to be kidding me. What the hell does he want?"

"No clue, but I will say he's smelling mighty ripe."

"Sometimes I hate this lousy job. I'll be right there."

It took Beau about ten minutes to muster up enough stamina to handle the stench. Hopefully this was a waiting-room question, where the airflow was better.

"Larry, what can I do for you today?"

"Obviously I need to talk to you about something, which is why I stepped inside."

"Okay, well, I'm here now."

"What? Ya just wanna stand here and have me tell you what I'm 'bout to say? I think ya might wanna sit down or take notes or somethin'."

"Sounds important, then, Larry. Let's go back to the interview room."

"I'll follow you then," Larry said.

Beau was grateful he was in the lead and not downwind of Larry. Beau sat on one side of the table, offering Larry the chair on the other side. Larry sat down and pulled up as tightly as he could to the table and leaned in, which caused Beau to sit as far back in his chair as he could.

"So, Larry, what would you like to talk about?"

"I need to confess to a crime."

"What kind of crime, Larry?" Beau asked and all the while thinking that maybe he stole some money or liquor to get high.

"I need to confess to a murder," Larry said matter-of-factly.

This sounded more serious, so Beau perked up and said, "A murder, you say. Who, Larry, who did you kill?" Beau thought maybe he was having a psychotic episode from Vietnam or something.

Larry, still not roused by what he was saying, said, "That bitch Abigail Barrington."

"Abigail Barrington," Beau repeated slowly. "But Audra Barrington is the one who went missing and turned up dead. Abigail Barrington just recently got married. Do you mean Audra Barrington?"

"No, you need to listen to what I am telling you, you stupid clown. Abigail Barrington is the woman I murdered. And I enjoyed it, too. Couldn't stand that whore."

"And why do you think it was Abby and not Audra?"

"Because I just told you so. What the hell. I know that slimy, spoiled bitch. Horrible savage of a human. Deserved to die, and I love how it was done," Larry stated, his tone now sounding annoyed. "Look," he said. "I committed the crime—now I must do the time."

At that, Larry started to laugh uncontrollably, and for a moment, Beau wasn't convinced he was straight and with all his wits about him. His knees started going up and down while he clapped his hands, all while belting out, "I commits the crime, now I's do the time. I commits the crime, now I's do the time."

"Okay, okay," Beau said while motioning his hand as a gesture to settle down. "Let's get back to the story, but before we do, I'm letting you know I will be recording our conversation. Then you'll need to write out your statement. Will you be able to do this, Larry? Can you write?"

"Of course, I can write, you moron. Do you think I'm dumb or something? I can probably write better than you, so piss off."

"Okay," Beau said, not wanting to get him annoyed enough to the point at which he would stop talking. "I just needed to ask, is all. Have you taken any narcotics or been drinking today?"

"Nope."

"Would you like anything to drink? We could be here for a while."

"Some whiskey would be nice."

"No whiskey, but I can offer you some water, coffee, or soda."

"Coffee, black, will do just fine."

Beau stood up and walked out of the room. He needed to get his head clear on what he just heard, and he needed to think about whether Larry was really in his right mind or intoxicated. Most of his speech had sounded normal, and he wasn't slurring his words.

There was just that moment of strangeness when he started singing out. Then the other thoughts collected in Beau's mind. Why did he suddenly decide today to come into the police station to confess? What was in it for Larry? He knows that by confessing, he will live the rest of his life in prison, and he knows he can't get alcohol in jail. Is he screwing with me and doing this for some attention, or maybe he needs a place to stay for a while now that he was getting older and thought a prison cell would do just fine. After all, it is in the cool and dry with television and three-square meals a day. And it even has an infirmary. To a bum such as Larry, prison isn't so bad, Beau thought. But surely, he considered that since South Carolina is a death-penalty state, he would face electrocution or lethal injection. What was his motive? These would be all the questions that Beau would present to him. Nothing in the investigation was leading them to suspect Larry Wycliff, the town drunk. While Larry was definitely verbally abusive to people, he had never been physically abusive, or at least that Beau was aware of.

Beau returned to the interview room long enough to drop off the black coffee to Larry, then stepped out again to gather up the tape recorder, a blank cassette tape, notepad, and pen, and then headed back to the interview room. Beau asked one of the officers on duty to stand guard outside the room now that Larry was confessing to a crime.

As Beau was walking past the front desk, the sergeant looked up and said, "Anything interesting?"

"Quite," Beau said. "Seems he's here to confess to the murder of Abigail Barrington."

"Him? Abigail? Well, that's interesting, since it's Audra Barrington who's dead."

"Isn't it, though? And Larry? Not seeing him as a killer. I think it's a hoax. Will keep ya posted on the outcome. And if I don't come out in an hour or so, come and check on me. I may have passed out from the stench." At that, he gave a quick chuckle and headed back to where Larry was waiting.

No intimate details of the death of Audra Barrington had been disclosed to the public other than she was found dead in a car in a swamp, so anything Larry was about to tell Beau would likely clear his name. There were so many unique details, there was no way he could make up even half of it. Beau thought the only correlation was that the car was found on Seacroft Lane, and Larry was reported to live on Seacroft Lane in a run-down trailer. Beau had spoken with the owner of the cottage, Nancy Reynolds, who lived in Upstate New York and said she had not been to the cottage for several months. She did not know the Barringtons, since she was not from the area and did not know why the car would be found on her property. She mostly rented the cottage out but hadn't recently, since she was doing some much-needed maintenance and updating on it.

Back in the room, Beau set up the tape recorder, tested it, and then asked Larry to speak slowly and concisely when it was his turn to speak. By now he was becoming immune to the stench.

"This is Monday, August 21, 1995, at 1.34 p.m. I am Beau Crenshaw, detective for the City of Charleston Police Department. I am here at the request of Larry Wycliff, who is confessing to the murder of Audra Barrington. Larry, please state your full name, date of birth, and address."

Larry was being very careful to obey Beau's comment about speaking slowly and concisely, or was mocking the process as he said, "Lawrence Horace Wycliff. I was born on March 9, 1933. I live at 389 Seacroft Lane."

It took about three minutes for him to get this out, so Beau told him he could just use his normal tone and pace.

"Make up your mind. First you told me to go slow, I go slow, now you want me to speed it up."

"I know, Larry. Just use your normal inside voice. Please tell me about the day you murdered Audra Barrington."

"Okay, and like I said, it's Abigail Barrington that I murdered, not Audra. I live near the swamp where y'all found the body in the car. Actually, I live back behind the cottage, ya know, in a trailer that's sitting back in the woods on the left side, ya know, where the pine trees are. I put the trailer back there far enough to keep the snakes and alligators away. Sometimes it works, and other times they end up crawling around nearby, anyway. They don't bother me, ya know. I guess I've lived with them long enough now that they just don't. I know some people hate snakes and alligators, can't stand the sight of them, but I don't. I knew who Abigail Barrington was and what kind of car she drove. Ya see, I come into town, you know, get some liquor or whatever else, and then I hang around town just people watching, let's say. I'd been followin' her for some time to know her whereabouts, only she didn't know, so on the day I knew I wanted to murder her, I left her a note on her windshield and said I was Audra Barrington and to meet me at the swamp. You see, I knew Audra had been missing for some time after seeing it all over the papers, ya know, so I decided to use her name to lure Abigail Barrington to the swamp. It's not like I wanted to murder her, but I just had no choice. I told her to come alone and that if she showed up with anyone, the deal was off."

"What deal?"

"Well, I had no deal, stupid. I just made that shit up. I wanted her to think I knew something 'bout her sister."

"So, what were you intending to do with her if she drove to where you told her to go?"

"I don't know. I was fixin' to figure that out when she got there, but I did bring supplies just in case."

"What kind of supplies?"

"Aren't you getting ahead of yourself?"

Beau's interest was piqued. "Okay, so why did you end up murdering her?"

Larry looked agitated, and then spewed out as he slammed his fist on the table. "Because she was a spoiled, nasty brat, a pretentious snot that didn't care anything about the people, especially the people she represented. That bitch didn't have to work a day in her life, just suck off her mama's tit. That's all she had to do, but no, she wanted to run around pretending to be a lawyer like it's all a big game to her. She played with people's lives, and she played with people's emotions, and she had to be stopped. She didn't care who she hurt or how she hurt 'em. She was interested only in winning the case. That's it. She didn't care how she hurt people, just win the case. That's it. That's it. I had to do somethin'. I had to stop her from doing it to others. She needed to be stopped. You hear me? She had to be stopped. Nasty bitch."

"Did she do something specific to you?"

"You're damn right she did!" Larry's voice was growing more insistent. "Because of her, they denied me liability insurance. Ya sees, the court ordered her to take my case pro bona, and she lost the case. Can you believe it? Look at me. How do ya lose a case like that with someone like me? Do I look like I can work to you? I'm a veteran and have served my country, and yet, here I'm being denied liability insurance at my age. Something had to be done. I had to do somethin'."

"You mean disability insurance?"

"Whatever. They owed me insurance money."

"Okay, Larry," Beau said. Beau jotted down a note to check out whether Larry had ever really served in the army. Everyone just assumed he had because of his crazy actions.

"Tell me what happened next."

Larry took a deep breath and then said, "Like I said, I'm not afraid of no snakes. I was hidin' behind the cottage near the swamp when I saw her drive up. She parked exactly where I needed her to. I waited a minute to make sure she was alone, and that no other car was gonna come up the driveway. You see that bitch may have been clever enough to drive up alone, but then have someone drive up behind her once I showed up or have someone crouched down in the back seat. Nope. She was as stupid as she looks. Didn't even have the sense to do that. See what I mean about pretendin' to be a lawyer? This bitch ain't smart. She's a dumbass." Larry suddenly chuckled and slapped his hand on his leg. "Can you believe that?" he said. "She parked exactly where I needed her to, so I knew right then this was a sign, that everything I was about to do was the right thing to do. She turned the engine off and just sat there in the car. I waited to see if another head popped up in the car. It didn't. After a few minutes, she got out and started walking toward the cottage.

"Then I heard her say, 'I know you're there, Audra. Come out and let's talk about this. I don't understand why you're doing this. Come on, Audra. Stop this.'

"I let her get a little closer, and then I came out from behind the cottage just then and startled her. I knew she recognized me, even though she wouldn't admit she knew me. A panicked look came over her face, and I knew I had her right where I wanted her.

"I said, 'Y'all remembers me, don't you, bitch?'

"With that squeaky, shitty voice of hers, she said, 'Of course I do. I got a note to meet Audra Barrington here. Do you know where she is?'

"Yeah, I said, 'she was inside the cottage,' but she wasn't in the cottage. Then she said, 'Well, can you ask her to come outside?'

"'No, she wants you to go inside,' I said. 'She's having a hard time walking and getting around. Broken legs'll do that to ya.' I made this up, you know, so she would be more willing to go inside."

Larry laughed again and slapped his hand against his leg.

By now, Beau was absorbed in Larry's every word and had his full attention on Larry. He started to see that maybe he wasn't the harmless bum that everyone thought he was all these years. The negative reaction to him may not have been all about the stench but about the evilness.

"So," Larry continued saying, "she ended up buying into that story and headed toward the front door of the cottage. I let her walk ahead, which she seemed glad to do. I don't think she liked my cologne, but do you think I give a shit? Do ya? I pretended to have a leg that dragged behind me to make me appear slower than I was. I let her linger on the porch for a while looking for her sister. She knocked a few times and then paced around a bit, looking in the windows."

"She hadn't really noticed me shuffling up the stairs behind her. She was only a few steps from the door again when I grabbed her from behind and covered her mouth with a cloth I had in my pocket that had ether on it. It didn't take her long to pass out. I dragged her back to the car and eventually set her up in the driver's seat after I, well, added some special touches to her. She was starting to come out of the ether as I was sewing the last stitch. I had to quickly get some more in her face so she'd pass out again. Guess I wasn't as quick as I used to be."

"I tidied her all back up and even put the seat belt back on. Pretty clever, huh? Y'all remember how I said I don't have a problem with snakes. Well, I had gathered one up, a water moccasin, and put him in a potato sack. This was the prize. I was going to love watching this. That son of a bitch was a fighter, ya know. I almost got myself bit. I almost thought I should ether him." Larry started to chuckle, amused by his own story.

"I tied the sack tight at first so he wouldn't get away and then loosely when I tossed him in the back seat. I knew he would be mad as hell but would eventually work his way out of the bag. In the meantime, I put a winch over by the tree on the other side of the swamp and hooked the car up to it and then started winding it up, so it pulled the car into the water. I took my time pulling it into the swamp. Then I waited. It took awhile, but I waited. I was like a kid in a candy store. I wanted to watch the show. It was exciting."

"What kind of show were you expecting to watch?" Beau said, almost afraid of what the answer was going to be. By now, he wasn't sure whether he was in shock, disbelief, or both.

"I don't know. Something just snapped inside me, and I found myself getting really riled up. So, I don't know. The kind of fucking show that gets revenge!" Larry yelled.

"What did you mean when you said you added some special touches?"

"I decided to have a little fun and carve up that perfect body she thought she had. It wasn't so perfect when I was done with her. And did you find my little prize? Just like in a Cracker Jack box."

"Larry, tell me exactly what you did to her."

"Let's see. First I chopped some hair off. That'd surely piss her off. Then I took some lipstick and prettied her up.

"She was still passed out from the ether. I made sure she got a good dose of it. I took my huntin' knife, ya know. Thems got the sharpest blades, and I created a map on her body. I tore that bitch from throat to her privates, then I sewed her back up again because I wanted her to suffer everywhere when she woke up, and knew if I didn't sew her up, she'd bleed out, and then I wouldn't be able to watch the show. What about the prize? Did you find the prize?"

"What prize, Larry. What prize?"

"I shoved the tube of lipstick up her private parts and sewed it shut," Larry said as he started to laugh uncontrollably, clutching at his stomach.

"You are one twisted motherfucker, Larry," Beau said in disgust.

"That bitch ruined my life, and I was going to ruin hers. I wanted to see her squirm and be in pain. I wanted to see the look of fear in her eyes when she woke up. I could see the look of fear in her eyes, and she was yelling at me to help her. Ya see, I timed it so once she hit the water and it started getting into the car, the snake would be out, and she'd be waking up. All I could do, hell, all I wanted to do was just look at her. You see, I also had time to pull off all the door locks and put compound down inside, something I learned in my army days, so there would be no way she could open the doors. No way in hell. The compound would set and harden. It didn't take long, ya know."

"I figured by the time the ether was wearing off that the snake would be ripe and would have figured out a way to get out of the sack. He'd be slithering all over that car to escape and she'd be groggy but then frantically trying to get the snake away from her, but no escape. Can y'all believe what a great plan that was? It worked. It actually worked. I was at the car looking in the windshield at her, laughing my ass off. She was screaming and flailing all over. She had this look of real terror on her face. I've never seen anything like that before and that snake was just a-nipping away, mad as hell. I saw it lunge up and strike at her. I'm surprised they didn't hear her in Georgia."

"Then I went in for the finale. I ran over to the tree and started winding the winch so the car would be completely submerged. Son of a bitch, though, if it didn't get caught up in some undergrowth and the back end stayed sticking out a bit. Oh, and I forgot to tell you that when I put her in the car, I also put all her things in the back seat, nice and neat like, and then I put the car in neutral. This made it easier for me to crank the winch to drag it into the swamp. I bet that sorry bitch wishes she never took me on. She hurt me, so I hurt her back. I heard others didn't like her, either. Did you ever hear that? Did you ever hear that even though they thought they were the almighty, there were people that hated their guts? Did you hear that? I did. Her and her pompous mother. Too bad I didn't get her, too, but she didn't do anything directly at me, just that bitch of a daughter of hers."

"Is this the only crime you are confessing to today, Larry?"

The deaths of Mary and now Audra were so similar in nature that Beau suspected he now had Mary's killer, or Larry had read enough about what happened that this was a copycat.

"Yup, just this one. Don't you be tryin' to pin others on me."

"What did you do next?"

"Whatta ya mean? I went home. Fixed me some dinner and went to bed."

"And then what?"

"And then I waited a day or so, went into town, and made a 911 call. Told 'em to go and check out the swamp for a shiny object in the water."

"Why did you do that?"

228

"Well, I got to thinking 'bout it, and I decided I wanted people to see her all messed up. I wanted people to see her without her hoity-toity attitude or hair all done, makeup all done, and clothes just right. I wanted her to be embarrassed for how hideous she looked."

Beau was shocked by all he'd just heard but kept his composure. In all his days at the police force, he had never heard anyone confess quite as methodically and with such pleasure as Larry had. Everything Larry told him was on point for exactly how it happened. There was not an ounce of remorse in this man's voice. In his mind, he was absolutely in his right to kill as viciously as possible. Had Vietnam done this to him or was he always this sick? What kind of monster was this man sitting across the room from him; this same man he had passed on the street a million times and paid no attention to. This was no rendering of fiction but a proclaimed admission of Larry's truth. How could Beau have been so wrong about this person? How could he have thought the town drunk was not capable of such violence? Why had he not found it odd Larry was hanging out at the police station more than usual, and then there was the run-in with Oliver? A coincidence? An eerie sensation crept over him, an eerie, sick feeling. Maybe he did all that so he could hear how the case was going, whom the police suspected, and whether Beau was getting onto him.

He was in the room with a madman. Suddenly, Beau felt as if he needed some air, so he told Larry he needed to get a new tape and that he would be right back. Beau asked Larry to write everything down on the notepad that was in front of him. He picked up the tape from the recorder in case Larry did something with the tape and left the room. Beau told the officer outside the door that under no circumstances was Larry to leave the room, none, and to occasionally look inside the window to check on him.

Beau spotted Eddy and told him to stand guard with the other officer outside the door.

"I'll explain later," Beau said. "But treat Larry as hostile and dangerous if there is any attempt to get out."

Beau's mind was spinning, and he almost didn't make it to the men's toilet before bringing up his lunch. He had started to perspire more than usual, beads of sweat forming on his forehead and upper lip. He splashed cold water on his face, hoping to cleanse away any evil that may have attached itself to him. Then he leaned over, hands on his knees, and breathed in long, deep breaths. Listening to a psychopath happily talk about murdering someone was beyond comprehension. It all felt so surreal.

# THE LOCKUP

"Simon, come with me," Beau said on his way back to the interview room. The tone was final.

Simon's chair screeched across the tile floor as he rose quickly in pursuit of Beau's request. *What's going on,* he thought.

Both men walked into the interview room, Simon closing the door behind him.

"Larry Wycliff, I am placing you under arrest for the murder of Audra Barrington. You have the right to remain silent. Anything you say can and will be used against you in a court of law. You have a right to an attorney. If you cannot afford an attorney, one will be appointed for you. Do you have any questions?"

"Abigail Barrington."

"What?"

"Abigail."

"Sorry, Larry, you got the wrong twin. Audra is the one that was murdered."

"Whatever you say, boss."

"Simon, please handcuff Mr. Wycliff and get him processed. He just confessed to killing Audra Barrington."

"Abigail."

Simon was wide-eyed as he pulled out his handcuffs and placed them on Larry Wycliff. He was face-to-face with a sadistic killer. This would be one to tell the boys at the bar that night. The only shining light was that the disgusting odor would finally be forced off the town drunk whether he liked it or not. What they couldn't do was wash away the foulness of his insides.

Beau couldn't take any more. He felt as if he wanted to strip right there and scrub himself raw. He headed back to his office and closed the door. He just needed a moment to catch his breath. Something was still itching away at him, though. Why did Larry confess?

He realized he didn't ask such an important question, so headed to the cell Larry would remain in until bused to the prison.

"Larry, why did you confess?"

"Isn't that what you wanted?"

"You must have a reason."

"Thought it was the right thing to do. I've been watching you scurry around like a rat getting nowhere and that sorry father of hers looking all gloomy and doomy. Kept asking you whether you had anything, but nothin' developed. Doctor says I have cancer, so don't have much time left, and wanted to go out with a bang. Could become famous, ya know. Might even write a book about me. And thought I'd help ya out so ya don't keep looking like the loser cop who can't solve a crime."

That was like a knife to the chest. Larry was right. He'd been right there this whole time, and Beau never saw it.

# 34

# TYING IT ALL TOGETHER

As Beau Crenshaw drove to Sutherland's Crossing, he was still processing everything that had just gone down in the last forty-eight hours. Larry Wycliff walked in off the street and confessed to killing not Audra but Abigail Barrington, yet Audra was the one missing, or was she? Who was at the house now tending to Oliver, who had taken ill just days after his wife was buried? Beau did not want to cause Oliver any further angst, but knew the man needed to hear they had the killer in custody. Beau would spare the gruesome details of what Larry did to his daughter, as no good would come of that. Oliver did not need that in his memory. Jail talks and rumors would soon spread, but Beau could pass it off as people just wanting to glorify the situation and embellish the story to make it more interesting.

After only a few knocks, Molly greeted Beau and told him to follow her upstairs. Head hanging low, he obliged. They stopped in front of one of the many bedroom doors. The housekeeper knocked and then stepped inside, announcing Beau's arrival. Beau's jaw nearly dropped as he looked over at Oliver, who appeared to be withering. A once vibrant, strapping, handsome man was shriveling away. Beau also noticed that Abby was not in the room.

"Beau, you look like you've seen a ghost. I know I'm not looking my best right now, but the doctors say I will get through this. Looks like I'm going to survive. How's the saying go? 'What doesn't kill you makes you stronger?' If that's true, I should be Superman soon. Now, please come in and have a seat. It's good to see you. You're the only real friend I have right now that understands what I'm going through these days. I wished we had met under different circumstances."

Beau smiled and took a seat beside the bed.

"I wish we had met under different circumstances, too, Oliver. Sorry you have taken ill, but with everything that has gone on, it's certainly understandable."

"I know I will rally and be up and running around soon. I'm not sure I ever gave myself time to grieve for Audra, since I had every hope in the world she would come home. With finding her body, burying my baby girl, and then Charlotte dying, it has all been too much for me. I just need a wee bit of time to rest. To take care of the family, I need to get stronger. I have to, for the kids' sake and Ruby. I know the kids are all grown, but they have lost so much, they don't need to lose a father, too. Lying here has given me time to think about a few things and what I want to do with the rest of my life. I've always wanted to go back to England to see where I came from, so I might do that sometime soon. I would take Ruby, of course, if she wants to go, but I think she will be over the moon at the idea of it. Something fresh to look at, a change of scenery, is what we all need right now. Maybe she can look up some family while we are there.

Richmond has been leading the company for a while and doing a great job, so I'm confident in giving him more reins to lead the way. Anyway, I appreciate you checking in on me."

"I'm here for a different reason," Beau said, looking down as he ran his fingers around the brim of his hat.

"Oh? Has there been a development in the case?" Oliver asked, sitting up in bed.

"In fact, there has been, Oliver," Beau said. "A man came into the police station and confessed to the crime."

"What? Who is he? Did he say why?" Oliver sat up higher in bed as if a shot of adrenaline had just kicked in.

"Just walked in off the street and asked to speak to me. His name is Larry Wycliff. You know, the town drunk who's been around as long as I can remember and who accosted you not that long ago."

"That guy? Oh my God. Why would he do such an awful thing to Audra? What did she ever do to him?"

"He said she lost a case for him."

"Lost a case?"

"How could Audra lose a case? She was a doctor, not a lawyer."

"I know. That's where it gets crazy, because he kept saying he killed Abigail Barrington and not Audra Barrington, but I told him there were identical twins and he got them mixed up."

"Lost a case," Oliver kept mumbling over and over, looking bewildered.

"His mind isn't right, so he likely just got confused on who was who," Beau said. "He's behind bars now and being processed through the system to serve a life sentence. I just wanted you to know it's over, Oliver. Your daughter's murderer is now behind bars. Oh, and he's got cancer, so either the cancer is going to wipe him out or his stay will. The state will be going for life without parole."

"He's got cancer? That's why he did it, then. He didn't have anything to lose." Oliver broke down in tears.

"Prison is no walk in the park. He'll suffer plenty in there, Oliver."

"I need to visit him in prison. I need to know why he did such a gruesome thing to her. How could one person hate so hard."

It was a statement, not a question.

Beau wanted to be careful on how he answered, so he said, "I guess Larry held on to a grudge. He's a slippery character, and who knows that with all his drinking, his mind has likely deteriorated. Larry has always been known to be a bit crazy. He'll likely be miserable with cancer. Of course, the state will provide treatment, but it will be only enough to keep him comfortable. They are taking the death penalty off the table because of the illness. You could ask to see him in jail, but I wonder if that would be wise. He might say things to upset you more, to get a rise out of you. It may be best not to visit him, but it's a free country. Well, not for Larry."

Beau wanted to spew out that the son of a bitch deserves to rot in hell for what he did to that woman but kept that thought to himself. He didn't want Larry discussing any of the details with Oliver. That would shred him even more. Oliver looked at Beau and nodded in agreement.

"Visiting him isn't going to bring Audra back. You're right, Beau. Staying away may be best. I appreciate your coming and telling me this, Beau. My God, this is news indeed, and I am not sure I have completely comprehended. Larry Wycliff, I still can't believe this. This is so senseless."

Oliver put his face in his hands and began sobbing again. Beau stood by patiently, letting the man release his emotions. After several minutes, he raised his head and wiped his eyes.

"I know burying Audra provided some closure, but this is the final missing piece," Oliver said quietly as he continued to process everything he was hearing. "And thank you for everything you have done. I couldn't have made it through all this without you. You gave me the courage to keep going, and I appreciate this more than you know. I know this is your job, but you have gone above and beyond for me, and I now consider you a friend, so I have something for you I have been holding on to for some time now with all the recent drama. Audra would have wanted me to do this. She was kind that way. Since your news finishes this chapter, let's end with something positive. So, here's to Audra. Her killer is now behind bars, plus you and your wife can enjoy a little something special tonight. I'm sure she's been patient with you during all this, and I'm sure she would like her husband back. Enjoy her, Beau, because you never know when it will be your last day with her."

*If you only knew half of it,* Beau thought.

Oliver reached over and opened the drawer to the nightstand. He pulled out an envelope and handed it to Beau.

"Please take this as a token of my appreciation and enjoy."

"No, really, I can't accept this."

"Please, Beau, it's the least I can do."

"Thank you, Oliver, but it's unnecessary. I am just doing my job."

No one had ever given him anything for just doing his job.

"I know," Oliver said. "But I want to do something good. Please let me just do some good—put a smile on a sick man's face, Beau."

The envelope was in Beau's hand when the bedroom door opened, and Abby walked into the room.

"Sorry, I didn't know you had company."

"Abby, come in, come in. It's over. It's over, sweetheart. A man confessed to killing your sister. Beau came to tell us he is now in prison awaiting trial."

"Really? Well, that is good news, Detective. Glad to hear a killer is finally off the streets and we can all sleep more peacefully. Did he say why he killed her?"

"That's the strangest thing, because he actually got you two mixed up. Maybe I shouldn't be saying this to scare you, but I guess he was a client of yours at one time, and you lost a disability case. You were his target. You must remember him, stinks like high heaven, likely a pro bono case. His name is Larry Wycliff. Ring a bell?"

"Larry Wycliff, Larry Wycliff. Hmm, I don't recall the name, but then I've had so many cases, they all tend to blend together at some point."

"Of course," Beau said.

"Dad, are you okay? I'll leave you two and come back if you like, but you know it's time for your medication."

"I was just leaving. I can see myself out," Beau said.

"Good day, Detective," Abby said.

"Beau, thanks again for coming by. We'll be in touch," Oliver said.

Beau closed the door to the bedroom as the sound echoed down the hallway. *What an empty and hollow house,* he thought.

As he drove away from Sutherland's Crossing and headed back to the office, it dawned on him that he had stuck the envelope Oliver had given him in his suit pocket. Thinking it was likely a gift card to a restaurant or some tickets to a game, he didn't pay it much mind. Where his mind was going was back to the interaction with Abby and her father. "Something isn't sitting right with me," Beau said out loud. But what is it?

# A WIN FOR EVERYONE

"I've left some paperwork on your desk," Gerald said as Beau entered the front doors of the police station. "You need to sign off on Larry's statement so I can get it over to the prosecutor's office."

"Thanks, Gerald. I'll get it right back to you."

"Roger that."

Beau fell into his office chair and let out a big sigh. What a few days it had been. One case was wrapping up, and a new investigation on a cold case was about to begin. He ran his fingers through his hair, then picked up a pencil from the cupholder. He tapped it a few times on the desk as he decided what to do first.

Beau picked up his office phone and dialed a number he knew by heart.

"Doc, it's Beau. Listen, I'm going to drop off the evidence from Mary's murder. No one called Mary by her last name—just Mary, but everyone knew who Mary was. Can you compare it to Audra Barrington's? Larry didn't confess to Mary's murder, but the similarities are just too close. And have you been able to check into the other thing we talked about? Good. I'll swing by this afternoon."

Beau signed the confession documents and was ready to head over to the lab when he remembered the envelope in his pocket. He took it out and opened it. It wasn't a gift card or tickets. In his hand was a check for $100,000. That was twice as much as he made in a year.

"What the hell?" he said out loud and then snickered. "You've got to be kidding me."

Stuffing the check back in his pocket, he grabbed the paperwork and headed off to the evidence room. Maybe his luck was changing. A man walks in off the street and confesses to a murder, and then the murdered woman's father hands him a check for $100,000. This all sounded too good to be true.

# A PRISON VISIT

Larry Wycliff was now a resident at the Charleston Penitentiary. It was a top-security facility designed to house violent offenders with longer sentences and inmates who exhibited behavioral problems. The prison comprised single and double cells, and all perimeters were double-fenced with extensive electronic surveillance. Most of the inmates in the prison were under close supervision, and their activities and movement within the institution were highly restricted. Despite being old and sick, the state law mandated that Larry be placed in this facility because of the nature of the crime. As the alarm sounded, Prisoner Number 6892 entered the visitors area in shackles and sat in the chair waiting for his guest. Only minutes had passed before a young man sat down across from him.

"Thanks for coming by. So glad to see ya. The company's not the best in here," Larry said chuckling.

"Always making a joke. I wish I wasn't visiting you here," Callum said.

"I know. I know. But listen. I want to make amends for everything I've done."

"My life turned out okay. That's why I moved back here. So I could spend more time with you. You know I just started as a mechanic over at Pete's Garage, right?"

"I sure did. So proud of ya. Your aunt keeps me current on what's going on. Have you seen her lately? Ya need to make sure you stay in touch. She's going to be all ya have."

"Dad, I know, and I will. Stop talking like that. We'll have some time together. As long as they keep you here in Charleston, I'll stop by regularly."

"It's not that, son. There's something I've been meaning to tell ya."

"That you didn't do it? That you just had a psychotic episode, and you confessed because of that?"

"No, I did it. But what I wanted to tell you is that I have cancer, pretty aggressive cancer, the docs say, so I don't know how much longer I'll be around."

"Why, then? Dad, why did you do it?" Callum's voice choked, and his eyes began to water.

"I know it sounds bad. Listen, I wasn't the best father, ya know. After what happened to you, I kinda went off the rails. That's why I sent you away to your aunt's house. I didn't know how to handle you."

"Well, I was the one that witnessed it."

"I know. That's what made it worse. I wasn't there. I was out whoring around while your mother was getting murdered. I shoulda been there. Made me a little crazy. I knew you needed someone to talk to, ya know, a female."

"I really wanted my dad, but I get it now. I've been in therapy, and it's really been helping me. Did you hear that, too?"

"I did. Maybe I should have done somethin' like that instead of turning out to be the town drunk," Larry said sheepishly. "Who knows, but what I wanted to tell ya is that I'm gonna have some money deposited in yer account, so I'll need your bank info. And don't be surprised when ya see how much it is. I don't want ya talking with anybody about this, either, not even your aunt, and I want you to spend it wisely. Heck, maybe ya can open your own garage someday."

"Okay . . . well . . . how much money are we talking about?"

"Half a mil."

"Half a mil!" Callum said, jumping up from his chair.

"Be quiet and sit down, sit down. We don't need nosy people listening in."

"Where did you get that kind of money?"

"Never mind where I got it from. Been saving awhile. Now, you need to know this. It will come from an offshore account. Ya got it?"

"Offshore account?"

"Now promise me y'all will keep up your therapy and spend it wisely. Oh, promise you won't tell your aunt about this. Okay? Promise?"

"Okay, I promise."

"Callum, I don't know whether it's because I'm dying, but I had to tell how sorry I am. I know I was a sorry piece of shit of a father, so I'm hoping the money will help to make up for some of it. I'm sorry I wasn't there the night you saw you mother get viciously stabbed, and I'm sorry I sent you away." Larry started to tear up and put his hands over his face.

"I know you did the best you could, Dad. I'd give you a hug, but I think they would get pissy about somethin' like that," Callum said, trying to make light of the moment.

"Glad to see you got my humor."

A siren sounded, then a booming voice announced that visiting hours were over.

"I gotta go, but I'll bring the bank account information by tomorrow. Sound good?"

"I'll be here."

# 37

# A WOUNDED CONSCIENCE

Beau had one more stop to make before heading back to his office to return a call Doc made earlier. When Beau listened to the message, Doc's voice had been a faster higher pitch, which meant he had discovered something of interest. Thoughts flickered between what Doc may have uncovered and his marriage. It seemed the marriage counseling had been teaching him some things, and that was a hatred of his past. It wasn't Kathleen he wanted a divorce from. It was himself.

Beau rang the doorbell and was now familiar with the Gothic chimes.

"Hello, Detective."

"Good morning, Rosalie. Is Mr. Barrington home?"

"Yes, please come in. I will let him know you're here."

Rosalie returned shortly to say Mr. Barrington would see him in his office.

"Thanks, I'll find my way there."

"Of course, Detective."

Oliver greeted Beau in the hallway outside his office.

"Beau, always a pleasure to see you. Come in. Come in. Sit down."

"I can't stay long. I should have dropped this by sooner, but I've been busy wrapping up loose ends, and time got away from me."

"Drop what by?"

"I need to give this back to you. I didn't realize what it was the day you gave it to me, or I should say I didn't realize how large it was."

"No, I want you to have it, Beau. I want to do something good."

"Sorry, but I can't accept it. It wouldn't be ethical. I've spent the last year turning my life around and trying to be a better person to stay out of divorce court. You almost had me, though. I did think about gambling the $100,000, winning some extra, and giving you back the $100,000, but I knew deep down that was a crap shoot. I just can't take your money. I'd get into a lot of trouble, too if the precinct found out. It might seem like a bribe or something. I appreciate the thought, though. It's not a bribe, right?" Beau snickered.

"Bribe money? There's no bribe here. I have done nothing wrong to require a bribe," Oliver said inquisitively.

"I know. It just wouldn't look right is all."

Beau didn't want to keep dwelling on the issue. It already made him sick to be handing over a check for $100,000.

"If you insist," Oliver said as he took the check and ripped it up in smaller pieces, then walked over to a wastebasket, and tossed them in. *There goes my early retirement,* Beau thought.

"So, you're looking much better, more yourself," Beau said, shifting the conversation back to Oliver.

"I am. I too have made some changes. Seems I will take that trip to England with Abby and Ruby, so I'm looking forward to that. I've had nostalgia for a place I've never been to for far too long. We've been looking up long-lost relatives of Ruby's that we hope to connect with while we are there."

"Fantastic. I'm sure you'll have a great time. And good to hear you're getting away for a while. I'm sure the change of scenery will do you some good. Listen, I won't keep you. I just wanted to drop that by. Oh, and is Abby around?"

"Abby? Why would you need to speak with her?" Oliver said defensively.

"It's nothing, really."

"We have a confession and a man in prison. I think this settles the matter. We have all suffered extreme losses, and Abby doesn't need to be dragged into this anymore than she has to be. I can't imagine what help she could give you, and the only thing I see of this outcome is her getting upset," Oliver said indignantly.

"Sorry, Oliver, I didn't mean to rattle you."

"Quite right. I didn't mean to sound riled. Still trying to adjust is all. Thanks for everything, Beau, and if you ever need anything, don't hesitate to ask me. I mean that."

"Sure thing. I'll see myself out. When are you heading out?"

"Day after tomorrow."

"Have a pleasant trip."

# NOT AN EXACT FIT

Beau's desk chair creaked unapologetically as he settled in for a phone call with Doc. It was on the third ring, and he was hoping it wouldn't go to voicemail.

"Crenshaw, you were reading my mind. I was just about to call you again."

"What's up, Doc?"

"I'm glad to see I'm the brunt of your entertainment for the day."

"How can you not love a little Bugs humor every now and again? You must have something good. Sorry I couldn't talk earlier. Had to make a pit stop at Sutherland's Crossing."

"How's the old man doing?"

"Looking better than he did the last time I saw him. Says he's planning a trip to England to see some long-lost relatives."

"Listen, I'm trying to tie up all the loose ends and close out these cases. Something's not sitting right with me," Doc said.

"These cases? Oh, you mean Audra and Charlotte. I agree.

Something's not sitting right with me either. Everything just fell too neatly together."

"Let's start with Charlotte. We just finished her autopsy. I think you will find this fascinating. The toxicology reports came back showing signs of strychnine in her system."

"Strychnine?"

"Yup, rat poison."

"Now how on earth would she get rat poison in her system?"

"The better question to ask is when did she ingest rat poison."

"Okay, when did she ingest rat poison?"

"The night of the wedding."

"What?"

"See, you have to understand how rat poison works. Strychnine is odorless and tasteless. With the proper dosage, let's say adding to a glass of champagne, a person could die within an hour of ingesting it."

"What the hell? She was murdered too."

"I think that would be accurate, given that no one else was sick or died that evening. It would seem logical that it was planned just for her. Now whether they just intended to make her sick or actually kill her remains the question."

"Doc, I have a strange feeling about who may have done this. What else do you have for me?"

"I went back over the evidence you had for Mary, which wasn't much at all, but I found some things we could test on now that we didn't have the capability to back then. We look for saliva samplings, blood samplings, and so forth. We were able to compare a DNA sample with one from the Barrington woman's crime scene, and while there was a match, it was not a complete match. It's odd because the test came back similar, but not exact."

"What does that mean?"

"Well, it could mean there is a genetic coupling such as mother, son, father, daughter, sister, brother, and so on. Even grandparents, aunts, uncles. You get the picture. And we tested the fingerprints from that wooden cross you brought in. No match to Larry, and no matches from the database."

"So, you're saying that the person who killed Mary, then, was not Larry Wycliff?"

"Correct. That is what I am saying. Larry Wycliff did not kill Mary, but someone connected to him likely did."

"Son of a bitch."

"Son of a bitch, indeed. And this next finding should have you even more perplexed. You have an odd fascination for trash cans, I will say, but you always seem to find some interesting things in there. That water bottle you retrieved from Sutherland's Crossing the other day and asked me to check for DNA, good catch."

"Yeah, that was a stroke of luck that I was there at just the right time. I don't know what came over me. I saw the water bottle in the trash and thought, why not? Oliver thought I had just dropped something when I bent over to retrieve it. I love trench coats. You can hide plenty under them."

"Turns out the DNA isn't a match for Abby, but you know the person it belongs to."

"You've got to be kidding me."

"Science doesn't have a sense of humor, Detective."

# WHERE THE WATER MEETS THE SAND

The car service pulled up to the curb to deliver its three passengers. A valet waited with a wheelchair for Ruby, who wanted to preserve her strength for the big trip ahead. She was elated to be finally going back to her home country with Oliver and Abby in tow. Once inside, the Charleston airport was abuzz with excited and exhausted travelers all dispersing in different directions to get to their final destinations. It was a whirlwind of energy.

"Let's get checked in, and then we'll head to the lounge," Oliver said.

"Sounds good, Dad."

Flying first class made the process comfortable and timely, and within minutes, they were settling into the lounge.

"Oliver, please leave me over by the window. I just love to watch the planes," Ruby said.

"Okay, Ruby. Abby and I will be just over there," he said, pointing to an area of empty chairs. "Do you want anything?"

"No, I'm fine."

"Well, Ruby is in fine spirits. This is the happiest I've seen her in a long time," Oliver said, smiling as he looked lovingly toward her.

"Dad, there's something that's been playing heavy on my mind. Something I need to tell you. There's something I need to do."

"Shh, no," Oliver said, placing his index finger on her mouth, then he took her hand in his and gave it a squeeze.

"No, Dad, there is. When we return to the US, I need to speak to that detective-what's his name-Crenshaw. I know more about the murder than I've let on, and it's time I got it off my chest."

"No, there isn't anything you need to say. This is one of those moments where the water meets the sand. We know there is sand beneath the water, yet the water keeps the sand's secrets safely covered with whatever the sand is hiding. I remember saying many times that I would do anything if only to have a second chance. There is nothing you need to tell me, my child. We have all been through so much stress in our lives and such tragic events. This last year has been excruciating. We need to put all that behind us and forget the past. This is our second chance. Sometimes, our deep emotional pain drives us to do unheard-of things. I can attest to that. There is nothing you need to say to Ruby either. Do you understand? Tell me you understand. She's so fragile, and I want this trip to be the best for her. From this day forward, we are starting a new life together. Got it? From this day forward, the past doesn't exist. I just want us to enjoy our visit there, finally back where we came from. Now, the minute we get there, let's have a real English supper, just like the one I've been waiting for my entire life."

"Okay, Dad, let's go do that." She smiled to appease her father, but her mind was already made up about what her next move would be.

Oliver let out a sigh as he squeezed his daughter's hand.

"You've set us free, baby girl. You've set us free."

# AN UNEXPECTED TWIST

"Simon," Beau yelled as he got up from his desk and hurried down the hallway. "Let's go. We don't have much time."

Simon bolted from his desk and scurried along behind Beau as they headed to the car. Beau threw the car into drive, screeching out of the parking lot, with the siren blaring and lights flashing. Simon knew something important was underway.

"I called Oliver, and he said they were flying to England today. He first told me he wasn't leaving until tomorrow. We have to get to them before they board that flight."

"Okay, sir."

Cars were inching off the road, making way for Beau and Simon to race through the city until they ground to a stop at a traffic light where people were bottlenecked. Beau lowered his window yelling at people to get out of the way, honking the horn and waving his arm outside the window, gesturing to move aside. They inched along until they were freed from the congestion and headed in the direction of the on-ramp to the expressway. There they picked up speed, exceeding the speed limit by a good forty miles an hour. Simon held on tight, still not sure where they were going until they pulled into the Charleston airport and parked at the entrance to boarding. Beau had radioed for backup, so Simon knew something serious was up.

"Let's go," Beau yelled, getting out of the car and running inside. He headed to airport security with Simon right behind him.

"Charleston police," Beau said, breathing heavily and holding out his badge. "We need to get to a plane that's about ready to board."

"Sir, we can't just let you into the boarding area without TSA approval."

"Then get it. We have a murderer on the loose."

"I'll see what I can do."

"Make it happen."

"Do you know what airline and flight number?"

"Atlantic Air, flight 954."

"Sir, that flight's boarding now."

"Then you better get us there, or you'll be charged with obstruction of justice."

Minutes ticked by before there was a response from the boarding agent.

"Hold that plane," security said. "We're on our way."

"Tell her she holds that plane, or she'll be in jail with you."

A golf cart showed up to take them to the gate. Simon hopped in the back along with the security guard.

"Get us there fast," Beau belted out.

The driver honked the horn and dodged pedestrians as he tried to get to the gate as quickly as possible. This was the most excitement he'd had in years and wanted to see what all the action was about.

In the meantime, Beau had radioed the backup with his coordinates and where to meet him. Gate eleven was now within sight, and Beau was eager to get there. Upon arrival, the airline captain met them at the gate entrance, upset that his plane was being delayed.

"Detective Beau Crenshaw, Charleston police," Beau said, waving his badge out for the pilot to see. "This is police Constable Simon Miller. You have passengers on board your flight that we need to have removed. We can't let them leave the country. I need them off this plane."

"Detective, what are you saying?"

"Exactly what I just said. I need you to have three passengers removed from this flight. Here are their names. One is an elderly woman," Beau said, handing the pilot a piece of paper. "Either you get them off, or I'm going to go and get them myself. Do you have an air marshal on board?"

"We do. All our international flights have air marshals."

"Then call the air marshal and ask him to escort them off."

A crowd was now forming after seeing Bruce and Eddy running down the hallway to the gate.

"Get this crowd out of here," Beau yelled out to the officers.

"Detective, the air marshal is going to escort them off the plane. They are on the way," the pilot said.

Beau stood nervously waiting for the familiar faces to exit the plane.

Three very startled faces soon appeared with Oliver leading the way.

"Beau? What on earth is going on here?" he said.

"You'll know soon enough. Bruce, Eddy take Ruby back to Sutherland's Crossing. Use this cart to get all of you down to your car."

"Oliver, what's going on?" Ruby asked.

"Ruby, we'll get everything worked out. We'll see you soon at home," Oliver said awkwardly.

With Ruby out of sight, Beau beckoned for Oliver and Abby to move toward a quiet area before speaking.

"Larry Wycliff was killed in prison."

"I'm not sure why you think I would care about knowing this, and this is why you jerked us off our plane for that bit of information?" Oliver said.

"Because I think your daughter knew more about Larry than she is letting on."

"Why would you think that?"

Beau turned to look directly at Abby.

"At your sister's funeral, there was a young man who was terribly upset about her death. Seems he was a patient of hers. I took his information that day and went back to visit with Callum to ask a few more questions. Seems Callum received a large sum of money from his dad. This was meant to make amends for him being a lousy father and sending him off to his aunt's house when his mother was murdered. Do you find it odd the town drunk would deposit a half a mil into his son's account?"

"He appeared to live a frugal life and evidently saved well," she said.

"I'll bet you'll never guess who the aunt is."

"Why stop here, Detective, do tell."

"The aunt owns the property where your sister was found. She keeps it as a rental but lives in New York."

"What a coincidence indeed."

"You know what else Callum told me?"

"I'm all ears."

"He said he was getting therapy. Apparently, he witnessed his mother getting murdered when he was a child. Lots of lacerations. I immediately thought about what a coincidence this was, so I went back and reviewed the records. She gets cut up. Your sister gets cut up. Same style, same pattern. And to top it off, you'll never guess where he was getting therapy. Newhaven, and your sister was the therapist. He said she was the only person to ever help him feel better."

"Wow, that is a revelation, Detective, but what does that have to do with me? Larry Wycliff confessed. So, what is this adding up to?"

"Yes, Detective, what does that have to do with Abby?" Oliver chimed in.

"Well, I had to ask myself. Small world how a father and son could be so intertwined yet not know what was going on. And why would a father, then, a father who was trying to make amends with his son, to a son who had moved back to Charleston to reacquaint with this father, kill the son's therapist? The only therapist that was making a difference? This makes no sense."

"What exactly are you trying to say?" Abby asked.

"Let me cut to the chase. You are not who you say you are."

"That's absurd. And why would I pretend to be Abby? I wasn't fond of my sister. Why would I want to be her?"

"Oh . . . I don't know . . . maybe it was the awful way that your mother treated you that stirred the pot and started the ball rolling. I believe you planned your disappearance to get everyone thinking it was you that was found that day in the swamp. It was a grand plan. I will admit I wasn't totally convinced until I asked around about Roger. Now that's a story and a half. Your father's CFO, had an affair with your mother, but it ended after she got pregnant and had an abortion. She paid him to go away to avoid a scandal. He was quick to talk with me about his meeting with you and how you planned to uncover them both. What I found interesting is that he kept saying it was Audra that was going to rat them out and not Abby. Then there was the pregnancy. We found a pregnancy test in the trash at your apartment, and I will admit I believed it belonged to you, especially when the dead woman was confirmed to be pregnant because we all thought it was Audra, but it was Abby, wasn't it. Did she test there so she could share the happy news or rub it in your face? Did she find out you were having sex with her boyfriend and came over to tell you to back off? At first, I thought Joshua was the father, but then when Sterling admitted to sleeping with you too it all made sense."

"What?" Oliver said in disbelief.

Abby cleared her throat.

"The judge did at long last offer up that warrant so we could gather all your patient records. Quite interesting. Callum's in particular."

"This is insane. My daughter did not kill her sister and then pretend to be her. The town drunk killed my daughter."

"Hold on, Oliver. I'll get to you in a minute. So, getting back to the story. I think you paid to have your sister killed because you loathed her that much and because you wanted your mother to suffer. I think Larry was more than happy to do the deed for you for that amount of cash. This was the perfect way for him to make amends to his son and for you to take revenge on your sister and your mother. I take it her dying wasn't in the plans, but an added bonus or maybe you were both in on it. Her autopsy did reveal something quite interesting. Oliver, this is where you come into play."

"You certainly have thought of everything, Detective. There is just one problem. You have a signed confession from a person who is now dead, and you have no way to connect me to the crime scene or to those funds. And what does Dad have to do with this?"

Beau moved his gaze from Abby to Oliver.

"Oliver, it seems your wife was poisoned—strychnine, to be exact. It seems she ingested it about an hour before she died. One of the waiters recalls you stepping outside to get some air, with a champagne glass in your hand, and when you came back in to make the toast, you handed your glass to your wife and picked up her glass to toast with. He remembers this, since all eyes were on you as you said your speech. I had to ask myself why someone would do this unless you went outside to put the poison into the champagne flute. We ran comparisons of strychnine found on your job site, and it was a match to the type that killed Charlotte. Building sites always have a problem with rodents, so it made sense for you to have an abundance of rat poison. It was certainly easy enough for you to obtain without any questions asked. I questioned one of your staff about the whereabouts of your suit from the night of the wedding. She said she had just taken it to the dry cleaner. We were lucky enough to get a warrant to pick up that suit before it was cleaned. When the lab tested it, they found trace amounts of strychnine in your suit pocket."

Oliver slammed his fist against the wall. "Are you trying to tell me that you are accusing me of murdering my wife?"

"That's exactly what I am telling you, and I think the random gesture of handing me a hundred-thousand-dollar check was to keep me quiet about it."

"Detective, my father did not kill my mother, and I did not kill my sister."

"We'll let a court of law determine that. Audra Barrington, I am placing you under arrest for conspiracy to commit the murder of

Abigail Barrington. Oliver Barrington, I am placing you under arrest for the murder of Charlotte Barrington. You both have the right to remain silent. Anything you say can and will be used against you in a court of law. You have the right to an attorney. If you cannot afford an attorney, one will be appointed for you. Do you have questions?"

"Dad?"

"Shut up. Don't say another word," Oliver snapped, looking toward his daughter. "My attorney will crucify you. You're going to regret this, Detective. This will be the end of your career."

"There's a lot of things I regret in life, Oliver, but getting two murderers off the streets isn't one of them. Sometimes money can't buy you everything."

# THE END

# AFTERWORDS

If you enjoyed Sutherland's Crossing, please leave a warm review wherever you purchased the book. This helps more than you know! I would also love to hear your ideas and comments so please email me at gwenkellyauthor@gmail.com or sign up for my newsletter at https://gwenkellyauthor.com

—

Please remember that a portion of the net profits, of your purchase, is donated to Georgia SPOT Society. We help pet owners, who otherwise cannot afford to spay and neuter their pets. We are a non-profit covering the state of Georgia, USA. We are 100% volunteer based and your donation is 100% tax deductible.

If you would like to make a donation to the cause, you can do so on our website – https://spotsociety.org

# ABOUT THE AUTHOR

I am an award-winning author who's passionate about animals and writing. I love to share stories. I'm always evolving to become the best fun version of myself. As I follow my path, I will continue to write stories, foster dogs, help shelter dogs find beautiful loving homes and aid individuals needing financial assistance to spay and neuter their pets.

My ultimate goal is to one day have a small farm called Sutherland's Crossing Sanctuary for animals needing a place to be loved, to feel at peace and eventually die with dignity.

I have many stories still brewing in my head and will continue to write books in many genres - murder mystery, children's book, historical true story, comedy book and whatever else formulates.

Please join me on my journey as I produce more books for you to enjoy and so together, we can continue to get lost in the world of words all while helping the animals!

Stay tuned for whatever may be next!

Made in United States
Orlando, FL
12 September 2024

51440265R00162